Jasper Beamon, a one-percenter, receives an ominous e-mail from his soul mate that she is publishing a tell-all book about their relationship. This threatening news sends Jasper into a neurotic tailspin where he is forced to examine his life. But will he?

Jasper's journey takes him from the tobacco fields of North Carolina to the bloody sands of Vietnam to post antiapartheid South Africa. Throughout life travels and hardships Jasper's constant companions, Jimmy Mack, his fateful appendage, and Lulu his loyal Chinese Water dog, urge, cajole and plead with him to alter his lifestyle before it is too late. But can he?

Upon returning to the United States, Jasper's troubles mount. He is hospitalized for PTSD and loses ten million dollars in the economy downturn but expects President Obama to relieve him from greed, restlessness and irresponsibility.

90 Percent: A Memoir of My Demise and Rise is humorous, political, passionate and timely.

With a voice that places her readers into a dream-like world, Kathryn L. Harris, has written a remarkable literary novel told in the first person.

ACKNOWLEDGEMENTS

I would not have finished writing this book without the support and assistance of many people. Following is a list of as many as I can remember.

Foremost, I thank God for his guidance and the vision to write this book.

To my therapist, Ms. Kathleen Nicol, who supported me through all of my angst, fears and emotional maladies. Her discussions and analysis helped me not only understand myself better but to create more distinct characters especially Jasper Beamon.

I am grateful to my editors, Grace Edwards Martha Bowman. I am appreciative of their reviews, suggestions and for recognizing my talent.

Thanks to Misha Crizer, my former writing partner, who advised me to write a trilogy. She also suggested that I write *90 Percent: A Memoir of My Demise and Rise* in Jasper Beamon's voice. It was a brilliant idea.

I am also indebted to all of the people I interviewed including, the staff of the Psychiatric Institute of Washington, John Greco at the Navy Historical Command Center, Mrs. Alma Gravely, widow of Vice Admiral Samuel L. Gravely, Dr. Anna Trouth, chairperson of the Department of

Neurology at Howard University, and other navy officers and to anyone else I interviewed but did not name.

I am grateful for the use of the Howard University Law Library directed by Ms. Rhea Ballard-Thrower as well as the kind assistance from the Information Technology Department headed by Mr. Frank King, Jr.

My sincere appreciation goes to my self-publisher, CreateSpace, particularly team number one and April Bogdon.

Thanks to all of my friends who were steadfast in their belief in me, even though they have not yet read a word of my book—Leanne Nurse comes to mind.

I wish to thank, Annie Mahon, owner of Circle Yoga for my yoga scholarship.

A special thanks to my interns: Nicole Raz and Yasmine Brown.

I thank my former lawyers of Hogan & Hartson, (now Lovell) Ms. Debbie Boardman, and Mr. Adam Levin.

Last but not least, I thank James F. Garret for the inspiration and the "You know what." How do you like me now?

PART I

Women

"Ninety percent of all men are involved with three women simultaneously. Hallelujah! I am happy to be in that number."
— Deacon Jasper F. Beamon

CHAPTER 1

"In a moment of decision, the best
thing you can do is the right thing
. . . The worse thing you can
do is nothing."

Theodore Roosevelt

A stubborn, slow-moving fog bank over my manicured lawn. It is as stagnant and polluted as the Anacostia River. I gaze at it out my window, the tiniest room of my $2.5 million, eight-bedroom brick McMansion in the trendy suburb of Washington, DC. I feel like a Bazooka bubble.

My cell phone chimes. Lulu, my Portuguese water dog, leaps on my chaise lounge, crawls up my chest, then licks my nose. I fumble as I pick up the phone, timidly touching the MENU button. It's an e-mail message—something that I rarely receive. An ominous feeling comes over me, but that's nothing new. I feel like that most of the time, especially during the holiday season. In fact, from mid-November until January 2, a cloud of deep depression descends on me like a sheet over a dead body.

I run to my private bathroom and lock the door, glaring at the little envelope icon as it spins and twirls out of control. I hold my breath, but bathroom fears invade my nasal passages like spores of anthrax. With each rotation of the envelope, my heart spins like the spokes on a bicycle wheel. Sweat droplets pop up on my face like a serious case of the shingles. Outside my bathroom window, I hear baby birds bawling.

I open the message, an infrared MRI beaming through my body. Fear rips through my Piggy Wiggly like lightning ripping out a tree stump. A sickening scream from the pit of my soul escapes my throat. Lulu is a cannonball bouncing off the bathroom walls. I grip the edge of the toilet seat.

Oh my God! Who . . . ?

Who is sending this to me? And two days before Thanksgiving! I am a snake-trapped chicken in a barnyard coop. My heart churns like a draining hourglass. Blood flutters through it, faster and faster, like a rocket on its way to Venus. Only this time the clotted contraption is en route to me, Jasper Fisher Beamon.

Dear Papa Beamon,

You got me pregnant.

WHAT?

How . . . ?

Are you serious? I ask, as if I were conversing with the person who wrote this bizarre message.

By immaculate conception? Through osmosis?

No. With the power of my pen.

On May 30, 2008, I gave birth to an 8½ by 11, 400-page novel. In your absence, I named her Fire Dancer.

I didn't impregnate anyone . . . or did I?

Who did I sleep with? Why is she—whoever she is—picking on me? I'm a nice guy, aren't I?

Fear not, for I bring you tidings of great joy. Your daughter is funny, exciting, and passionate. Very much like her mother.

"I like it," I say as I unconsciously rub my hands gently on Jimmy Mack, my trusted appendage and companion. Jimmy Mack a nickname given to me years ago by my big brothers on the Omega Psi Phi line, the "Que" line as we call it. One of the most important lines I've ever stood on.

My publisher is ready to roll our bouncing baby girl right off the press, but first Fire Dancer insists on meeting her daddy. Below are a few lines to help you get better acquainted:

I'm aiming for all three, but one will suffice, because my daddy taught me not to leave anything on the table.

I gaze into his eyes and feel a come coming on. He drinks in my eyes—not only for the lifesaving, water-diluted electrolytes,

but also for the nourishment that his starving body, soul, and
spirit have been craving for forty years.
  Gobble gobble. Happy Thanksgiving!

                                              Howard Girl

"Oh . . . my . . . God . . ." I moan. It's from Jeanette. She's
written a book.

I recite my mantra: *Calm down, calm down, calm down.*

A nauseating sensation invades my body, from chest to
groin. I slump to my knees, drop my overall and pull out
Jimmy Mack. He sings his song, missing the high note by a
millimeter.

"Don't let Mr. Uppity Charles Anderson get wind of it,"
says Jimmy Mack "with his slew-footed self."

"God forbid," I reply. "My reputation will be over. He'll
leak it to the whole congregation . . . and Martha."

"Wipe it all in your face . . ."

"I'll be kicked out of church . . ."

Afterward, my heart is still a defibrillator, but I read
the message again. *What is this?* It's more than twelve
months since I quit her, like an immature jackass, over the
telephone.

"She wrote a book? Ohhhh, Ludicrous! Is that what she's
saying?" I ask Lulu, my loyal and sympathetic companion.
Her real name is Ludicrous. "I shoulda apologized or done
something a long time ago, shouldn't I, Lulu?" When will I
ever learn?

"Woof."

My rambling heart drowns out the sounds of Lulu romp-
ing around like an amphetamine nut. I read somewhere
that pets are supposed to relieve stress—something about

providing unconditional love. Me and Lulu, we're a pack; though, of course, I'm the omega dog. I remember a familiar saying: "If you want a friend in this town, get a dog." Since I don't trust easily, Lulu is a perfect solution for me.

I look at her hopelessly. "But Lulu, I didn't do it." *Oh, I'm losing my mind.*

Dumbfounded, I watch Lulu sitting majestically on my terracotta bathroom floor. "What are you doing? You're not . . . urinating on my floor?"

"Woof," she answers.

"You animal," I say. But I can't be too hard on her. "You're nervous, too, aren't you? Jimmy Mack," I say, meandering on, "what did she write about? Not me, I hope!" I read the message again. "A 400-page novel . . . *Fire Dancer* . . . and I'm the—the *father*!"

I'm shocked, although I must admit that I'm proud of her, too. I remember how often I told her (fool that I am), *Jeanette, I want you to succeed.* I said it so often, it became my good-bye preamble.

"Calm down," says Jimmy Mack, lying like a piece of Moroccan flatbread in my overalls. "Why get so insanely upset about it? It's just a book!"

"Maybe she's trying to blackmail me," I reply. "You know women. Maybe she's gonna to threaten to tell Martha about our affair. I mean, Jeanette—she was real nonjudgmental. I told her some . . . some unsavory things I've done."

"Like what, for example?" asks Jimmy Mack.

If I interviewed a woman with large breasts, Lord have mercy, I would spend the whole interview wishing I could do some of my favorite things. *Uuummm.*

"I confided in her about . . . everything. And you know what she said to all that, Jimmy Mack?" I recall it like it was yesterday. *Jasper,* she would say, sounding sweeter than peach cobbler, *what matters to me is how you treat me.*

"Bow-wow," barks Lulu.

I didn't appreciate her like I should've. I kept harping on this success thang. I shoved it down her throat each time I broke up with her:

Jeannie, I want to see you succeed.

"Well, what is success if it isn't writing a book?" I ask Lulu now.

"Woof!" she barks excitedly, looking directly into my eyes.

"Is that a *yes*?" I ask.

"Woof, woof!"

Success is a good thing. But not at my expense. *Write a book, okay? Just not a book about me!*

All this ranting is making my head feel as if a squirrel family is using my scalp for a basketball court.

I know she's as smart as the "Iron Lady," Ellen Johnson Sirleaf, the first female president of Liberia. Still . . . *I didn't know she had it in her,* I think. On the other hand, I'm not surprised at anything Jeanette does.

"Never ever underestimate a Howard University woman," says Jimmy Mack.

"Now I know."

"Remember the slogan on her T-shirt? What did it say?"

"Howard Girl . . . Out of Your League."

"I rest my case," says Jimmy Mack.

Jeannette is a shock jock—a tease. But we sure did have some good times. I know that much. But really, I don't know a thing about women. I couldn't judge one from the other in a cotton-picking contest.

"You know, women like attention." says Lulu, right on cue. "Maybe she's trying to get some."

"Are you out of your mind?" asks Jimmy Mack.

Doggone, I'm so scared. "But I loves her, I sho' 'nuff do." It's what my Mama would have said.

"Confused, man, CONFUSED!" Jimmy says.

A therapist—that's what I need. I'm a highly educated man, but I can't keep my heart from jingling long enough to see a good coach. All this lollygagging is enough to make my mother puke—if she were still alive. But she's not my problem anymore.

"Why did you settle for Martha anyway?" asks Jimmy Mack.

Wrong timing, I think.

"Wrong everything," says Jimmy Mack, reading my thoughts.

"She acted like I was the last man on earth. All that attention—I ate it up. I never had that before. I learned—too late—that it was extreme jealousy."

"Tell it like it is, man—you married her for status and to get some respect."

"You think so?"

"I can't do anything now. I would lose my money!"

"And what would you be without money?" asks Lulu.

"A bastid," says Jimmy Mack.

"Isn't he one already?" says Lulu.

"I'm an old dog."

"Woof?"

"So I can't learn new tricks. I've got to stick with the familiar."

"Oh, forget it!" says Lulu disgustedly, rolling away from me.

"Don't get me wrong—you know I adore Jeanette. I idolized her." She's a classy woman. Dresses like an *Essence* model. Carries herself with a Michelle Obama comportment.

Martha, on the other hand, reminds me of a hippopotamus: bow-legged, stout, and stubby, with a face to match. She has passed her prime.

"Never had one," inserts Jimmy Mack.

The difference between Jeanette and Martha is the difference between filet mignon and a hog maul.

"But suppose Martha finds out?" I ask Lulu.

Twitching her tail back and forth across the hardwood floor, Lulu looks at me, puzzled.

"Overreacting, Jasper, huh?" is Jimmy Mack's comment.

"Calm down! When Martha goes grocery shopping…"

"Go ahead. Do it," he insists.

"Thank you, God—she's gonna give me some space and time."

"No," I reply. "Not yet, anyway." I ruminate for a moment, like Romeo over Juliet.

"Yeah, yeah, I hear you," says Jimmy Mack.

What would I do if I didn't have him and Lulu? I can't talk to anyone else about my feelings for Jeanette.

I've been in this bathroom too long. *Tomorrow morning. You just wait and see. I'm gonna call. I'm gonna do it.*

* * *

CHAPTER 2

"What worries you, masters you."

Haddon W. Robinson

We're making our annual Thanksgiving pilgrimage to the beach house, like the rich Rockefellers. It's a perfect NFL day.

I drive every year. It is exactly 387 miles door to door. It takes me seven hours. I get the opportunity to do something I like and do it well. If people would leave me alone . . .

Before I can back out of my driveway good, though, the phone rings. My gray Lexus ES330 came with OnStar, so it flashes the identification of all my callers. Reading the number, I take a deep breath, brace myself, and pick up the phone. Martha is nagging me about things she wants me to do, but I switch her off. Even contacting Jeanette takes a back seat.

Mr. High-and-Mighty—Charles Anderson, one of the church trustees—is calling. Charles Anderson is my nemesis. A ferret look-alike—not that I should talk. After all, I'm no Shaquille O'Neal either. Charles's claim to fame (and his point of nuisance, from my point of view) is this: His family has been members of Mount Mariah Baptist Church for generations. He loves to brag about how his great-grandfather was one of our founders. "Laid the first brick," he says proudly, and too many nauseating times. I've been a deacon for more than thirty years, but he still acts like I'm an encroacher. He uses any excuse to belittle me.

I drift into my dream world and concentrate on how I will drive the first 108 miles of the trip: From Parental Guidance County (that's Prince George's to us "locals") to Indian Head Highway. Then merge into Interstate 95, which leads to I-295, and exit at 84A. I'll scout for signs of I-95, and then my mood will change drastically when I merge back onto it.

I'm jolted back to the present by the voice of Charles Anderson. "Jasper, I called to remind you of the church meeting on Friday," Anderson says, his accent like a British lord's. It's so annoying, I've missed my turn, and now I'll have to drive seven miles out of the way.

"Concentrate on driving, will you?" yells Martha.

Damn that woman! "What do you think I'm doing?"

"Getting us lost."

"I'm on my way out of town, Trustee Anderson," I say, forcing myself to give him his dues.

In less than a millisecond we are growling at each other like two pit bulls.

"Oh! Off to that beach house again, huh, Deacon?" His voice dribbling with sarcasm and singeing with jealousy.

"It's Thanksgiving."

"I know it!"

"Just telling you."

He laughs. "Don't eat the whole turkey." Then he bangs the phone down before I can strike back or digest his sarcastic comment. That man's greatest pleasure is torturing me. I'm edgy anyway, and now I'll feel offended by his crack at me for days.

The sun is brilliant and the air is brisk. But it doesn't feel like it to me.

I'm still hoping this all—the depression, Jeanette's book and Charles Anderson—goes away. *Maybe it was only a nightmare.* That's been happening a lot lately, especially with Martha overpowering me like a blood-sucking mosquito in a Mississippi swamp. I hate to admit it, but she is abusive and intrusive. Overbearing and condescending. And insanely jealous. One Christmas, Jeanette had called to thank me for her present—$5,000—while Martha and I were driving to the beach house. My wife and I got into a convoluted argument that lasted all seven hours until we got there. Like I said, she's a pain in the—

"Don't forget just plain crazy!" says Jimmy Mack.

"Woof!" adds Lulu.

I still remember the first time I saw Jeanette. It was July 3, 2003. She entered my office, wearing a navy blue waist-hugging suit, and I felt like a volcano had erupted. She turned me and everything in my office inside out.

"You almost lost it," teases Jimmy Mack. "Blew your mind, captain!"

I could tell right away that she was much younger than I was, about twenty years.

"Michael Jackson's PYT?" teases Jimmy Mack.

It was supposed to be an informational interview, only twenty minutes at the most. But before the two hours and fifteen minutes were over, like a Nigerian PhD professor, I had given up my complete curriculum vitae. From that day on, I pursued her relentlessly. I called her for no apparent reason, begging her to contact me if she needed anything. I was a crazy man.

"Money?" quips Jimmy Mack.

"Anything," I reply. I instigated and pleaded with Jeanette for more than a year until our relationship metamorphosed from a beautiful, fun friendship into a powerful, emotional love affair.

"Soul mate?" asks Jimmy Mack.

"*Yeah, the whole sweet potato pie. Yummy.*" One Friday night when Martha was out of town, I got up the nerves to call her. Did you call me? I ask. I heard my telephone ring, I said. To impress her, I even told her we have three phones (which we do) and I couldn't tell which one was ringing. The story wasn't true, of course.

"What did she say?" asks Jimmy Mack.

"She said, 'I don't even have your home phone number."

"Gotcha. What happened after that?"

"She said that she was gonna to a gala with a friend, and quickly hung up the phone."

"You were crushed."

"Man, I adored her, worshipped her, idolized her. She made me feel soooo good."

"I see that."

"She spent countless hours consoling me, cajoling me, and listening to me bellyaching about my marriage, about my personal and business problems." Man, I used to call her up, moaning and whining about how much I wanted to see her, touch her, and kiss those luscious lips. The prettiest set of lips a woman could ever possess.

"She possessed you."

"She helped me discover the playfulness in me. Took me back to the few happy days I had in my childhood and my college days."

The day I showed Jeanette I'd programmed her number in my OnStar, I was as excited as the day I made my first million dollars. But if Martha sees a message from her, or from a*nyone else she doesn't know, a nuclear war will break out.*

"God forbid," I say mistakenly out loud.

Martha says, "What?"

"I'm praying."

Since retiring, settling for Martha, and spending my days around the clock in her presence, I feel like I am slowly losing it. Decaying from the inside out.

"Brown lunging—inhaling shreds of cotton," says Jimmy Mack quietly.

"Oh. Well, keep it to yourself," blurts Martha. She doesn't say a pleasant word to me the entire trip. Nor does she inquire about my somber mood.

Today, though, I'm on a sojourn to Purgatory instead of a family holiday. I chant and pray feverishly to myself: *God, don't let Jeanette call me while I am driving. Not today.*

I enter North Carolina: my home state. I take my first breath of air after being born again. My heart speeds up at this crossroads every time. One road leads to my hometown, and the other to Jeanette's. It's the inevitable fork in the road, the symbol of my life. Fate has been cruel to us. We were born, she in the east and I in the northeast —too many years, too many miles, and too many dollars apart but— as Gladys Knight sings, "If anybody should ever write my life story, for whatever reason there might be. She'll be there between each line of pain and glory, because she's the best thing, the very best thing that ever happened to . . ."

"Me."

"What'd you say?" asks Martha.

"Nothing," I reply. My hands are clammy. As I grip the steering wheel, they tremble. *Am I gonna to urinate in my pants?*

The Carolina scenery is endearing. In my mind I see the neatly planted rows and rows of farm crops that will spring up and ripen next spring and summer. In reality, I see only the dead dry tobacco stalks.

"Must have been a large crop of tobacco," I say.

"Tobacco kills too many people."

It is taxing to talk to a woman who keeps me in thrall.

"People should quit smoking," I reply.

"Just like that, huh?"

"Never mind." Why did I even open my mouth? Still, I am jostled by the realization that this plant will kill more than a million people in the U.S. this year alone. I harvested this poison as a youth. I feel guilty.

I focus instead on the appetizing vegetables. I can almost taste the juicy, ripe tomato on my tongue, slipping and sliding down along my windpipe. I recall the many delicious meals my grandmother prepared. One of my greatest pleasures still is roasting Carolina peanuts and eating them straight out of a bottle of Pepsi Cola.

But the agonizing memories soon seep in. I'm still embarrassed by the thought of having to sell fruits and vegetables door to door. But I have a talent for selling, which I later perfected. Little did I realize that it would come in handy in the future.

But those days are over. I have my houses and my cars. Just thinking about my bank account gives me an erection.

I roll the window down as Route 264 becomes I-795 South. The smell of pine trees swishes up my nose. I breathe in deeply. It is pure and refreshing, like a cool glass of sugary lemonade. Southern comfort. Just smelling and seeing the green trees and foliage alone is worth the ride.

I gaze at the Southern country homes and the mansions sitting a half mile from the main highway, surrounded by acres of landscaped lawns, dilapidated tobacco barns, and abandoned tractors. The panorama is as beautiful as it is familiar. It makes me nostalgic. I am home.

I thank God when we finally arrive. I don't want to spend the *holidays alone with Lady Macbeth. At least this is a chance to see my children, and my son-in-law, too. That is, if Jeanette's message doesn't leak out and cause a tornado.*

Sunday, I can escape into a full day of football fantasy.

* * *

I sneak out of the house the next morning, pretending I am just looking to walk Lulu. For a few peaceful minutes, I watch my cheerful dog frolic up and down the chilly beach. I envy her happiness. Lulu barks, and I jump like a firecracker. But I'm living the fears of Jeanette's book and the memory of Charles Anderson's ribbing over and over again in my brain.

I try to work up the courage to check my phone. Did Jeanette send another e-mail? I whistle "Night and Day" as I trot behind Lulu. The tune is fitting; I can't think of anything else but her.

"You're gonna crazy, man," sings Jimmy Mack.

I sit down on the dunes, pull off my shoes and dump out the sand. Lulu comes up to me, shaking the sand from her body.

"These gritty pebbles in my shoes aggravate me," I say to her. She licks my face just as I bend over to tie up my shoes. Then we trot on.

I sold my business at Martha's insistence, with trepidation, because I dreaded retiring. I haven't been the same since. I remember discussing my retirement with Jeanette one day, over several cups of coffee. I am still grappling with the gravity of it, even after two years. The day the transaction was final, I felt like a man who'd been diagnosed with a terminal disease. In a very real way, ever since, I have been dying—just fading away. Since my retirement, Martha's been treating me like a monkey on a string, without a tambourine. My main goal is to hold it together, one day at a time.

"Bojangles!" says Jimmy Mack.

I feel like I'm in prison—as Jennifer Hudson sings, in "maximum security."

"Woof, woof," Lulu says.

"Ohhhh! Well, would it have been better to meet Jeanette *before* I tied up all my money?"

"Excuses, *excuses,*" Jimmy Mack taunts.

"Is she gonna to send me another message?" I ask Lulu.

But Lulu is having so much fun, she hardly notices me at all.

* * *

Thanksgiving Day, three p.m. We eat a soulful dinner. Martha is a good cook. Maybe better than the Neelys, that down-home cooking couple on the Food Network. This I don't mind saying. Today, the square oak table that she inherited from her grandmother is laden with all the traditional dishes: a thirty-pound turkey, collard greens, snap beans, candied yams, barbecued ribs, mashed potatoes. Enough to feed Martha's Table, a homeless shelter, for a week. Poor souls.

Sitting at the table are my children, Rodney and Melanie; my son in-law, Matthew; and various uninvited relatives—at least, I didn't extend an invitation to them. They're mostly Martha's and a smattering of my own: a brother, a sister, and a couple of grateful distant cousins. Right now, I can't tell where they fit in or to whom they are related.

Like millions of Americans throughout the country, my son says grace, thanking God for all we have. *Meanwhile, I'm daydreaming—watching Jeanette's titillating butt dancing the Zampoogie.*

"Oooo-weeeee!"

Everyone looks at me as if I have lost my mind.

"What?"

"Hmmm?"

"What'd you say?"

I lower my head and slyly reply, "Nothing."

Underneath the table, my bare feet are playing footsies on an Oriental rug that Martha bought on the Internet. She had it shipped directly from Delhi, just in time for this homespun moment.

I announce a ritual—a distraction. Everybody must tell something they are grateful for.

"My new Steinway piano," says Martha, true to form.

"Madam has two pianos," says Jimmy Mack. "One at the beach house and one at home."

She plops her matronly flapjack on the stool and strikes a key, as if she were the Great One, Mary Lou Williams, herself. That is another thing I can give Martha—she's not half bad at tickling the old ivories—because I wouldn't want anyone thinking she is totally evil.

"Hurrah!" says Jimmy Mack.

"Being alive. Surviving uterine cancer," says Melanie.

"Yes, baby, you did it," says Matthew as he grabs Melanie in a heart-warming embrace.

"Thank God the doctor was able to get it all out," I say.

"It happened only a few months after we moved to Jacksonville." Matthew says, dropping his shoulders.

"Just after we got married," says Melanie pitifully.

"Family. What's that Pointer Sisters' song?" Rodney says, jolly. "*We are family, I got all my sisters with me.* Uh-huh. And my new BMW."

"Bought with daddy's greenbacks," interjects Jimmy Mack.

"And Dad, while we're at it, when you gonna give me the money to start my business?" asks Rodney.

"Today's not a good day to talk about business. Be thankful, son."

My son picks this day to pressure me into underwriting a business for him? It ain't gonna happen. I came up the hard and backbreaking way. I think he should do the same.

Am I a good father? Well, I'm not close to my kids. But the reality is, it's all about my money—keeping my money. To tell the truth, I'm ashamed to admit it, but I resent their requests. My goal is to keep as much of my money as I can for me, so I can maintain my image.

"Arf," barks Lulu.

"Dad. Dad!" Melanie and Rodney are calling me. "HELLO? DADDY!"

It's my turn. I hear Lulu whimpering.

"Hmmm . . ."

Among all this opulence, I feel impoverished. Lost on a deserted island.

I wave my hands across the table, just as Martha gives me the disgusted look she's been waiting for throughout the entire holiday.

"For all of this," I say, and my fake smile fades away.

An hour later, while I'm watching football with Matthew, my cell buzzes, *You've got mail.* I can barely breathe. Is it a text from Jeanette? But I can't answer it, because Martha and Melanie are washing dishes and could come in the room any minute. Matthew might understand, but I can't take that chance. I wait until halftime when he goes to the bathroom.

My underarms are soaking wet like puddles, and my fingers shake. I gaze at the text icon as if it's a medical X-ray of cancer enlarged in my throat.

Dear Jasper,

Happy Thanksgiving. Hope you weren't frightened by the e-mail I sent you—I was having a little fun. Just want you to check it out. Contact me as soon as you get back.

Jeanette

Whew! My lips are twitching and my fingers race across the keyboard like ants after sugar. She must know I'm frightened to death.

I answer:

Will contact as soon as I return.

…Jasper

Thank God, I say silently, easing the cell phone back in its place on the right side of my pants just as Matthew comes back. I act as if I'm concentrating on the game.

"What's the score?" he asks, drying his wet hands on a paper towel and pitching it in the trash can, like Kobe Bryant from the free-throw line.

"The Redskins are fourth down and gonna for a field goal."

"Whoa!" shouts Matthew.

I'm peculiar: I like sports, but when it comes to true male camaraderie I'm on the fringe. I look at sports because that's what real men do. It makes me feel a little better. So I pretend to be excited about the quarterback's next play. But really, I can't wait to get back to the city. I need to talk to Jeanette about her book. I want to read it, despite this uncontrollable fear.

* * *

The very first day we're back home, I muster up my courage and answer Jeanette.

"Did you really write a book?"

* * *

CHAPTER **3**

"The cost of liberty is less than the price of repression."

W. E. B. Du Bois

Why is Martha such a heifer?

She is crowing like a barnyard rooster hell-bound. "Get these boxes in the car! You know the traffic gonna' be heavy. We need to get on the road. What have you been doing?"

There she goes, nagging and complaining again. I don't respond. What's the use?

I pick up the boxes like an obedient boy and push past her through the doorway. I pitch them in the trunk of my Lexus like a pro baseball player. She always has something for me to do. And it's always something negative.

"That's a good boy," mocks Jimmy Mack.

We are driving back to Carolina five days before Christmas.

She forces me to use my car more than a good mechanic or traveling salesman would ever recommend.

"I drive my car down here every time."

"Jasper, I'm not gonna wear out my Benz," Martha says boldly.

I ignore her, reaching down to knead Lulu's coarse bronze fur. I am hoping to solicit Martha's sympathy.

"That's what *your* car is for," she continues.

"Blah, blah," I mumble under my breath, but I respond sheepishly, "Yeah, I'm coming."

"Poor jackass," mocks Jimmy Mack.

"Me or her?" I ask him.

"Take your pick," says Jimmy Mack.

Martha ambles out of the house.

Two weeks after Thanksgiving Jeanette e-mailed me back. In the meantime I got myself worried sick, still hoping and praying she didn't write any book.

Dear Jasper:

Yes, I did. Sorry it took me a while to get back to you. I lost my phone and had to haggle with the company before they sent me a free replacement.

I answered that same afternoon. I asked her again.

Jeanette, you didn't. Did you? You really wrote a book?

"How many times you gonna ask her?" shouts Jimmy Mack. "It's not gonna to change the fact: SHE WROTE A BOOK!"

I hesitate this time to answer her immediately, and I start to procrastinate. Maybe I'll deal with this next year. . . I have too much on my mind right now.

"Next year is here already," says Jimmy Mack.

"Almost," yaps Lulu.

I smile now, my eyes on the road but forcing myself to focus on Lulu as well. "You know you're gonna on a trip, don't you, girl?"

"Woof, woof!" She sounds as happy as a playground full of children.

At least someone *in this household is happy.*

"No getting lost. When we get there, we need to decorate ASAP," demands Martha.

"I need some rest first."

"You tell her," Jimmy Mack eggs me on.

"That's all you do now, is rest."

Tuning her out again, I try to enjoy the driving. But I know that I will not sleep well tonight.

Once we reach Carolina, we pass through several one-horse towns. I see lonely, isolated, unoccupied, abandoned farmhouses.

That's precisely how I feel right now. *Abandoned.*

"By whom?" Jimmy Mack says, curious.

"By Jeanette. I wish she could spend Christmas with me."

"Yeah, right. It was your decision."

"Don't remind me."

When we reached the turning point that leads to her home town and mine, I take the low road, the highway leading to the luxurious beach house, but I feel so tired.

My folks and friends back home think I'm a hero. They judge by how much money I have. For a millisecond, this idea makes me feel good. But if they could only spend a night in my household . . . feel the bruises on my soul . . . view the splintered prism of my spirit. If they could do all this, that envy would turn to deprecation.

Poor, sorry me.

But Martha interrupts my daydreaming again.

"What is wrong with you?" she asks.

"Would you leave me alone?"

"What in the hell is wrong with you?" she repeats.

Is she trying to agitate me?

"Give me time . . . and *I'll* leave *you* alone!" I whisper to Jimmy Mack.

I imagine leaving her, but a sundry list of problems creeps into my skull. I'm worried about the book that Jeanette wrote. She told me in no uncertain terms she's written a book. It's up to me now to read it. I'm beginning to dread this holiday. I used to call Jeanette every time I left town, longing to take her with me. I wish I'd done it this time.

The long driveway leading to the beach house is lined with palm trees. At Christmastime it's decorated with lights and looks like the Champs-Élysées. The overlapping branches almost touch the shiny top of my luxury car. Even without the lights, it is a spectacular view—in the summer months, more beautiful than any lane of palms on the Bermuda Islands. It looks like the entrance to paradise. Yet driving in, I always feel like I'm on the last mile to Alcatraz.

I purchased this $3.2 million second home because I want to feel as though I've overcome my past—the homelessness and the shotgun homes. I want to feel that I've arrived at a place of happiness and left memories of the past behind me. But they cling to me like a wet bathing suit to a naked body.

I think I know how the balladeer feels when he sings "A House Is Not a Home."

"You bought it for outside show," says Jimmy Mack.

Christmastime is depressing anyway. The lights, the decorations, the frantic shopping—it all weighs my heart down. I feel like the dejected child I was growing up, when my family didn't have money to buy me anything—and didn't want to if they had it. But my siblings, my grandparents and I gave each other whatever little we had. Having money now doesn't alter my feeling at all. Even the Christmas carols are dispiriting. Jingle bell, jingle bell, jingle bell rock! The lyrics only remind me more of Jeanette and how much she likes to dance. And that doesn't make me feel merry. When most people are dreaming of a white Christmas, I'm terror-stricken, having dreadful nightmares. The Christmases I know certainly aren't snowy-white or Norman Rockwell–picturesque.

"What did you expect?" asks Jimmy Mack.

The weather—bristling cold, clammy, and overcast— makes me feel gloomy, too. Instead of feeling like I stepped out of a Currier & Ives painting, I long to crawl up under a bed and sleep until the New Year turns old.

Everywhere I go, I smell gingerbread like my grandmother used to make. But this recollection plunges me into a downward spiral, too. I cry so often that I have to avert my eyes from strangers, constantly dab my face with a handkerchief, and pretend I have a cold when Martha is around.

"One day at a time," says Jimmy Mack.

* * *

My job today is to find a Christmas tree. Not just any tree but the perfect Christmas tree. I take Lulu, Jimmy Mack (who goes everywhere I go), and a frat brother of mine (a fraternity brother for all of you out there who don't know) named Levi Johnson, to hunt for the perfect pine. Johnson is a real estate agent, an Omega man, and a sports fanatic. Sold me my house on the island—got me a good deal, too. That's one of the reasons I became an Omega man. We have an extensive network of businesspeople—people in all walks of life that can help you out. Not only that, but it's the most elite black fraternity that ever existed. Johnson and I generally get together to watch football and talk about fraternity business whenever we come down here. I'm pressured as usual, with Martha's voice grinding in my ears: "Don't forget to check for freshness. And make sure its six feet," she says. "A Carolina pine."

"On and on . . . !" exclaims Jimmy Mack.

He's right. The way she talks down to me, you would think she's the only grownup in the state. I prefer a Fraser fir, but what the hell, let her have what she wants. A Carolina pine. It's easier this way.

We drive several times around Emerald Isle, an exclusive beach off the coast of North Carolina just 89.41 miles from Jeanette's home town, as if finding the perfect tree is a matter of life and death.

"Johnson, do you remember the day you became a *lamp*?"

"Yeah, I couldn't forget that day—it's second only to the day we got to *go ovah*."

"I was happier than Jesse Owens winning his four gold medals at the 1936 Olympics."

"Me too, man," says Johnson.

I must admit, I was a frightened soul that day. I was a boy-man on the edge of the diving board, about to plunge headlong into treacherous waters. I remember thinking, *I'm joining a fraternity of men—whose very gender makes them part of a suspect group—with irreversible consequences.*

"Remember the chief beater?" says Johnson.

Of course I do. He was a molasses-toned giant who chose that job for a reason. His face, in my memory, is grimace registering his sadistic satisfaction. When he would slap the palm of his hand with a black leather strap and pat his feet to the rhythm of an R&B record, he was terrifying.

"He loved to trade some wood," I say.

"I can still feel it now . . ." Johnson's face contorts as if he's in pain. "His favorite expression was *It takes a man to take a beating.*"

"I just decided he was a psychopath, man."

"*Becoming an Omega man is serious business*—that was Kevin what's-his-name's motto. And we took a lot of ridicule, hours of humiliation, and hazing-like physical abuse to get there."

"I don't remember that, but he was right," says Johnson. "Made sure we learned the four Cardinal Principles of Omega Psi Phi."

"Manhood, Scholarship, Perseverance, and Uplift," we recite together. These principles are responsible for helping me to achieve my primary goal: becoming a rich man. They are the steps to the Kingdom . . . and I'm not talking about the one in the sky.

It takes us an hour to find one that meets Martha's specifications. Before I buy it, I ask the guy to trim the stump until the sap is visible.

"I don't want my wife complaining about it not lasting long enough," I say.

"She'll be satisfied with this one, Mr. Beamon," the Christmas tree guy says.

My cell phone rings, and I flick it open. A familiar voice is on the line.

"Hi Jasper," she purrs. "It's your old *friend* Rebecca."

What she's calling me for, I don't know. But it's against my stated wishes.

"Your Hoochie Momma," laughs Jimmy Mack.

As my anxiety shoots up fifty notches, I scream at Rebecca, "Why you calling me down here?"

"Just want to wish you a Merry Christmas," she says.

"Consider it done," I growl.

She ignores my attitude and my disinterest, and continues to prattle on far too long. I feel awkward. I'm afraid Johnson will catch on. He's standing within earshot, pretending he's looking at the trees while kicking dirt. Lulu yaps on and on, playing on the last fragment of my nerves.

I've got a little tiger in my tank, too. Rebecca is my bed partner. Our "sexcapades" have been gonna on for almost thirty years. I met her in 1980 when I was running for political office in PG County, Maryland's Eighth District. I was hoping to win a seat on the Public Safety and Fiscal Management Committee. She was young and very attractive—a Harvard lawyer, too. As Lionel Richie and the Commodores sang, "She's my brick house . . . The lady is stacked and that's a fact . . . knocks a man to his knees." Her family was pretty well off—they own several summer homes on Oak Bluffs, and she worked for one of the leading law firms in the United States.

I met her when she volunteered at my campaign office. Her job was to review newspaper articles, magazines, and other news pertinent to my political campaign. I took her to dinner. Later that night, in the bedroom of her suburban home, I gained her vote. Thereafter she retired from news junky to sex junky. Her appealing good looks and our sexual cravings are the foundation of the relationship.

I end the conversation and pay the Christmas tree vendor as quickly as I can.

"Come over for some coffee and biscuits," I suggest to Johnson.

"I'm not really hungry," he says.

"Homemade biscuits and country jam. I guarantee they're good. I made them myself . . from scratch."

"Naw, man, I got to get home. The game is coming on—I don't want to miss the kickoff."

"Come on, Johnson, you can look at the game at my house," I plead sadly.

"You need company . . . bad," says Jimmy Mack.

Martha is volatile as usual. I'm afraid she is gonna to explode any minute. I don't want to confront her by myself. Since we arrived the other day, I feel the tension mounting. I want to ward it off as long as I possibly can.

"That bad, huh?" asks Johnson, relenting. "Okay."

My eyebrows unfurl. The slaughter is postponed for tonight. "You can help me trim the tree, too."

"Putting me to work? What's gonna' on, Jasper?" he asks suspiciously, turning around in the passenger seat to look me directly in my face. "Remember, you can tell me anything."

"Nothing, man. It's nothing. But thanks." No true confession for me. I choose to float down "de nial."

"Sure," Johnson says. "When you wanna talk, I'm here."

* * *

CHAPTER 4

"A house is a home when it shelters the body and comforts the soul."

Phillip Moffitt

B ack at the house, we finish decorating the tree—under Martha's supervision. The living room is nestled and aglow with the heat of the built-in fireplace. It looks like a feature in *House & Garden* or *Architectural Digest*. In fact, the whole house, from the dining room to the basement, looks like something out of a magazine. The table is set formally, adorned with the best china that my money can buy, accompanied by every conceivable piece of silverware.

Later that night, after Johnson leaves, I stare at the six-foot Christmas tree. A beautiful black angel, divinely anchored at the top, looks down from its perch. The lights are blinking amid a hundred presents sprawled underneath. It's my childhood dream come true. It's idyllic, but there's something missing. I feel like a stranger in a foreign land.

I walk to the window and listen to the ocean roar even while an earthquake is shaking my heart apart. I've accumulated all these exterior things—anything money can buy. But looks are deceiving, as Grandmama often said. This house is a showpiece. When I bought it, I thought that it would wipe out the anxiety I felt when I was a homeless child. I thought giving Martha a leg up in the Millionaire Wives' Club would help make her a warmer, more loving woman. No such luck.

Far from becoming more loving, Martha has made it clear that her disdain for me has only increased. I'm not gonna to stew over buying the house, but without a thought for *my* feelings, she demands money for her relatives—more money than I give my own relatives. Even though it's Christmas, a time for love and happiness and giving, we have an argument about it—the biggest one yet.

"You've got to support seventy-two of my relatives," she demands.

"How can I do that? Let 'em work and take care of themselves," I say.

"You'll see, Jasper F. Beamon, you'll see" is her reply. "I can take your money and these houses, too. Don't let me have to prove it to you."

I have no doubt without the slightest provocation; Martha will do exactly what she says. There have been too many unexplainable and explainable incidents in which she has used her formidable wrath against me and others. Her voice alone, causes the hairs on my scalp to rise like the dead. *I can't let her take it all away!*

I clasp my hands over my head to stop the words from coming back . . .

* * *

"This ain't your house, and never will be." The oldest of my four stepbrothers, John—broad-chested, brazen, and bow-legged—is blocking our only exit to the house. He's jumping bad right away by standing defiantly in front of the door.

"Let the door hit you where the good Lord spit you!" screams Levi, his lanky, hateful-looking brother.

But, Martha, I love my mansion, I cry inside. I don't wanna lose it.

I'm a slight kid of diminutive stature—seventy-five pounds in wet Navy boots.

Until today, we've lived scattered about off and on with various relatives like Biafra refugees, or with my maternal grandparents in a four-room shotgun house, all rooms connecting like train cars, from living room to kitchen and onward. The bathroom, located on the back porch, was only accessible through the kitchen.

This day, the day we move into the Grimes house, leaves an indelible scar on my heart. I'll never forget it. Little do I know, the abuse I take will manifest itself in emotional problems of unbearable magnitude in the years to come.

It is September 22, 1952—my birthday. The sky is overcast. The front steps are crooked. The porch is cracked. My despair is as malleable as barb wire. Perched on the edge of a bony and leafless pine tree, a blue bird is humming a melancholy tune.

I make a decision: When I grow up, I'm never gonna to live in anyone else's home.

We walk into the Grimes' house. "This your new room," says Mama gaily as she pushes us into a dark, dreary, and sparsely furnished room. A single light bulb is dangling from the ceiling. A lonely double bed and dresser, sorely paint-neglected are the only two pieces of furniture.

I vow: *I will be rich someday. I swear I will buy as many houses as I want to.*

I am thirteen.

* * *

"Martha, Martha, Martha." I know she hears me. "Let me see what I can do."

"You better." says Martha venomously.

Meekly, I reply, "I promise."

* * *

CHAPTER 5

"As human beings we all want to be happy and free from misery. We have learned that the key to happiness is inner peace."

Dalai Lama

We return to the suburbs late Sunday night after spending a miserable holiday together. I still haven't made an appointment to read Jeanette's book.

The traffic is heavy, and the torrential downpour matches my gloomy and anxious mood. I am a rider in a funeral procession, in my mind, trolling to the burial site of my maternal grandmother. On the other hand, the awful weather is advantageous, allowing me to focus my mind on the road and not on Jeanette. I almost forget Martha is riding beside me like a mannequin, in obscurity.

But not for long. As I pull into the driveway, I remember I need to read that novel as soon as I get a chance.

As soon as the car comes to a halt, I let Lulu out to stretch her legs. She lifts her left leg and does her business, then runs wild in the backyard.

"Woof, woof!"

Maybe she spots another possum, or maybe it's Martha lurking around the house like one. It's disgusting when dogs don't even take to you.

I furtively check my cell phone. The message light is blinking like an orange traffic signal. I stop immediately under an amber tree and open the e-mail.

It's from Jeannie.

My heart quickens as if I'm negotiating a billion-dollar business deal.

Jasper,

I hope your holidays were fine but you need to read this book ASAP.

That's all her message says—terrifying words.

"A book about whom?" I ask Jimmy Mack.

"About you, fool."

"Am I in it?"

"What did I just say?" Jimmy Mack raises his head, like a cobra bracing to strike.

"Not a time for you to get sexually excited," I scold.

"We can't control our desire, even under the worst circumstances," says Jimmy Mack.

What in the name of God does she mean? I ask myself. But I know what she means. She really did write this book about me, and I better read it before it is published.

Lulu runs up, yapping away, her antics remind me of comedians on *Saturday Night Live*. I love this dog, but when I'm nervous, she gives me the willies.

I'm confused and light-headed. I grab my Bible and go outside to sit in the gazebo. First, though, I fumble in my pocket and pull out my cell phone again. Stop. Then read a few chapters in Psalms.

"You should have thought about praying and reading the Scripture a long time ago," says Jimmy Mack. "What did Spike Lee say? *Do the right thing.*"

"God, if you help me, I promise I *will* do the right thing." Then I type my message to her, my hands moving across the keyboard like spider legs.

Dear Jeanette,

You're too much for me, really you are. I still can't believe you wrote a book! I'm gonna to do my best to read it like you said, ASAP.

Jasper

"You oughta get it together, man," says Jimmy Mack. "Who you think you foolin'?"

He's right I make promises in a crisis. I pray, read the Scripture, and attend church. I serve as a deacon and an elder at that! But when the crisis passes, I'm back to living the same old lie, committing spiritual and emotional suicide.

I finish just in time, hitting the send button as Martha voice echoes across the lawn.

"What's taking you so *long,* Jasper?" she yells.

"Waiting for this silly dog to relieve herself. You know how she is." My words sound like gobbledygook.

"You need to get in here and unpack this luggage!"

"I'll be there in a few minutes. You don't want her pissing on your rugs. I know that." I mumble under my breath. But I respond so quietly, I'm sure she doesn't hear me.

I call Lulu with an ear-splitting, "COME HERE, DOG!"

Lulu runs to me as if it's dinnertime, and she hasn't eaten in a week.

"I've been thinking more and more about it, Lulu," I say. "About getting out of this relationship. I know it's been more than thirty years . . . but those are thirty-plus years of my life I can't get back, right?"

Lulu says nothing but looks agreeable to my proposal.

I go on. "I've got plenty of money. It wouldn't take long—if I plan it right. I can disappear and spend the rest of my days on a lovely tropical island. Where the women know how to treat you and don't mind show-ing their appreciation for a job well done. Right, Jimmy Mack?"

"Amen," Lulu and Jimmy say in perfect harmony.

"That's a deal," I promise.

I woke up this morning feeling jumpy and irritable. I feel like hot coals are burning my throat. But I'm not angry at Jeanette—just my life overall. In her heart, she's not cruel. She has been trying to get me to read this book since November. Now that I'm back in the city, I'm gonna to investigate. Figure a few things out that will help me live the life I deserve.

* * *

CHAPTER 6

> "I didn't pledge Omega, but every now and then I need to look in the mirror and say: Bow, Bow, Bow."
>
> *Rev. Matthew L. Watley*

Martha is *mad*!

My mind is a 3D movie playing negative words—"never gonna mount to nothing," "bistard," "no good"—and scenes of horrific images: Vietnam carnage, yelling and arguing in the Grimes' household. I feel like running and crying.

I'm driving back home from the shopping mall, and my cell phone rings. It's Rebecca calling. Martha is dozing at first.

"Hi, lover," Rebecca says. "When are we gonna to get together?"

"I don't know. Can't talk now. Someone is in the car," I whisper.

"I don't care."

"Let me call you back," I plead.

"Come on now," she says in her sexiest voice, smacking her lips. "I've written a compilation of Zane-ish poems. Come on over and let me read them to you?"

"Zane-ish?" I whisper.

"Yeah, baby. Erotica, you know—the kind you like."

Martha hears our conversation and she reaches across me like a construction crane and yanks the phone from my hand.

"This is my husband. What are you doing calling him?"

Rebecca must have dropped the phone. All I can hear is a loud dial tone.

Martha is an enraged gorilla. "Who's that, Jasper?"

My lips twitch and quiver. I don't say a word. I feel like a victim trapped in a fire. What can you say to an irrational, jealous woman? I drive on, praying silently. By this time I am all too familiar with Martha's jealous outrages . . .

* * *

I meet Martha while I'm in college; her attention is intoxicating, but I confuse possessiveness for love. While serving in the Navy, I date several (well, many) women; after ten years I still am not ready for marriage. But I feel undone. I'm having severe night sweats, horrible nightmares, and flash-backs. My dreams are flooded with the blood of the Viet Cong and the mangled bodies of women and children. My sleep is fractured with the grisly details of the injured and the dying. The smell of gunpowder nauseates me, and the sound of bombs thrusts me back to the Grimes household like it were yesterday. Instead of seeking therapy to heal my emotional illness, I cope with my constant symptoms and Martha's pressure by marrying her.

It's the mid-70s, and radios all over the city are blasting the hottest R&B single: "Sexual Healing," by Washington's own son, Marvin Gaye. Sexual healing strikes a central vein in Jimmy Mack and my reckless soul, too. How sorely we are in need of it! The newness of sex and exhaustive jealousy of the past few years with Martha has worn Jimmy Mack down. And the birth of our two children doesn't help either, not to mention that my wife's behind is quickly spreading and her peckerwood hair is turning grey and unmanageable, just like she is.

Somehow I've become the typical reckless and bored male government worker. I cruise the halls not only for the paycheck, the beanies, and the beauties, but also to get away from Martha and these dogged horrific memories of war and childhood.

The best time of the day is lunch. The intoxicating odors drift from the cafeteria to my office: fried chicken, pork chops smothered in gravy, mashed potatoes, string beans, iced tea, and coffee. In addition to the pies and pastries, I ogle the beautifully dressed women, my forbidden co-workers, and the waiters as I pass through the lunch line. The latter reminds me of the affectionate cafeteria workers of my college days, the former are fine fine women! What more do

I need to tell you? Because of them, good food, especially good soul food, music and attractive women are forever intertwined in my mind—especially since Mama often fed me leftovers. Sniffing their perfume and fantasizing about making love to my share is the highlight of my day.

Insanely jealous before, Martha is even worse after we marry, to the extent that she does not want me to speak with or even so much as look at other females. This attitude has not waned with the passing years. Once, when she found a woman's telephone number in my BlackBerry, she harassed and badgered the woman, as relentless as bed bugs on a motel mattress. She called that poor woman every hour, insisting she stay away from me—or suffer the consequences.

Before my retirement, when I used to travel to my offices in California and Florida, Martha would call several times during the flight and then, when I'd arrived, again at odd intervals during the night. She even called before sunrise each morning. I never got any sleep.

When she travels, as she often does for musical gigs, she insists I go with her. If I can't go—for business reasons or whatever—her tiger-eyes bore into me like a radar. Like a charging bison. Then she leaves me enough work for a maid brigade to do.

Once, she made me haul furniture downstairs and set up a bedroom suite on the first floor for her aunt, who'd suffered a stroke. I wanted to hire a moving van and a decorator, but she wouldn't even discuss it. My son helped me out though: moving and arranging the furniture and painting the walls. While Martha was out of town tending to her aunt, I was tending to Jeanette. We spent many hours together, playing like kids on the first day of summer vacation. Being the furniture mover was well worth it.

"The Bengal was away . . . and you played, man," says Jimmy Mack.

I smile, "Yes."

"Always checking on your whereabouts," scoffs Jimmy Mack. "What did Clarence Thomas and the chief justice sing? *Got to satisfy the dog in you.*"

"Now Jimmy Mack, why you think so little of me?" I ask.

For a short while in the middle of our married life I was better. I had structure—but it was too much and too soon, thanks to my job and Martha's rigidity. The green-headed monster reared her head, and suddenly I understood the difference between nourishment and punishment and the difference between a mother figure and a motherfucker.

Memories of mother seethe through me like lotion on parched skin . . .

* * *

We are unwelcome. It's clear from the outset that this isn't gonna to become a blended love family. They despise us for intruding on their space and into their lives. Pete's sons, my stepbrothers, are pissed with their father for marrying Mama just seven months after their own mother's death. We'll pay for it—that's for sure.

We do our best to settle into our "new house," quietly laying out the blankets and quilts my grandmother made for us. My brothers Richard and Johnny are sitting on the edge of the bed, sucking their thumbs and clutching soiled teddy bears. Barbara is carrying her precious 45 rpm record player and putting her saddle shoes in the closet.

No sooner do we finish unpacking our battered, weary suitcase than the room begins to shake like an old building in the hands of The Dynamo Demolition team. My stepbrothers are kicking the walls. The doors are rattling and the windows tremble. My stomach is churning like the blades on a hand-driven lawn mower. My sister and brothers begin to scream and cry.

Without a word about the turmoil, though, Mama says, "Y'all were playing, huh?"

"Playing?" I ask. "We were trying to put our clothes in the dresser, when John and Levi started messing with us."

"Oh, shut up, boy! Don't start lying," she says angrily.

* * *

"I'm asking you a question, damn it! Who is that woman?" Martha asks hotly.

"I don't know," I respond. "*You* snatched the phone." And then I blurt out, "A friend."

Martha's eyes are blazing red-hot, and her nostrils flare as if she were a bull facing a matador. "A FRIEND?" she says. "A WOMAN friend? What *friend*?"

"A friend . . . Someone I'm helping out."

"Tell that woman not to call you anymore. And if you don't, I'll do it for you," she says icily.

She's still ranting as I pull up into the garage. I jump out of the car like a convict escaping from prison, practically before it even comes to a complete stop. I race straight to my private sanctuary: my basement office.

I lock the door and push an office chair under the doorknob for extra protection. She's right behind me, running down the stairs. She bangs on the door pacing back and forth like a lion, screaming, yelling, and cursing without the slightest restraint.

"I told you before to stop messing with these women! Didn't I?" she demands.

SILENCE.

Does she expect me to argue with her? Defend myself? Yes, as crazy as she is, she does expect that. But I've learned that not talking can quell her anger faster than arguing can. These tirades frighten me. I know she'll eventually go away, but I'm getting a headache. I look in my desk drawer and find a bottle of aspirin. I shake out two pills and swallow hard.

Martha is trying another angle: threatening me with all manner of things. "I'm gonna to cut off your cell phone! I'll burn your fingers off, so you never answer a phone again!" she screams.

I don't take that one seriously, because I pay my own bills—and hers, too.

"The law is: No more phone calls! Do you hear me?"

I've tuned her out.

Her rampage continues. "I will take all your money!"

SILENCE.

Why does she keep saying that over and over again?

As things cool down I remember something important: *I am starving.*

I open my mini refrigerator. I keep it in this office for times just like these. I pull out some bread and peanut butter.

"I guess we'll eat this tonight?" asks Jimmy Mack.

"I'd rather eat a sandwich for dinner than face her rage."

During the commotion, I can hear Lulu barking and whimpering outside my door. I'm afraid to open it until I'm sure that Martha is not lurking around, waiting to attack me by surprise.

Finally, an hour later, I hear her cursing as she labors up the stairway one step at a time.

Thank God.

A few minutes pass. I hear her stomping on the kitchen floor, banging pots and pans. I guess all that bitching is making her hungry. She's clearly trying to make me angry, but she's not gonna to succeed. She must be on the phone; I hear snippets of her conversation. She is talking to our daughter, then to our son, yakking like a monkey.

"Let that bitch just try calling him again," I hear her say.

Trying to put the chaotic scene behind me, I open my computer to see if Jeanette has e-mailed. Although I'm still procrastinating about seeing her, it is times like these I need to hear from her most. I need her cheerful and energetic spirit. I rely on her to calm my nerves and help me make some sense of my chaotic life. All through the past year and a half I've been longing for her every day. Even though we broke up, I am still pining for her.

"You complain to her. Tell the truth, man," says Jimmy Mack. "You ventilate, that's all you do. You need to get serious, man."

"Jimmy Mack you always tells it like it is."

I really need to read that book of hers. But I'm afraid of what she might have written, so I procrastinate. Even though I know I'm making another stupid mistake, nearly as bad as the first: breaking up with her.

The next morning Martha nearly corners me as I am heading to my bathroom. I manage to skirt through the door and slam it behind me, then bathe as fast as I can. I grab a scone and a glass of juice, which I drink standing at the kitchen counter. And that's where she finds me.

She walks right up in my face and lays down another of Martha's Cardinal Laws, what she calls the "rules of the house" (never mind that I paid for it): *No women calling on your cell phone.*

This goes along with all the other rules:
You must report your whereabouts to me at all times!
We will eat dinner together every night!
Socialize with whom I tell you to!

And my favorite, *I promise you, I will take every penny you have!*

I feel I have no alternative but to comply. What's a man to do?

"Cuss her out," says Jimmy Mack.

I start to hyperventilate. Lulu runs up and rubs her head against my pants leg. *Damn! I'm a prisoner,* I think. But I don't say anything, just stare at Martha. My goal now is to get out of the house as quickly as I possibly can.

So I turn and dart to the garage as if my pants were on fire. I jump in my car and speed away. I'm fuming inside, barely able to grip the steering wheel. I dial Rebecca as fast as I can and escape for some S and S. I'm trying to be Christian but, taking a quote from Maya Angelou, Martha makes me sin eighty times a day.

"Having an affair? You're sinning," says Jimmy Mack.

"I know, but what am I to do? I need to have some fun. What's wrong with that?" I ask.

"Don't you feel guilty?" asks Jimmy Mack.

"It's just sex—what am I gonna do?"

* * *

Two days later I am in my home office. Instead of staying in her own office, Martha is hanging around mine as usual. My cell phone rings. As soon as Martha hears it, she bolts right up out of her chair and hovers over me like a buzzard over a dead carcass.

"Hello?" I say into the phone.

"Is this Jasper Beamon?" asks an unfamiliar male voice.

"Yes," I answer suspiciously.

"Are you free to take a telephone call from Jeanette Priceless?" the man asks.

The hairs on my chest and arms prick up like a needle on a porcupine. It has now been more than fourteen months since I heard her voice.

"Yes, I am." I don't know his voice. But neither that nor Martha's intrusion in any way diminishes the thrill I feel at the chance to talk to Jeanette again.

"Hi, Jasper," says Jeanette, bubbling with so much enthusiasm that I can feel it permeating through the phone. "Can you talk?"

"For a minute or two."

"Martha is eavesdropping, man," says Jimmy Mack. "Look at her ears perking up like a hunting dog on the trail!"

She leans close into me. I feel the hairs rise up on the back of my neck.

"I contacted you several times about reading my novel since November and you haven't done it yet. You said you were gonna to read it ASAP."

"I messed up."

SILENCE.

"Your wife answered the phone when I called the other day, you know," she continues.

I know it all too well, I think as I recall how emasculated I felt—Martha said she knew it was one of my women.

"Do I hear someone?"

"Yes," I say feeling like Joe Frazier dangling on the rope.

"Like a boxed-in prizefighter," says Jimmy Mack.

Martha coughing. I can only hope Martha thinks I'm talking to a man. What will she do to me if she finds out . . . ? The thought terrifies me.

But the paranoia doesn't stop there. Jeanette has written a book, and I think she wants to blackmail me! I've got to discourage her from publishing it.

One of the other phones rings, and Martha reluctantly shuffles out of the room, shuffling and coughing, to answer it. *Lucky me.*

"I'm an old retired man now," I say. "My life is an open book."

"'It is now sho' 'nuff," says Jimmy Mack.

"You got that right, Jasper," she says. "You hit the nail right on the head." Jeanette bursts out laughing in that trademark cackle of hers, and I imagine her throwing her head back at the same time.

"What's the best way to communicate with you? Call you on your home number?" she asks pulling my leg.

"E-mail me."

"E-mail you, okay," she says. "While I have you on the phone, though, I'd like to ask you to call me Thursday between four thirty and nine p.m. at (202) 555-1212."

"Yeah. I will."

I quickly say goodbye and place the telephone back in its cradle, as gentle as a mother placing a newborn in a crib, before Martha returns with her nose poised and sniffing for the kill.

I toss and turn during the night. I dream the worst. I envision a "tell all" book in which Jeanette uses my name and discusses the intimate details of our former relationship.

"I'm just a prisoner—a prisoner of love!" Jimmy Mack imitates James Brown, singing the song of the same name Karaoke-style

Instead of waiting until Thursday, I call her the first thing in the morning as I head out to the church.

"I'm gonna to Texas next week," I tell her, "but I'll call you when I get there." Again, I am avoiding setting a date to read that book.

"What are you gonna to do out there?"

"Take a course on how to train business executives."

"Really?" Jeanette says, and I can hear the smile in her voice. "I think you know how to do that." She's always making me question my actions and reflect on myself, which is disconcerting but a necessary practice for me. She has more confidence in me than I have in myself. The end result: She gives me the confidence I lack. "You *were* a successful business owner, or have you forgotten?"

"No, I haven't. This is different. It's an organized program."

"I see," she says. But I know, just by the intonation of her words, that she thinks I can do this myself. She's right again.

We chitchat like old friends. "What've you been doing?" "I'm relaxing in my room—away from the pressure of being under the twenty-four-hour surveillance of Ms. Martha."

"My best friend got married," she says.

I have pressing issues to talk about with Jeanette. I'm trying to be polite, but I'm really not thrilled to be talking about weddings. I had to finance my daughter's a couple years back. That set me back $10,000. After her wedding, I had to help her move a house full of furniture to Florida. I begrudge her for that, too. At least I'm doing more than my father did for me. I kept a roof over their heads and made sure they have plenty to eat and clothes on their backs. My own father never did as much when I was a child.

I'm not entirely selfish, though the truth is, Jeannie doesn't talk about her family as much as I talk about my money and other troubles. In facts, it's usually *she* who listens to *me*. I keep her ears stinging with news about my problems. And I'm itching to tell her about a couple of things gonna on right now. But for the moment I can forget about that darn book! I do my best to hold back, slipping into the conversation like it's a pair of comfortable pajamas.

"I've hired an architectural firm to construct the new addition to our church," I say. I'm the interim pastor—the church administrator. That makes me responsible for basically running the whole church. But I'm afraid of making a colossal mistake. It has taken me more than two years to select the new pastor. I keep making the same mistake over and over again. I don't know why I'm so afraid of making decisions, both about the church and about women. I avoid it like most men avoid marriage.

When I was a CEO, decision-making was easier—I had my partners to help me out. I feel more pressure now, though.

The wrong decision could bring a wave of criticism and ridicule down on my head from my haughty church members . . . like Trustee Anderson. I fear a throwback to being abused by the Grimes boys.

"Huge burden, but you wanted it, big boy," interjects Jimmy Mack.

Decisions scare the hell outta me. The good Lord knows I'm not good at deciding who to marry, either.

"You thought she would add something to you," says Jimmy Mack.

Shaking my head wearily, I say, "You're right. I thought she would improve my image." She's caused me a lot of sleepless nights.

Most people join a church to establish a spiritual relationship with God. I joined Mount Mariah Baptist Church because of its status in the community. Mount Mariah is highly regarded for its historical background and its large rich congregation of which I'm proud to belong. Like becoming an Omega man, it makes me feel better about myself, at least on the surface. I've been a member for thirty years, and currently I rank in the hierarchy of the church as a deacon. I feel this position was bestowed on me because of my wealth, which just reinforces my attachment to the Almighty Greenback.

"When will the church addition be finished?" Jeanette asks.

"Over the summer, in July. At least, I hope so," I say nervously. "Another fiasco like the one this winter . . ." I don't want to even think of it. It made me feel like resigning from the deacon board. I was so afraid.

"What fiasco, Deacon Beamon?" she laughs playfully.

"You know the one I'm talking about. The incident of the missing church funds—you heard about it? When the church van driver stole a large sum of money from the church?"

"Oh!" she says. Then she quickly switches to the subject of most interest to her now.

"Jasper, all this talking is fine, but you have got to read the book."

"Read the book . . . ," I say noncommittally.

"I don't know why you're taking so long!" she replies.

I am afraid. Maybe she wrote about my secret life with Rebecca. And if Martha finds out—there goes my money and my reputation. Because of the intimate knowledge Jeanette has, I might have to face a lot of stuff I've refused to deal with: my abusive childhood, my hypocritical lifestyle, my affair with Rebecca, the love between Jeanette and me. So much, it give me a migraine headache.

"Man, you're afraid to face YOURSELF," says Jimmy Mack.

"*I can't do it. I can't.*"

"I know you're afraid, but I want to protect you, so readers will not be able to know who you are," says Jeanette impatiently. Almost as an afterthought she says childishly, "I thought you would be proud of me."

"You know I am."

"Oooo-weeeee," says Jimmy Mack.

"Listen, I just turned into the church parking lot. Let me get back to you in a day or two. I promise I'm gonna to read it," I say anxiously. I'm dog tired from worrying about it all night long.

"When?" she asks, perturbed.

"Soon," I snap back. *I wish she would stop pushing me. She's scaring the life out of me.*

"You crazy," says Jimmy Mack. "She's trying to help you, man."

"Don't wait until it's too late," says Jeannie.

ZING!

"Sounds like a warning to me," says Jimmy Mack.

* * *

CHAPTER 7

"Before you run, check to see if the
bulldog has teeth."

Les Brown

"**B**ASTID!"

*I bolt upright in my bed. Where am I? With my
pajama top I wipe the sweat off my face, trying to
orientate myself. It has been many years since I lived with
my stepfamily, many years since I was in Vietnam. I'm still
having nightmares about both experiences. The carnage I
witnessed in the Nam, and the ridicule and harassment the
Grimes' put me through, haunt me every night and day. Add
that to Jeanette's manuscript, and my life is a living hell.*

How do I cope with all this? By behaving worst than
before, exceeding my previous avoidance tactics. I run like

an escaped convict, traveling like a roadrunner and attending church like a religious zealot. I travel so much, I feel like James Brown on his 1999 whirlwind tour through the Bible belt. Augusta, Georgia. Kinston, North Carolina. Raleigh, North Carolina. Waco, Texas. I'm traveling from place to place, ducking and dodging Jeanette, trying to outrun this bullet aimed right at my back.

Time goes by. The more I run, the more insistent Jeanette becomes and the more scared I get. If I am not traveling, I am planning church meetings or attending retreats—anything to run away from that book. My track and field talent has certainly come in handy.

I drag my fatigued, frightened body and soul to church seven days weeks, like I'm a Pentecostal Holiness preacher. On Sunday I am there all day, from morning until night. I attend every possible church service I can, including Bible study, and even teach Sunday school when a teacher is needed. I even start a finance ministry to talk about the global economic crisis, secretly hoping it will relieve me of my fears about my own bank account.

"And to avoid being locked up again," says Jimmy Mack matter-of-factly.

"Don't remind me."

Oprah Winfrey said, "If you are willing to deal with the past, you can make the moment you are in rich." But I'm not sure how to deal with my past, so each moment is a mystery to me. But soon, I'm tested like never before.

"Soon and very soon . . . you are gonna to see the King," sings Jimmy Mack teasingly.

* * *

It is Memorial Day weekend, last year. As soon as I hear Martha's car back out of the driveway, I race around my fifteen-thousand-square-foot house with Lulu right on my heel, I let out an ecstatic, "WHEEEEEEE!!!"

Martha has left for the beach. Every year she spends at least one week with a group of friends at my beach house on Emerald Isle. She returns with several pounds of butterfish, and believe me when I say I don't know who smells worse, her or the fish.

Unfortunately, my jubilance at her departure is short-lived. Two days later, tragedy strikes. As best I care to remember, I hadn't even sat down good in my investor's office before he said, "I . . . I don't know how to tell you this . . ."

"Tell me what?" I shouted.

"Mr. Beamon, I'm sorry. Your portfolio has decreased by ten million dollars."

"You lost my MONEY! Tell me you're joking! TELL ME!" I scream.

* * *

For my financial ministry sessions, I consult a professor of economics from Howard University to give a talk on the current economic crisis in America. I'm delighted to make this connection because Howard University is the higher educational home of the woman I adore. Furthermore, Omega Psi Phi fraternity was founded on the Howard campus. In fact, it is a charter member of the exclusive "Divine Nine," an association of the most influential African American fraternities and sororities in the United States, the majority of which were founded on this illustrious campus. I guess that's one of the reasons why Howard is called "the Mecca."

Our sessions are held once a week, which is out of the norm because most ministries hold meetings only once a month, but I've got to keep busy. I facilitate the twelve-week course based in part on *Washington Post* financial columnist Michelle Singletary's book *The Power to Prosper: 21 Days to Financial Freedom.* We discuss tactics for saving money as opposed to spending relentlessly using credit cards. It helps participants save money—at least for the twenty-one days. The most enjoyable workshops I hold are on the topic of how to get rich. I use Dennis Kimbro's book *Think and Grow Rich.* These keep my mind off things, since I think about money like I think about Jeanette: ninety percent of the time. I spend most of that time thinking about why I became rich and worrying (needlessly, some may say) about keeping it, even now.

In 1950s and 1960s the South where I grew up was mainly an agricultural economy in which the overwhelming majority of sharecroppers were blacks; of course, I knew that personally but it's also true according to Dr. Henry Gates, Jr., in his book, *Finding Oprah's Roots.* Blacks were highly skilled farmers—using skills learned from their slave ancestors—but most of them, like my stepfather, did not own land and had no assets or money. Consequently, they were obligated to sharecrop, a system controlled entirely by white landowners, to make a living.

Sharecropping, which literally means "sharing crops," was an unequal and ruthless business practice. In fact, the more accurate term would be "slave cropping," because the landowners made all the decisions and kept practically all the money—up to ninety percent of the profits. Although blacks were technically free, they were still enslaved to a devastating economic system. Landowners dictated the crops black farmers could plant, the price of labor for harvesting the crops, and the amount paid for the harvest. In order to farm, most black farmers had to obtain cash advances to buy seed, farming equipment, and other necessities, with interest up to thirty percent and terms more unscrupulous than today's check cashing stores. The sharecropping system was backed up with threats and terrorist tactics: lynching, beatings, burning of homes, and the enforcement of Jim Crow laws.

I remember vividly the fall my stepfather Pete made me go with him to the tobacco auction. The flat beds of autumn leaves, the pungent smell of tobacco, the rumbling voice of the auctioneer—it was all so fascinating and unique to me at first. The jingling sound of money was joyful music to my poor ears.

Sadly, it all turned sour.

Pete's crop of tobacco was always underrated and judged substandard although most of the time it was brilliant, golden, and cured just right. That fall the auctioneer, Melvin—a white, freckle-faced young man with a tongue faster than Cassius Clay's—stared down at Pete's harvest, and faster than a Pentecostal preacher he said, "Your crop's alright, but you could do better."

Melvin deliberately counted the money quickly into Pete's hand. "Fifty dollars!" he shouted.

Pete's eyebrows shot up, then he bowed his head in shame and stuffed the money into his pants pocket, walking away with misery written all over his face.

I was stunned. "You know you just got ripped off, right?" I asked Pete.

"What you talking about, boy?"

"He took you," I repeated. Do I have to make myself clearer? I thought.

"Shut the hell up, boy! You don't know what you talking about."

Okay, whatever. But I knew that Pete had been cheated. It was easy to do since he couldn't read or write or add sums. When the news got back to my classmates, they called him—and me—dumbo. I learned my lesson. At that moment I knew for sure I must get an education and keep account of my own money, which I did. I obtained a Master's in business from the now-defunct Southeastern University in DC, where I once was chairman of the board.

* * *

When Jeanette calls me I'm anxious to tell her my latest traveling news. "I'm leaving on Sunday for Waco for several days." To her, it sounds like just another one of those *I promise I'm gonna to read your manuscript* conversations.

"I see," she says sarcastically "Yeah, you told me," she says sounding disappointed. "You also said you would call me when you got there."

"Yeah, if it doesn't interfere with my football game," I say, and laugh.

"Dr. Phil is right," she says, "Nothing takes the place of football. Nothing."

"Sports addict," I say, but she laughs, too—she knows how much I like football—and it's music to my ears. I feel more like myself. My depression lifts and my nightmares subside.

Just the thought of traveling makes me feel as excited as Michael Jordan hitting the boards.

"As soon as I get settled in, I'll call you," I say.

"Wait until after the Packers game," she insists.

"Her voice is tinged with a little revenge and disappointment," says Jimmy Mack.

"You're probably right," I reply. Man, she is also a big tease. I like it sometimes, but it can get under my skin, too.

Waco, Texas, here I come . . .

* * *

CHAPTER 8

"If thy right eye offends thee, pluck it out."

Matthew 5:2

I have a good flight. I arrive in Texas and take a taxi to my hotel. My argument with Martha has just about flown from my mind, like a chicken from what my stepfather called the "coop." We seem to always end up fighting about two things: my money (like this time, about giving my hard-earned cash to her relatives) and my whereabouts. I am gonna to Texas, so she is losing control of my movements and my whereabouts for a few days—and my money, too. For the hell of it I might just spend a bunch of money; after all, it's mine, isn't it? But I stick to the twenty-one-day spending fast I've been preaching, reminding myself that I'd rather watch my money grow than spend it ruthlessly.

"You go man," says Jimmy Mack.

My training conference in Waco is productive. Or as productive as it can be, under the circumstances. A couple of times, I don't even show up (like when I was in college) for the morning sessions. Really, one of the biggest benefits is just being on my own. Alone in my hotel room, I have more privacy. I fantasize about my getaway scheme and even do a little research on the Internet (now that Martha isn't breathing down my neck) on the possibility of disappearing to that tropical island somewhere. *Do I have the nerve to carry it out?*

I have this compulsion to worry all the time. Thoughts of Jeanette's book are milling around in my head. I don't know what to do. Researching exotic locales and faraway places— island countries I might escape to—eases my anxiety. I also consider places I can go to right here in the States. I even get some tender loving care.

I check the local television stations and tune into the Sunday football game. Any last bad feelings still lingering in the corner of my mind, I blow away like smoke from a pipe. The game is about to come on. It is thrilling to watch the tackling and combat in the hotel, all by myself. I feel as if I've just been paroled. I eat what I want when I want and where I want—on the sofa or in bed watching TV. I leave the dirty dishes on the floor and pig out on french fries. I prop my feet on the coffee table. I even sleep late. I could live like this forever. In fact, it feels like the first day I entered A & T University. The worst of my life, a nuclear meltdown, is over.

* * *

Droves and droves of cars are parked all over the campus, filled with suitcases and college necessities. Melancholic parents are dragging laden trunks in through heavy doors. Excited students struggle with arms loaded full of bags and books. Grandmothers tote grease-stained brown bags filled with fried chicken, potato salad, and collard greens—something to keep those chilluns from starving.

I feel emancipated. I just hightailed it from a communist-occupied family to a democratic university campus. Boy, oh, boy! I feel like running and jumping and singing the five verses of the "Hallelujah" chorus.

Before I left home, my mother begrudgingly said, "Jasper, if you really need me and Pete to take you, we can."

"No," I reply, "I can make it there myself."

So I've arrived, sans my "affectionate family," in my beat-up blue Ford Mustang, a car I bought with the money I saved this summer selling vegetables from my grandparents' garden. I'm never gonna back to the Grimes home again. Not one holiday. Not one summer vacation. I feel giddy and relieved. I've escaped, even if it's just to a local haven situated only thirty miles away. I've left behind the chaos and the craziness of my dysfunctional family.

"Welcome to the dorm," the resident assistant says. "Glad you're here."

Gazing around the room, I giggle to myself, shamefaced. "Thanks!" I linger in the doorway of my pint-size palace. Then I rush around the room, opening doors and pulling out drawers and unpacking my clothes. I put what few garments I have in a dresser the size of a bank vault: socks in one drawer, underwear in another . . .

College is all that I have been waiting for and more!

* * *

I watch the game, which is heavenly, and then finally I call Jeannie about reading her novel, which I dread.

We exchange greetings, and I get right to the point.

"You asked me to call you today, so I am," I say. "Calling you."

"What's gonna on?" she asks.

Does she think I'm Marvin Gaye? I think angrily. She contacted me first. What does she want? First Martha, now Jeanette.

"How was your trip?" she asks.

"I'm calling about the book," I say, testily. "I'm calling because I said I would call you. About the book."

"Stop acting like Doctor Jekyll," says Jimmy Mack.

Impatiently Jeanette says, "For the hundredth time, when do you want to read it?"

"As soon as I can—I'm not sure right now. Like I say, I'm gonna to be down here in training several days." She's always yakking and yakking about reading that book. Darn it! I feel like turning off my phone and never contacting her again.

Cool it, I say to myself.

"You are pissed with yourself," says Jimmy Mack.

I throw my shoes across the floor. "You're right again, Jimmy Mack. I have mixed emotions."

"Lord knows I would be very angry with you," says Jimmy Mack.

"I came here to get away from all this stuff!"

"You can read it while you're down there," she says.

"I'm not sure. They keep us busy from seven in the morning to eight at night." The truth is, I'm still trying to buy time.

"You're blaming them?" says Jimmy Mack.

"Oh," says Jeanette. She knows me well, and I can tell from her tone that she knows I am vacillating.

You're nickel slick," says Jimmy Mack.

I say nothing.

"Is there something wrong?" Jeanette asks.

"No!" I snap. I realize that I'm taking out my anger on her. I am angry with Martha . . . and myself. And I am taking it out on Jeanette. So I try again. "So what's this book about?"

"It's about me . . . and our relationship," she says.

Even though I don't believe that she's telling me the whole truth, I pretend I do. I *need* to believe her—for my own sanity.

"I'll call you when I get back, and we'll set up a definite time, okay?'

"Okay," she says.

I hang up the phone and fall on the hotel bed, lying beneath the western-style sheets, feeling depressed and angry. Memories, memories—hurtful, painful, unbearable memories. Shame and ridicule accompany images of the Grimes boys taunting me, images that flash and hum like a cold refrigerator in my head.

"I didn't handle that right," I say to Jimmy Mack. He feels warm and comforting, like a teddy bear, as he crawls around in my PJs.

I'm too scared to believe anything. It's just me.

The thought of returning makes me feel like I am drowning in a rainstorm. I have to face Martha. I have to face this book.

* * *

As soon as I arrive back in town after the conference, I send Jeanette this e-mail:

Hi, Jeanette:

   I'm back in town for a few days . . . but I'll be leaving again very soon.

                                            . . . Jasper

"Sure," says Jimmy Mack.

A few days after getting back from Texas I call Jeanette again. It's Monday, and I'm in the church basement. Alone. I figure this is a safe place. I let her phone ring three times—she's not home. "Lucky me," I say gleefully to Jimmy Mack. *Don't have to deal with that book . . .*

Before I go to bed that night, I sneak down to my office and send Jeanette a quickie.

I'm in town for one more day. Call you soon.

> *... Jasper*

Wilson and Raleigh, North Carolina, here I come.

* * *

CHAPTER 9

"Waiting too long to take
corrective action could
be dangerous."

David Frost

M y time is up.

On Thursday, March 26, I receive another e-mail
from Jeanette. She has reached her breaking point. I
don't blame her. She lays me out with one final punch:

Dear Jasper:

*As you may have guessed, the reason that I've been want-
ing you to review my novel is that it is an account of our*

relationship. You are one of the main characters. I want to give you the opportunity to read it and suggest any changes to things that could identify you as Jasper F. Beamon.

Because of my concern for your well-being and my desire to conduct this in a professional and respectful manner, I have not discussed this over the telephone. But since November 26 I have tried to get you to read this book. I have texted, and telephoned you, I have cajoled and nudged. All to no avail. I am burdened and bothered by your indecisiveness and irresponsible lack of response to my requests.

In addition, I am under a deadline. I need to hear from you by 2:00 p.m., Friday, March 27. If I have not heard from you nor received a firm timeline or a commitment to review my manuscript, expect to receive an official letter, after which I will know that you are not concerned about the contents and are not interested in reviewing or making any changes therein.

Again, I only want to protect you. Herewith is my availability for the three days in question:

- *Friday 5:30–10:00 (after that time I will be in slumber land and not available for intelligent, lifelike, or earthly communication);*
- *Saturday 9:00–noon;*
- *Sunday until noon.*

I expect you to make a firm commitment to read it on one of these days.

Jeanette Louise Priceless

She's signed her whole name and sent me a copy of the e-mails from back in January saying I was gonna to read the book. I know I'm in trouble now. I feel like a miner trapped fifty miles underground.

"Oh my God," I moan to Lulu and Jimmy Mack.

Lulu slobbers all over my face. I don't even notice the saliva dribbling down my neck.

"I told you so," says Jimmy Mack.

I can't answer right away because Martha swoops over me like a buzzard over a carcass. Finally *I* e-mail her back:

Dear Jeanette,

I know I have postponed it too many times—it's my fault. A little frightened, you know. I'll try not to be so anxious.

That night, I don't sleep a wink.

The next day, Friday, March 27, at 9:27 a.m., as soon as Martha goes to the bathroom, my fingers are airborne the minute I hear water running in the sink. I peck and hunt as if I'm on a rescue mission. This is the note I send to Jeanette:

Hi, Jeanette:

I'm in Carolina and won't return until next Thursday, April 2. When I talked to you last about this, you said the book was not about me. Are you mentioning my name, or is the character known by a fictional name? I definitely will make every effort to review as much of it as I possibly can on Friday, April 3, or Saturday, April 4. Which is better for you? Shall we meet during the day?

PLEASE DON'T SEND IT as I am afraid that Martha might get a hold of it—or worse.

...Jasper

When I say "or worse" I'm thinking of that weasel Trustee Anderson. I know I sound mentally unstable. In these back-and-forth communications with Jeanette I'm paranoid, one step from becoming a suicide bomber.

Martha enters my office like a CIA operative scanning the room. She strains her neck like a long-necked Canadian goose, hoping to see whom I have written. I hit the send button like my fingers are on a coal burner.

"Have you seen the grocery store flyer?" she says suspiciously.

"No."

When she leaves for the store, I check my messages. There is one from Jeanette.

Hi Jasper,

I got your message. You are making me very nervous. That is why, among other reasons, I don't like to talk about important things on the telephone and via the Internet—so much is lost in the translation. No, this is a novel. No, I do not mention your name. Again, I want you to check it out so it doesn't identify you. I'll discuss the details when I meet you. Either day is fine with me.

Jeanette

I am very scared, so scared that I send her another e-mail saying I don't know whether she got the first one.

Hi, Jeanette:

I'm sorry for making you anxious. I apologize. You naturally raised my curiosity when you said I am the main character in the book. But, like you said, so much can be lost in e-mails and phone calls.

I plan to come start reviewing the book on Friday morning, April 3, from 9:00 to 1:00 or 1:30. I have a meeting to attend in the afternoon. If I don't finish, which I doubt I will, I will make another date to read it ASAP.

Jasper

I check my messages many times after this, typing furiously to get into my mailbox while Martha is out. My fingers are cramping—I think I might have carpal tunnel syndrome.

Saturday morning I check my messages again. My heart is skipping beats, and the blood is rushing to my brain. *Oh!* She has returned my message.

If you read fast, you should finish maybe some of it but I doubt you will finish it before your meeting. So, Friday it is. I look forward to seeing you. You won't finish it in four or five hours.

Jeanette

Friday. I can't even think about it. If I could get back down there and read that novel any sooner, I would.

Maybe it's like she says: She is concerned about my privacy. She wants me to review the manuscript before an editor sees it and makes final decisions on the content. She wants to be sure that I am not identified, that the book shows no evidence of our intimate relationship. I'm still very nervous, though.

"No man, you're so paranoid. She told you to read it a thousand times before? I hope you get it straight now," says Jimmy Mack.

* * *

CHAPTER 10

"A brother is a friend given by Nature."

Jean Baptist Legouve

’m headed for Raleigh, North Carolina, to my brother's house. I call Jeanette, singing as free as a butterfly. "I've been visiting Martha's relatives in Kinston, North Carolina," I explain when she answers. "Her aunt is very sick again."

"Oh!"

"What does she care about anything having to do with Martha?" says Jimmy Mack. "I told you about that before. Keep on . . . and one day you are gonna to regret it. You need to use some common sense. "I sent you an e-mail," I say to Jeanette.

Her reply is "I didn't get it."

My heart thumps like a musician playing the tuba. *Where in the world did it go?*

"I really did send it."

"You're in Carolina?" says Jeanette. "Mr. Travel-a-Lot!"

"She's disappointed with you, Jasper," translates Jimmy Mack, "but happy to hear from you because she knows she'll see you soon."

I don't know what Jeanette thinks of my telling her about my in-laws' business. But I can only procrastinate for so long.

"I'm gonna to follow up as soon as I get back," I say to Jimmy Mack. I promise I will keep my appointment.

"Okay. She's cool for the time being."

"I know she doesn't trust me."

"Who would?"

"My brother's sick, too," I tell Jeanette. "He had a stroke two weeks ago."

"Oh!" she says, her compassion audible.

To garner more sympathy, I say, "This is his second. He had one when he was fifty."

"Oh, wow," says Jeannie.

"I'm on my way to see him now."

"You're in your car?"

"Yeah."

"Isn't it dangerous, driving and talking?" she asks.

"I have my telephone speaker hooked up to my dash-board," I tell her. "You remember?"

"Yes, I do," she says, her voice nostalgic.

"Jeanette sounds like she wants to see me!" I say to Jimmy Mack.

"Sounds a little like that, but I think she wants money or your help in some way," says Jimmy Mack. "Maybe she thinks the book, once you read it, will make you be a better person. Or maybe she is trying to protect you, like she said. I've got it—she is nurturing feelings for you. She wants you back. How would I know?"

"How's your class coming along?" she asks, then clarifies, "The business training you took in Waco?"

"Fine. I haven't done any work with it. With all these folks sick . . . " I say.

She pauses. "How long will it take you to get to the city limits?"

"About an hour and thirty minutes," I say.

Another pause. "Have you been doing anything interesting since you retired?" she asks.

"Nothing in particular. My wife makes all these appointments and . . . we go out to dinner almost every night."

"Uh-huh," she says. I detect a slight bit of sarcasm in her voice. She's probably turning up her nose and making an ugly face right now, which I find amusing and cute as a baby's babble. Disappointed, Jeanette asks, "I thought you were gonna to call me to make a follow-up appointment? What happened, Jasper?"

"So I have to make another appointment with you now, huh, Jeanette? I'm . . . I'm just so busy . . . with church stuff and . . . and Martha's relatives," I say, banging my fist on the steering wheel. I'll do it when I come on Friday, April 3.

Lulu starts barking. She knows I'm insulted.

"Quiet, quiet. Why should I have to make another appointment to see you?" I say indignantly. That's not the way it used to be. Then I touch Jimmy Mack for comfort.

"Because you take too long, and I'm not always available," she says.

My throat tightens like a pair of latex gloves. "Yes," I gulp. *Oh my God!* My head starts pounding like 'Jack' wedging a sledge hammer. I try to keep my mind on the road.

"Jasper? Are you there?" "Let me read you a few pages. SILENCE.

"Yes. Okay," I say, leery of what I will hear.

"Whaddya think?" she asks about the part she just read. "You like it?"

SILENCE.

"So . . . give me some feedback on the part I read."

"Okay, just give me a minute. I need to check something," I say. I can't let Jeannie know I'm frightened. My Lexus swerves to the right. I brake and miss an oncoming car by a nostril hair. My car hits the frozen shoulder of the road, like a basketball bouncing out of bounds. I jump out of the car, rush down a long ravine, and jerk my head around, watching the passing cars swerve overhead. I heave violently like a pregnant woman with morning sickness.

"Everything okay?" she says, her voice full of concern.

"Yes, everything is fine. I was checking my front tire. I thought I was losing pressure. But it's okay now."

"Good. Now back to my novel. *Whaddya think?*"

"Good. Good," I manage to say. "You're some writer."

"Thank you. Oh, and guess who I have as my legal representative and literary agent? He's a powerful attorney who's represented some famous authors. William Blackwood. You heard of him?" Teasing me again.

"No." *And I don't want to,* I think while massaging Lulu, who's on the passenger seat beside me. But still I ask, "Who's William Blackwood?"

She's really scaring me now. Somewhere inside, I manage to feel proud of her writing talent—but I don't want to know any lawyers. I don't want to have anything to do with them. I have nightmares about battling Martha in divorce court with a cadre of lawyers working on her behalf to take my money.

"I wrote him, and he answered me back in less than ten days. He thinks highly of my work. I'm really proud of it. I must be a good writer, huh?"

"Yeah, you must be," I say, feeling all sorts of things: sad, sincere, proud, conflicted.

"Would you like to see a copy of the letter he sent me?"

I hesitate. But Lulu jumps up, as if she wants to read the letter herself. *What can I say, huh, Lulu? I don't want to see.* I think to myself, scratching the scruff of her neck. "Sure, e-mail it to me." I can read it quickly so Martha won't catch me.

But the thought of reading even a letter makes my stomach queasy. The list of problems I'm gonna to have play through my mind again: My name and reputation out there for all the world to see. Things I have to face up to: my sexual relationship with Rebecca, my hypocritical life as a deacon, the inauthentic life I live. I feel frightened about getting any communication whatsoever from a woman, because Martha has some vigilant eyes. I visualize her hovering over me like a secret service agent. Once I finish reading it, I'll have to shred it like a paper-cutting machine.

"Jeanette, I'm near the city limits. Gotta concentrate on the driving." I hate to hang up but I am anxious to stop talking about the book. "I'll call you soon. You have done a lot of work on this book. I will be in touch soon."

* * *

I pull into the state capital, exhausted from my drive and from thinking about this damn book. I feel like letting loose, but I know now is not the time. "Big brother" is needed.

Richard is my most fragile and youngest sibling; this is his second stroke. He was the quiet one and probably one of the most frightened (besides myself) whenever there were fights in the Grimes household. He used to run and hide in the closet for safety and, I suppose, to shut out the violent noises. Come to think of it, though, I used to dash to the closet faster than he did. The thought makes me feel ashamed. We're probably all still suffering from growing up among the Grimes family terrorists.

I pull up to Richard's 1950s ranch-style house, a mere hut compared to my mansion, dreading what I might see.

Walking into his small living room, I spot posters on the walls: Dr. King, John Kennedy, and Malcolm X. I drop my tired body down in his burgundy rocking chair, close my eyes, and rock back and forth, trancelike. Humming to myself, I watch Lulu out of my left eye. She is inspecting Richard's house like it's a dog's arboretum.

My cell phone pings—I have an IM, an instant message. *I can't believe my eyes*. It's from Charles Anderson. On the subject line are three terrifying letters: FYI. He has forwarded me the last e-mail message I wrote to Jeanette. It went to him accidentally.

"*Could I have done that?*" I say in horror. My fever shoots up like a bad case of malaria. I feel like whooping and hollering. *What does he think? Does he know who Jeanette is? What is he gonna to do?* I try to control myself by grabbing hold of the creases in my pants.

Richard is a Pentecostal Holiness preacher who's been on sick leave these past six months. His church, in a small village just outside Raleigh, has a congregation small enough to fit in a corner store. He's a younger version of myself, though several inches taller (height I wish I had). When he shuffles into the living room with his cane, he's wearing preppy, red-striped flannel pajamas and smoking a foul-smelling Cuban cigar—a gift to him from a church member who hoped to encourage him to quit smoking cigarettes forever.

It reminds me of the dreadful tobacco auctions that cheated my stepfather out of large sums of money.

Richard looks better than I thought he would, thank God. I don't know whether I'd be able to take it if he looked otherwise. No harm, but I can't stand looking at sick people. Even if they are my relatives.

"You're looking pretty good," I say. "You're looking good."

"How's everything?" Richard asks.

My thumping heart drowns out Richard's next words. His mouth is moving, but I can't understand anything he is saying. I reach forward and hug him. I've never been too good at giving affection or receiving it from people, with the exception of my three blood siblings and, of course, you know whom. But I do love to hug. I stand quickly and put my arms around him like he's a POW. I know his financial condition, so I slip an envelope stuffed with cash in his PJs pocket as we hug each other tight like blood brothers do.

"Not too bad," Richard says. His right hand flies automatically to his head, getting caught in a curl of his beautiful kinky hair—still black, even at his age. He puffs on his cigar, to my dismay, drawing on it three times as I imagine Castro would.

"Oh, Richard, those cigars stink . . . Please."

Lulu runs up to Richard and sniffs his heel.

"And who is this cute fellow?"

"My dog," I say. "Say hello, Lulu." Lulu barks excitedly and skips around him in a frenzy.

"You got a dog?"

"Yeah. You know, that's what they recommend these days."

"*They* who?" asks Richard, his brown eyes smiling and laughing at me as smoke billows in my direction.

"She's good company for me, Richard. Should you be smoking?"

"Oh, Jasper! Live a little, man."

"That's what I'm trying to help *you* do—live a little longer!"

"You know, you're my big brother and I admire your success. And we've discussed your moving to an island and getting a divorce all the time—maybe for the last twenty-five years. You say you gonna to do this and that—and yet you have done nothing but talk. But there's no point, so I give up."

"Richard, give your old brother a break, huh? I apologize for getting up here so late, "Martha's aunt, Joyce, is hospitalized again. The one who raised her."

"That one—the hypochondriac?" laughs Jimmy Mack.

I laugh too. "Yeah. Doctors ought to know better than to operate on an old woman."

"That's too bad. How's Martha doing?" asks Richard.

"Same old, same old. We argued about my coming here."

Richard sighs. "What's the problem *now*?"

"With Martha . . . or Aunt Joyce?" I ask.

"I know what the hell's wrong with Martha," he grins. "I'm talking about her aunt."

"Acute pneumonia." I give him a look.

He ignores it. "I'm not even gonna to talk about it, Jasper. I keep praying for you. But I don't see why you put up with that . . . that blank-blank woman. Lord forgive me! A woman like yours makes me lose my religion." He sighs again. "I just don't get it."

I sit back down, cringing, as I pat Lulu. She jumps up and licks my face. No sound comes out of my mouth. I am too embarrassed.

Finally I say, "I don't want to lose my money."

"Brother, ain't that much money in the world! I've *never* seen a man let a woman control him and his money, too."

"You just wait," I say. "I have a plan."

"Yeah, sure, Jasper, I've heard that one before."

I decide to change the subject. Quickly. "You're looking pretty good."

"Thanks, big brother."

"You said that already," says Jimmy Mack, always there to correct me.

"Have you eaten, Jasper?" Richard asks as he gathers his cane and shuffles into the kitchen. I suddenly notice that despite his stroke, he really does look good.

"Yeah. I'm fine."

Richard's stroke left him paralyzed on the left side of his body. I realize that I don't want to watch him eat anything. Watching him eat is repulsive to me. Watching the food drip down his face would make me want to vomit.

"Are you watching your diet?" I ask. *Not that I'm eating right myself.*

"I'm trying, but if food isn't fried and salty, it don't taste good."

"But you know you got to be careful. You don't want to leave before your time like Mama did."

"I'm trying, brother. You sure you don't want anything? Fried chicken? Ice cream?"

"I'll take some ice cream."

He maneuvers himself to the refrigerator and takes out a package of Neapolitan.

"Let me get it, Richard," I say.

"No, I can do it."

"A scoop or two is all I want. It's better than eating fried chicken."

"You're right about that." He drops two scoops in each bowl. "It's soooo good," says Richard.

"I don't know how you can taste anything."

"Why?"

"With that foul-smelling cigar taste in your mouth."

He abruptly changes the subject. "She's your wife. What can you do? Love 'em . . . or leave 'em."

"It's too costly otherwise," I say dejectedly.

"Yeah," he responds, shaking his head gloomily "You need to leave 'em. You're spending the night?"

I shake my head again. "She told me I had to come back tonight."

"Now, Jasper, I know you're not gonna to drive all the way back down to Kinston tonight! You just got here. She's still jealous, I see."

"Hasn't changed a bit."

"Never will, brother, never will. When you gonna accept that fact or move on?" asks Richard. "How long has it been now? Thirty-five years? Forty? Mama said you never had no common sense." He looks at me. "Sorry, big brother, I shouldn't have said that."

For the next twenty-four hours, I know that phrase is gonna to sound like tinnitus in my ears.

"What did she know?" I scowl. "Let's not talk about it. I'm getting depressed just thinking about both of them. Anyway, I'm working on something."

"Really?" he says, as if he wants to believe me. "Sounds intriguing. Could it be . . . another woman?"

I smile and put another spoonful of ice cream in my mouth. I don't dare tell him about Jeanette or my scheme I've been dreaming about. Instead, I look out the window just as the headlights of a passing car flash across the living room wall. I visualize myself relaxing in a nightclub, some romantic European destination known only to me, Lulu, and Jimmy Mack—and of course, Jeanette.

Just the thought of being a long distance from Martha, if only one hundred miles, gives me the courage to stand up to her. "Richard, you know the saying, 'Distance makes the heart grow fonder'? Sometimes it makes me grow a little courageous." So I call her. I may suffer later, but she's here and I am there.

"I'm spending the night," I tell her firmly. "Yes, yes, I'll be back there tomorrow."

"Are you at Richard's? You sure?" she asks. "I want to speak to him myself," she demands.

"He's sleeping," I say as I place my index fingers to my lips so Richard will be quiet. "I have my cell phone with me. Call anytime. I'll answer, I assure you, Martha."

"You better."

It's a relief and a pleasure to see my brother even though I'm worried about his illness. It is good to get away and spend some time with a real family member who respects and loves me. Later I will focus on my conversation with Jeanette, although Charles Anderson has taken that small pleasure away from me. All in all, I'm proud she's written a book.

* * *

The next morning I leave early. Richard shakes my hand as we stand on the porch.

"When you coming through again, brother?"

"Let me see where I'm at, okay, Richard?" I hug him tightly again. We stuck together when we were kids. When we wanted to spend the summer with our grandparents, we wrote a letter that persuaded my mother, over the objections of my sharecropping stepfather, to let us go. At first, she was gonna to let everyone go but me, but Richard refused to go without me. *I don't know who needs each other the most— him or me.*

I pull away from him reluctantly and slog down the steps. In my Lexus, I put my foot to the floor and head south, driving fast on the road again to Kinston.

With all that's gonna on in my life. I feel overwhelmed. There's Richard's stroke, Jeanette, Martha and her sick aunt, and Charles Anderson added to my list of woes. I need a rest.

* * *

CHAPTER **11**

"The key to change is to let go of fear."

Roseanne Cash

I t's Friday, April 3, at 8:15 a.m. An eighteen-wheeler honks its horn, and I bolt upright like I sat on a veterinarian needle. I'm approaching Washington—getting nearer and nearer to her place—and I'm horrified. Every bump in the road makes me jittery. I'm forty-five minutes early. I punch a button on my cell, and her phone rings. She answers.

Oh my God!

I swallow my terror and speak. "I'm on Fred Drive—close to you, I believe." I gag. "What's your address again?"

She rattles it off.

"Thanks," I say. "I know where I am now."

I am near her house. I know because the streets are clean, the lawns are pruned, and the air is light.

"I'm only ten minutes away," I continue. "I'm early. Do you want me to wait?"

"Yes, please. I'm not ready yet," says Jeanette.

"I'll stay in my car." I hang up.

To Jimmy Mack, I say, "She seems different. This frightens me."

Exactly forty-five minutes later, I walk up to the receptionist's desk, where a college-aged girl is chomping on a BLT sandwich. The aroma of fried bacon makes my stomach queasy. I remember that I didn't eat breakfast.

"Apartment three sixteen," I say. "Jasper for Jeanette Priceless." I watch the girl dial the number on an old-fashioned black rotary telephone.

"Jasper is here," she says when Jeanette answers.

After she hangs up the phone, she says, "Go on up," and turns around toward the television. The channel is switched to MTV.

"Thank you," I say as fear engulfs my spirit.

I take the elevator up and step out into the third-floor hall. My shoes squish on the carpet. My heart trembles. I feel like running away.

This is it.

Warily, I knock on her door. I hold my breath as I hear the chain being unleashed and the tumbler flipping.

She's standing there. And I can only stare, in awe of her beauty. Those come-get-me eyes, the full African lips, that brown-sugar skin.

We greet each other politely. Her long piano-playing fingers release the knob, and she opens the door wider. Her fingers remind me of Martha's and their common creative talents, which makes me more nervous. She moves back a few steps. Blood rushes to my head as her dancer's body mesmerizes.

"Let me take your coat. Make yourself at home," she says, invoking her intoxicating voice.

"She doesn't sound like a blackmailer to me," says Jimmy Mack.

"I hope you're right," I mumble in reply.

When she turns to hang up my coat, I look her over, trying to gauge her intent. I try to keep my mind on the up and up, but my feelings rebound like mattress springs, springing up and down. How am I gonna feel comfortable in the home of my enemy? We haven't seen each other in almost a year and a half. She hasn't changed one iota, as far as I can tell—still ripe as an apple.

I never looked that good in the first place. On my best days I look liked a racially mixed Pee Wee Herman. I've aged noticeably. My mixed gray hair has recessed several inches from my forehead in the past few years. My once-rugged face is now ugli fruit.

"Ooooh! "You feel that way about yourself?" asks Jimmy Mack.

"Yeah."

"Have a seat at the table," says Jeanette.

"Okay."

My love, my idol. How can she do this to me? I ask myself. Langston Hughes' words run through my mind: *Life ain't been no crystal star.* Suddenly, this poetic line rings like a tried-and-true testimony to my life.

"How? Just like you dropped her, remember, fool?" says Jimmy Mack.

We were hanging out in the Dutch Touch. A romantic but deceptive café—modern exterior. Casablanca interior.

One minute I playfully picked her up, hugged her tightly and swung her around. The next thing I remember was running out of that place like my pants were on fire. When she called two weeks later, I told her I couldn't see her ever again. Everything I owned was on the line. Money . . . EVERYTHING.

You need professional help, she kept repeating.

On the radio, Bob Marley is singing "Coming in from the Cold." I stagger across her living-room as if I am tramping on broken glass. I plop my favorite gold-and-purple hat on a dainty, heart-shaped mahogany table. I march directly to the dining-room table like the sailor I once was. This is the first time I've ever been in her place. And yet, I realize my fate is cast in a blazing fire.

"May I offer you something to drink? Tea?"

"Tea sounds fine," I mutter.

I watch her as she moves intently around the small kitchen, lacey curtains floating behind her in the wind. Colorful African baskets and a framed beach scene hang on the wall. Soon I hear the kettle sputtering. The aroma of chamomile drifts into the dining area. I take a few breaths to calm myself. I pray fervently to myself. I hope she isn't planning to do anything to dirty my reputation, to ruin me. I try to stay positive.

The book is sitting right in front of me at the edge of the maple table, a pile of white paper looking as venomous as a Black Mamba—I need to discern its purpose. I am about to learn this is only a fraction of the manuscript.

"I need to know what's on all those pages!" I say to Jimmy Mack.

"She already told you, Bozo," says Jimmy Mack, trying in his own way to reassure me.

"So, how're you doing, Jeanette?" I ask patting my feet like a drummer under the table.

"Fine," she replies with a little smile. I can see her dimpled cheeks even out here, far from the interior of her kitchen. "And you?"

"Oh, I'm fine." But it's not true. I feel like a vulnerable witness in a federal protection program.

She steps over to me and hands me an antique English teacup, so delicate that I'm afraid to touch it. I hold it gingerly as the steam rises up into my nostrils. Memories of the good times we had skip through my mind as I listen to Bob Marley. I feel horny, remorseful, and terrified.

I'm jostled back to the present by a shushing sound. I turn my head and see pages of her novel spitting out from the printer landing all over the floor.

My eyes bulge like I've stuck my finger in an electric socket.

How long is this thing?

I grip the edge of my seat and silently repeat my mantra: *Calm down, calm down, calm down.*

"Oh!" says Jeanette, bending over to catch the flying pages.

If I could only palm those warm cheeks in my hands . . .

"Man, her butt tantalizes you regardless of what's gonna on," says Jimmy Mack, "and that's a fact."

"I'm sorry. I should have done this last night. And the paper holder isn't in the right position," mutters Jeanette.

How did she find so much to WRITE about? "You have over 275 pages on the table already." I can't read all this today.

Looking at the papers falling all around me, I can't wait any longer. "Let me see it," I say, on pins and needles.

"Wait! I need to talk to you first." She pauses. "It didn't give me any pleasure to jack you up like this."

"It didn't give me any either." *God, she really knows me.*

"Why ya do it, then?"

I feel I can trust her enough to reveal my innermost secrets—the reason it took me five months to get here. "Afraid of the unknown."

She sighs. "You gave me no choice."

"I'm sorry."

"First and foremost, Jasper, I wrote this book because I needed an outlet for my grief. It was a way to process my feelings. A way to heal my broken heart." I hear anguish in her voice. "To get rid of my disappointment and pain and to heal you."

As she continues explaining, I get more and more anxious once again. Maybe her purpose *is* to get me.

"Shut up," Jimmy Mack says, even though I haven't said anything.

"I hope this book will help do that," she says. "Maybe more people will be encouraged by your experience."

"I've talked about this many times to you . . ."

I don't know what to say to this.

". . . and Jasper, I hope you can see yourself in the words and pages. Really see yourself clearly enough to get the professional help you need so desperately. I noticed your overwhelming anxiousness and fearfulness, and your habit of fleeing difficult situations. I want you to get a handle on your life. Therapy can help you deal with stress and solve your problems. Then perhaps you can be happy—I'm afraid you are headed for a stroke."

"I've been running from Charles Anderson, too."

"Really?"

"I inadvertently sent him one of your e-mails."

"Which one? What did it say?"

"He's trying to find out who you are, if we have a relationship."

"I'll pray he doesn't."

"Thanks for your concern, Jeanette," I say, as gratefully as I can manage.

"I hope you know that I didn't intend to hurt you."

"In my heart I knew that," I say, sighing. I feel like she has scolded me while hugging me. Which makes me feel more stupid than I do already. "I believe you."

"All this worrying for nothing," says Jimmy Mack. "I told you so."

"This is a novel, not a memoir or biography. It's a work of fiction. You understand what that means?"

"Yes." I shake my head. Now I really feel like an idiot.

"It's about me. You have the right to change anything that identifies you as Jasper Fisher Beamon."

"Anything?" I ask. I cannot believe my ears.

"Anything."

"Thank you."

"Take notes as you read. We can discuss and make the changes later."

I begin reading, fast and furious—like a Dale Carnegie speed reader. Suddenly I'm feeling mistrustful again. I scan every word suspiciously for something that reveals me. My nerves are back on a Ferris wheel. My face contorts in a grotesque grimace, so tight I feel as though I have Bell's palsy.

What has she written?

I expect some explosive revelation about me to jump off the pages at any second. *Lord, help me,* I pray.

"How long do you think it will take you to finish?" asks Jeanette.

I flip to the last page. *Four hundred pages . . .*

I think for a minute and then calculate in my head. "Maybe five or six hours if I just skim it. It's really long."

Surprisingly, more than twenty descriptions and scenes jump right out at me. Off the pages even. There is a reference to the type of business I owned, my residence, and my university and fraternity affiliations, too. People who know me would be able to identify me easily. With a little probing and snooping from the wrong people—like Trustee Anderson, for instance—my name and my reputation would be in every "Nook" and cranny.

"Way befoe God even gets to read it," says Jimmy Mack.

She captures the essence of me: my quirkiness, my fears, my obsession for money and status.

Even more surprising is that I think her writing is lovely. She has captured the essence of our relationship—the long talks over exotic dinners, our love of music and dance, and definitely my innermost feelings for her that I expressed to her every day. I wonder how she remembers so much about what we did and, in particular, what I said.

I adjust, discuss and delete several references to me. I am thoroughly absorbed in it all, in her book, but every so often I glance at *her*, moving around the dining room. Her body distracts me; her aroma arouses me.

I realize the magnitude of the moment. "Jeannie, you wrote a book!"

The situation seems comical to her. "Yes, I did!"

And she breaks out into her trademark hearty laugh. Her spirits seem to soar as she begins to tease and banter. "And I sure enjoyed writing it."

"I bet you did."

"Okay, let me see." She takes the manuscript from me and reads a few lines, then hands it back to me.

I start reading again, not even lifting my eyes from the pages. Writing it has finally given *her* the control and the power. I feel ambivalent about my new position. I am worried out of my mind but still happy about her magnificent writing talent.

* * *

It was callous, the way that I broke up with her back in November—two Novembers ago, that is. It was fear that made me do it.

I was sitting at my desk when she called.

"This is the Empress Jeanette," she teased.

"This is the Emperor," I brazenly replied.

"If the mountain doesn't come to Mohammed, then Mohammed will come to the mountain."

"Where are you?"

"On the train."

"How long are you gonna be in your office?"

"How long do you want me to be here?"

"Can we have a drink together? Maybe a glass of *juice or a cup of tea?*"

"What are we gonna do after that?" I asked provocatively.

"Mmmmmmm," was all she said.

"I'll meet you at the metro station, in the parking lot. Do you think you can recognize me?"

"Bet my money on it."

A few minutes later I was in the parking lot, driving around in a circle, when I heard an arresting voice.

"Emperor! Emperor!"

I parked the car quickly. "You're a crazy woman."

"But you love it."

I braced myself against the emotions bubbling up inside of me.

"Do you want me to walk behind you, Emperor Beamon?"

"Yes."

We talked and drank.

Twenty minutes later, my cell phone rang and, regrettably, I had to go back to the office. I hoisted her up and spun her around as we said good-bye. She felt so good.

"Oh-hoooo!" she squealed delightfully.

"I got to go," I said as the tremors set in. "I have to read the Scripture before a thousand people in my church every Sunday. Suppose someone spots me here with you. The whole church would know that I'm having an affair." Foolishly, I cried out in frustration because I was afraid of getting caught and afraid of getting a divorce.

"YOU ARE THE MAN," said Jimmy Mack.

* * *

"AN OMEGA MAN?" asks Jimmy Mack sarcastically now.

"Jimmy Mack, I never said it! I never said, "I'm breaking up with you!" I realize. "I just dashed to my car and took off like a meteor. Left her standing in the parking lot. I can see that bewildered face now. I never called her to tell her about my decision, either. Just let it drop, like our relationship hadn't even existed."

Maybe if I had acted more manly.

"Man, you sound like Teddy Pendergrass singing, 'Maybe if I had been a little more kind to her...' " says Jimmy Mack.

At least I could have made a dinner date, talked to her in person, been more respectful, and acted more courageously. Maybe if I had gotten some help instead of weaseling out, this would have never have happened. She wouldn't have written the book. I left her with all of these unresolved questions about our relationship. She knew I loved her. She was puzzled about why we couldn't be together and why I even broke it off. I was too. I wanted to be married to her, but I denied my desire and superimposed my feelings onto her. I remember screaming at her, "You just want to be married!"

"You were living in a fantasy—you were really talking about yourself," Jimmy Mack says, shaking his head.

I read continuously for three hours more, faster than a Hewlett Packard scanner, stopping only briefly to ask questions, make notes, and discuss changes. "You've made me a trustee," I comment.

"And a deacon."

"That's okay. No problem," I say. Then I tentatively suggest, "But I think it might be good to change the type of business I'm in. My wife, my daughter—they're so smart, they might figure this out."

"Okay . . . change it to what?" she asks.

I think about this for a moment. "A financial planner."

"There were several resemblances and references to you and your business, but it's your call.

"Fine. Change it, please."

I glance at my watch. "It's after one. I have an appointment. I need to go." *I feel like fleeing.* Oh! God . . . I'm running away again. That's what got me in trouble in the first place.

"Yeah, man! You rushed back to work and never called or did anything," says Jimmy Mack.

"Well, take the whole thing with you," she says. "You can review what you read. And you better not take long reading it."

"No. No, I promise this time, although I've only read a few chapters. I will get back to you ASAP."

"I hope so," she says. "It has been an ordeal for me, too—it took so long to get you here. I really didn't send it to you because . . . Well, I could have sent it to you, but you were afraid it would fall into the wrong hands, if you know what I mean."

"Yes." Into Martha's hands.

"And she really wanted to see you—I suspect maybe start over," says Jimmy Mack.

I get up and walk around, wandering near three large windows in the back of the room. Trying to calm my nerves. What a peaceful view! I see trees in the back of her building as large as those in Rock Creek Park, blowing in the wind. It feels as if I'm near a calm beach. On the windowsill I glimpse a photo gallery of family pictures. When Jeanette turns around and looks at me, though, I sense that I've intruded into her private collection.

"My son-in-law wants us to go to Africa this summer," I say casually.

"Oh yeah? How nice," she says, although her tone indicates otherwise.

"But I've got plenty of time to finish everything up. If I go, that is." I am thinking about the most secretive place to hide the manuscript from Martha. I'm glad Jeanette didn't send it. Martha is always checking the mailbox and hanging over my computer whenever she can. Her schedule is so unpredictable that she might have intercepted a FedEx delivery. "I've got to be careful where I keep it and when I read it."

"You got to be more careful," laughs Jimmy Mack.

I make an appointment to come back to Jeanette's the following week to finish up. Then I dash off to my meeting with the deacon and trustee boards. I dread seeing Charles Anderson.

* * *

We hold the meeting in the church's big conference room. We review reports of the fifty-four church ministries, which include topics on the progress, problems, and money for financing each of these. Luckily, Trustee Anderson doesn't get a chance to bother me today. I listen quietly in the back of the room and speak only when asked a question. It goes well, but I'm still scared.

After the church meeting, with the reminder of the manuscript in my briefcase, I head for the deacons' office, stopping by the administrative office on the pretense of saying good morning. But in truth, I'm trying to find out if the coast is clear.

When I finally walk toward my office, I almost collide with Pastor Wheeler, a tall, lanky, fair-complexioned brother, one of the few genuine people in my church.

"Good morning, Pastor," I say, feeling sneaky. I fake a smile, but I know my face looks like Dr. Seuss' *How the Grinch Stole Christmas.*

"Morning, Jasper," he says in his sermonic voice, stepping toward me with a smile.

He wants to talk, but we exchange a few words, and I scurry away with my time bomb.

I selected Doctor Wheeler out of a pool of fifty other candidates to become the next minister of Mount Mariah. He's a fellow Omega man and a Carolinian, too. We're "good buddies."

"Crown 'em," teases Jimmy Mack.

"Shut up, man," I say.

Forty-one years old, Pastor Wheeler has the carriage of an Omega man and the fiery voice of a traditional preacher. Furthermore, he graduated *magna cum laude* from Columbia University and received his PhD from the Divinity School at Yale University. Although he is married with two children, his cool good looks are an asset still. Black women of all ages are always attracted to a handsome, charismatic preacher—looking for love, spirituality, and God all wrapped up in a father figure. His credentials far exceed the demands of the church's "five-percenters," those rich, class-conscious members often referred to by Malcolm X in his time. The ones who got rich as contractors for the military industrial complex but consider themselves still black and proud—they travel to Africa, find their roots, donate to the Nelson Mandela Foundation, and (last but not least) volunteer at soup kitchens in southeast DC.

"You included," says Jimmy Mack.

"Me included."

In the office, which is a combined meeting space for all church officers but is mostly used by the deacon board, I take the brown bag from my briefcase and tuck it in a mahogany desk drawer, which was donated to the church by Trustee Charles Anderson who inherited it from his great-grandfather. I lock it. Here the manuscript will be safe from Martha's roaming eyes at least.

* * *

As member of the trustee board, Charles Anderson is also responsible for the fiscal health of the church. The next week he meets with the finance committee and accounting staff. After the meeting he jimmies the lock on my desk, rampages through it, and finds the manuscript. As I enter the office, I catch him like a possum, reading. I'm shocked!

"How did you get into my desk? You have no right to break into my desk and read my personal property!"

"This is church property, Deacon, or have you forgotten? My family . . ."

"Oh shucks! Here he goes again," says Jimmy Mack.

"Please, don't start with your family," I say angrily.

"I saw you sneak in here last week, hiding something in your drawer. I have to make sure that our church's reputation is always clean, Deacon Beamon. I thought it might have something to do with that woman, Jeanette."

"Don't keep calling me 'Deacon'!" I shout, then whisper, "You are getting on my nerves," remembering there are others in the church.

"I call the shots now, Deacon," he says indignantly.

"What do you want from me?"

"Let me give it some thought," he says nastily. "Maybe that beach house of yours. Does Martha know about this little affair of yours?"

"Listen," I say, losing my breath, "let's keep this between us, please. I beg you." I feel like falling on my knees.

"We need to talk about you and Miss . . . What's her name again? This is gonna cost you something!"

Just as his words fumigate the air, the church secretary opens the door. I snatch the chapter from Charles Anderson, pull the remainder of the manuscript out of the drawer, and ease out of the room quicker than a magician and as fast as these little feet can take me.

* * *

CHAPTER 12

"You cannot fix what you cannot face."

James Baldwin

F inally home, I walk gingerly up the stairs and lie down on our four-poster canopy bed. Something is wrong. My hands are sweating, and so is my forehead. I toss from side to side, not sleeping more than a few seconds at a time. *Do I have to repay the stolen church funds? Is Charles Anderson gonna to blackmail me? Is he gonna to tell Martha? Is he gonna contact Jeanette?*

"I was proud when the higher-ups selected me as church administrator," I say.

"Tickle you, Elmo," laughs Jimmy Mack.

"Now it's a burden—I don't know if they will approve of the way I conduct business."

"Man, give it a break, will you?" says Jimmy Mack.

I've had more than twenty years of experience selecting, hiring, and evaluating employees at my former company. I should have confidence in what I'm doing. But the thought of even a single inquiry, a comment, a criticism—the idea of someone asking me to justify my choices makes me nauseous.

Selected by Mount Mariah's Leadership committee to find a new pastor, I zigzag across the United States, for two long years, like a butterfly that has lost its wings. I meet many pastors, but with Martha pulling at me like a donkey, I'm too scared to decide on one.

"Scared enough to run and hide," teases Jimmy Mack.

That's why I always keep a pack of Tums in my pocket . . . I did the best I could, but some church clans can be so uppity.

While I can manage it, I review some of Jeanette's manuscript and send her my recommendations:

Hi Jeanette,

I'm not feeling too well but wanted to follow up on my promise. My recommended changes are enclosed. I will review further for any other recommendations; but, I at least I have covered some of it.

. . . Jasper

Suddenly a sharp pain detonates like a bomb in my chest and vibrates down my left side. My heart is jack hammering. All these decisions and problems—hiring a new pastor and an architectural firm, Jeanette's book, and now Charles Anderson—is causing me to get very sick. I've got too many stressors at one time.

Am I having a heart attack?

"Martha, something is wrong with me!" I call out.

Her voice floats up the stairs. "Why didn't you wait to next week to do all that? You just need some rest—you drove six straight hours," she says.

"No, this is different!"

I count the contrasting threads in my bedspread, hoping the pain will subside, at least enough so I can attend the church meeting tonight. My heart starts racing like Beauregard the racehorse heading for the home stretch.

I hear Lulu coming upstairs, taking the steps two at a time. She races into my room with her tongue hanging out. She rests her forepaws on the bed. She senses that I'm sick—I can tell by the forlorn look in her eyes. Smart dog. She jumps on the bed and nestles her warm body as close to me as she can.

By this time, my heart is doing painful cartwheels. I tremble. I sweat. I shake all over.

I'm gonna crazy, I think.

I manage to get up and close the blinds, hoping that darkness will alleviate my headache. It doesn't do me much good though.

I recall my conversations with Jeanette today and yesterday. For no good reason, a random vision of her in a negligee pops in my head. I want her so bad that I ache. I start to pray. My prayer becomes a chant.

"IIIIIIIIIIIIIIIIIIIIIIIIIIIIIIIIHHHHHHHHHHHAAAAAAA AAAAAIIIIIIIIIIIIIIIHHH!"

I don't know what I'm saying—my words are unintelligible, even to Lulu. She looks as though she is afraid for me. I am losing it rapidly.

"Sinner!" says Jimmy Mack.

Lisa, my guardian angel, says, *A heart attack has no warning. The heart pounds, skips, and palpitates. A desire to escape is present, and there is an overwhelming feeling of impending doom.*

"Thanks," I say, in excruciating pain. "My heart! It feels like . . ."

Jimmy Mack completes my sentence: ". . . like a hippo's ass hunkered down on your chest."

I'm scared as hell. I know my cholesterol is high, something like 235. I need to stop eating all those hamburgers and French fries. Like Richard said, *I know I shouldn't be eating these greasy fried foods, but they taste so good.*

SO GOOD. Yeah.

"Do as I say, huh?" says Jimmy Mack.

"Martha, call the paramedics!" I urge her.

"What about the church meeting tonight?" asks Martha impatiently, her voice ringing with as much compassion as she can muster.

"I can't make it!" I groan. "I'm too sick!"

My angel pays me another visit.

Jasper, Lisa calls in a soft voice, *one or more of your coronary arteries are completely blocked. And blood to your heart is cut off! A narrow vessel, located in the chambers of the heart, constricts during a heart attack. Excessive stress, high cholesterol, and high blood pressure are the primary risk factors.*

I hear you, Lisa.

"I'm not gonna to church tonight," I say aloud.

"I'll call the church," Martha says, "and tell them you can't make it."

"Never mind that!" I plead with her. "Call the rescue squad!"

Five minutes later, a county ambulance arrives in my driveway. The paramedics strap a mask over my face and plug in the oxygen tank. Martha tries to take charge—interfering with the experts. She is shocked, but like a dutiful wife, she accompanies me to the hospital.

Sometimes I think she only wants to keep me alive to torment me.

Jimmy Mack says, imitating Martha, "I told you not to eat those fattening foods . . ."

"Open your mouth, Mr. Beamon," the young paramedic says as he lifts the mask and slips a tablet under my tongue. "Just relax. We're gonna' take good care of you."

"Give him the nitroglycerin tablets every five minutes," says his colleague. "And an aspirin, too. Three hundred fifty milligrams."

En route to the local hospital, they put leaded adhesive backing on my chest, and I feel like a casket is closing in over me. They place small suction cups on each arm, and I feel like I am gonna to faint. They take a blood sample and hook me up to an EKG machine with so many wires, I'm like a patient in intensive care.

I'm not ready to see my maker yet.

We arrive in less than ten minutes. The paramedics rush me inside on a gurney. Thank God, I have good coverage. I only hope it will ensure that I get the best medical treatment possible.

Martha runs ahead and goes directly to the admissions desk, rummaging through her giant pocketbook until she pulls out my insurance card. She begins to register me, working like a gold medalist in training—hoping to keep her gravy train running, no doubt knowing she came up short in my most recent will. Even semiconscious, I hear her doing her best to give the admissions personnel the blues. "You're too slow and too darn inefficient," she barks. "Get me the supervisor!"

She even frightens the paramedics, who wheel me into a curtained area as if they're racing to win a 5K.

By this time, I am unable to do anything.

A short white man with a full head of unkempt gray hair walks up to my bed. He flips though my medical chart and looks me straight in the eye as he introduces himself.

"I'm Doctor Ginsburg," he says, staring at me as if he's been practicing medicine for a hundred years. "What seems to be the problem?"

I force myself to describe my symptoms to the doctor and his attending nurse. He bends down and gently places his stethoscope on my chest like my loving grandmother rubbing liniment over my chest.

"Mr. Beamon, have you ever had a heart attack?"

"No," I say weakly.

"How old are you?"

"Sixty-nine."

"Have you ever had a stroke?"

"No."

"Do you smoke?"

"No."

He turns to the nurse and says, "Give Mr. Beamon the usual set of lab tests. The troponine, the CK, and an electrocardiogram."

I'm hoping and praying that all these tests are negative. If I didn't have a heart attack, I'll take better care of myself the next go round.

* * *

The next day, I am about to eat my breakfast of fresh orange juice and a bowl of high-fiber cereal when Doctor Ginsburg steps into the room.

"Ugh." I wish they would give me my bacon and eggs. This food is gonna make me sicker.

"about eating right ..."

"Do what I say, Jimmy Mack, not what you see me do."

"Mr. Beamon," says Doctor Ginsburg as he pulls up a chair next to my elevated bed.

I hold my breath and squeeze the side of the thin hospital mattress.

"I've got good news," says Doctor Ginsburg. "There's no heart damage. You've had a panic attack, not a heart attack."

"No heart damage." *Thank God!*

Doctor Ginsburg goes on. "You have been under a lot of stress lately?"

I nod.

"Stress can cause damage to the heart. You need to develop coping skills to deal with the difficulties and challenges in your life, huh?"

"Yeah," I say.

I want to say, *I'm dealing with ingrate church members and a woman who has the audacity to write a tell-all book about me.* But I don't. I dare not share any personal information with this doctor. I hardly know him, after all.

"She let you check it out— it wasn't that bad. She told you that," says Jimmy Mack.

You're right, pal, I'uumm know. I just don't know.

"I just retired," I say aloud. I recently retired.

"Retired?" Doctor Ginsburg repeats.

"Yes."

"How is your life more stressful after retirement? It's supposed to be the opposite."

"It's a long story."

"Okay . . . tell me about it?"

"I can't."

"Well, that's your prerogative. But rest assured, Mr. Beamon, you could have a heart attack the next time."

I am as taut as a clam.

The doctor rambles on. "Panic attacks are not to be taken lightly. They generally keep coming back unless you change your lifestyle. I'm gonna to recommend several coping mechanisms I want you to use. First, do you go to church?"

Yeah, right, Doctor, I snort. "I'm a deacon, for thirty-some-odd years."

"Hmm. Long time," says Doctor Ginsburg, nodding. "Do you have a close relationship with God? I suppose it is not my responsibility nor my business to ask you that, but studies have shown that people who have an intimate relationship with God or a higher power of some sort cope with life's challenges better. They are healthier, experience less anxiety, and live longer. I want you to examine that relationship—see if the one you have is working for you."

Ha, ha, ha.

"I'll do that," I say. "'Cause I do have a lot of . . . a lot of guilt and shame."

The doctor creases his face like Groucho Marx and clears his throat. "I'm not an expert on emotional issues, Mr. Beamon, but I would strongly recommend you seek counseling if you want to live a long and healthy life. You need help analyzing these issues, analyzing yourself. A good therapist can help you improve your relationship with God and everyone else in your life. Please allow me to set up an appointment for you with a therapist. You have the best insurance that money can buy—coverage for everything."

Yeah, how well I know it.

My insurance company courted me like I was a high-profile celebrity. My son, Rodney, and I were invited on a mini-cruise with unimaginable amenities: a live band playing both classical and jazz music, waiters serving the most delicious food known to man, the best California wines and champagne flowing like the Congo River .

"You used it at Psychiatric Institute of Washington," Jimmy Mack says.

"Don't remind me of that day." Even with all my money and good insurance, they treated me badly. I was accompanied by the police, one a black fellow built like an NFL linebacker and the other a burly white guy, as the paramedics rushed me inside the front entrance. I tried to hide my face;

I didn't want to appear on the evening news looking like an FBI's Most Wanted criminal. I yanked my cuffed hands away from the linebacker and got several bloody nicks on my wrist. For two days my hands stung like alcohol poured into an open wound.

"It's important to talk to someone about your stress and anxiety, Mr. Beamon," says Doctor Ginsburg.

"Isn't that what Doctor Moore told you at PIW?" asks Jimmy Mack.

"Why don't you want to do that?" Doctor Ginsburg insists.

Shrugging my shoulders, I say, "I don't know. You're right. It's important."

"Jasper, you act so dumb," Jimmy Mack says, acting like he wants to throw up.

"Real men don't go into therapy—I've always believed that," I say. "Nor do they get committed to psychiatric hospitals."

"They pretend everything's okay and carry on," says Jimmy Mack. "Like you, they keep ducking and hiding until a crisis erupts. Like the day in your broker's office, the day PIW put you under a suicide watch."

"You want to get well?" says Doctor Ginsburg.

"Of course I do," I respond. I know I need to get help. Help coping with my feelings. I could start by asking why I've decided to suppress my love for Jeanette instead of escaping my humdrum life and hurling myself into her arms.

"Then you better do whatever it takes to live a healthy lifestyle. A deal, Mr. Beamon?"

"Yes," I say wearily.

When Doctor Ginsburg leaves, I shake my head down at Jimmy Mack. "I can't go to that therapist."

"Chicken Little."

"God and I are gonna to take care of my woes, all by ourselves." And I begin to pray.

"Jasper, you do that every time—call on the name of God to get out of trouble. If you really want to change, you would get a divorce, go into therapy. Do something besides whine. You know the saying: God helps those who help themselves," Jimmy Mack reminds me.

I know this all too well.

* * *

CHAPTER 13

"I am sick and tired of being sick and tired."

Fannie Lou Hamer

A few days later, I'm out of the hospital. I feel like I need to go back again. I am lying on my bed getting some badly needed rest and trying to calm my nerves, as Doctor Ginsburg recommended, by rubbing Lulu's head.

For several days I have been nursing a low-grade fever with alternating bouts of chills. My symptoms are intermittently accompanied by headaches and nausea. I feel as if I'm getting the flu: burning, itching, tingling. I spend the time on my favorite hobby: ruminating over not having taken the flu shot. To compensate for this oversight, I slurp up seven tablespoons full of a syrupy medicine, hoping to overtake the symptoms invading my body.

But what can I really do? I've done my research. I know what's really gonna on and I talked it over with Lisa. Listen to what she said: *Adjacent to your spinal cord and your brain is a bunch of nerve cells, called ganglia, that congregate for a specific purpose: to provide your body with sensory nerve functions. These are what make you taste things, feel pain, and cry. Basically, they control all your vital human emotions.*

My ganglia cells, I've decided, have been lying perfectly dormant since I was a child. But stress, depression, and the repeated loss of my soul mate *(oh, Jeanette!)* have weakened my immune system and caused a whole host of problems. My cells are agitated now, and they are waking up—like corpses in that movie *Night of the Living Dead.*

"You told me this would happen, Lisa."

In her angelic voice, Lisa says, "You didn't believe me. I am here to help you, Jasper."

The reason for the break-up was simple: I didn't want to get a divorce and lose half of my money. But Jeanette was the perfect woman for me. The frustration. The longing. The guilt. It's all killing me. I think of her every minute now. Depression is my daily companion. But I have no choice but to stick with the devil I know. Plus, I have an image to uphold, a bank account to protect. And I can guarantee you that I will do *anything* to avoid humiliation. Even the thought of it scares the hell out of me. And that, in turn, causes more stress.

To make matters worse, I haven't taken the doctor's advice. I haven't talked to a therapist, and I haven't followed-up with Jeanette.

To pass the time, I review the lengthy conversations I've had with Jeanette, and for some unknown reasons the scenes at PIW keeps playing in my brain, too. In my head, they play like a movie screen over and over, until I can't take it any longer. I screamed at the doctors when they asked me a simple question.

"Have you had a crisis lately?"

The images . . . the images are as vivid as if it were yesterday . . .

* * *

I reach across his desk with my hands in a death grip.

"Jasper!" Jimmy Mack screams as my hands are inches from strangling the last breath from my banker's obese body.

"Oh my God!"

I run to the bathroom, slam the door, and lock it.

"Mr. Beamon, Mr. Beamon!"

I hear them calling my name. They bang. They scream.

I unclip my serrated-edge Navy SEAL knife from my pants. I gently rub it across a vein and slit my left wrist. I gaze at the oozing, thick, red fluid dripping down my arm. The security guard, two police officers, and the paramedics arrive simultaneously. They knock the door down, just in time to witness the worst part of my suicidal episode.

The police subdue and handcuff me. My shoes dangle off the stretcher like two overcooked pigs' feet. They slide my body into their vehicle as if I'm a pan of pork chops. We speed off to the Institute as if in a presidential motorcade. I scream, thrash, and curse as I've never done before, all the way across town.

I act as if another human being has taken over my body. I get into a confrontation with Martha, and it is so cantankerous we almost come to blows. The entire PIW staff has to intervene.

I spit on the policeman, the one I've named Zealie. I kick the football impostor like I'm an opposing player. I'm hoping that Martha can overrule the medical crew and staff. I want to get out of here. But no way—they're used to bullying women.

"Mr. Beamon, you need to calm down! Please answer my questions. We are all here to help you," says Doctor Moore.

"Nobody can help me."

The policeman nails me, lifting me like a sack of potatoes, and drags me toward the elevator.

"There isn't anything wrong with me," I say, and suddenly, I jump forward and punch the wall.

I hear a quiet, professional voice say, "It's time to take him down."

* * *

Impulsively, I dial her telephone number.

"Hey," I say, pretending that I'm feeling fine. "What you doing?"

Before I get the words out of my mouth, she cuts me off. "Jasper, call me later. I'm getting ready to start my dance class."

Oh! It's like that, huh? I think.

"Okay," I say and hang up the telephone.

"Fooled you this time, hey, Mr. Beamon?" mocks Jimmy Mack.

Maybe if I deal with administrative matters instead of matters of the heart, I might feel better. To distract myself from thinking about Jeanette I call the chair of the church's search committee, which turns out to be a gross misjudgment on my part. Charles Anderson answers.

"Hi, Trustee Anderson. It's me, Jasper."

He instantly begins to nag me about Jeanette and the e-mail I mistakenly sent him. "Who is she, Beamon?"

"None of your business."

"I've got a sneaky suspicion about you, man. . . and Ms. What's-Her-Name."

"Oh, lay off me. I'm sorry I got you anyway."

"How're you doing?"

"Okay," I lie. The truth is, I feel like death is not only at my door but slamming into it.

"What's been ailing you this time, Jasper?" He says this as if I am always sick and always complaining about it. "I'll put you on the prayer list." His tone is judgmental, as if we are a list of hopeless sinners.

"Nothing too much," I say. I'm not about to give him the pleasure of gossiping about me to the other old buddies.

"Glad you're better, then, Deacon," he says.

"Thank you, Charles."

"Good thing you called, too. I canceled the church meeting, so you didn't miss anything." As he says this, I imagine his rodent-size neck sniffing the air, as if his place in heaven were already reserved. "There have been some . . . unforeseen complications . . . The meeting will have to wait until further notice," he says without giving an explanation. I know he wants me to probe him for details, but I refuse to give him that pleasure. He'll take it as another opportunity to insult me.

Rejected again, I gingerly ease the phone in its cradle and kick the bedside rail in frustration. I clutch my chest when the pain starts to come.

Oh my God!

"What did I do wrong this time?" I ask Jimmy Mack.

"Strike two," says Jimmy Mack sarcastically. "Poor baby."

But Lulu understands me. She is my substitute soul mate, albeit an inadequate one. She walks right up to me and licks my face.

Even so, I am anxious again. You'd think I'm getting ready to volley against Venus on the first day of the French Open.

* * *

Jasper . . .

My guardian calls me as she flies over my bed and deposits herself on the bedpost.

Your virus is traveling along your central nervous system.

"I can feel it," I reply dreamily.

Your axium picks up the coded information sent out by the cells. Your brain, that singular organ that affects your entire body, is sending information to the ganglia.

"What is the message? I beg you . . ."

When you're very stressed, the ganglia alert your immune system, which weakens as a result, while at the same time they also transmit messages back to the brain . . .

"They're talking to each other?" I ask incredulously. "What are they saying?"

WE ARE AGITATED.

"Oh, gracious me . . ."

Six days later, I am swollen. A cluster of painful blisters filled with clear liquid covers the meaty part of my behind. They look like a band of bean sprouts. These pus-filled blisters are my suppressed emotions—the physical manifestation of my love for Jeanette. They are raging passion flowers.

For the next five days, new blisters continue to appear. The shingles virus commonly presents itself in the chest area, but for some godforsaken reason, mine zeroes in on my rear end. Blisters scatter over my butt like a deadly mix of prickly poison ivy and a diaper rash. I am in intense and unrelenting pain. When I finally see my local doctor, four days after the shingles rash has appeared, it's too late for him to help me. He advises me to see a specialist and makes an appointment for me with Doctor Trouth, the first female chairman of the Department of Neurology at Howard University.

Doctor Trouth, who is also a professor, is every bit as busy as her rapid-fire tongue. She prescribes FAMVIR and warns me about its side effects: diarrhea, nausea, headaches.

"Nothing new to me," I tell her.

I am uncomfortable both day and night. Because of the excruciating blisters on my buttocks, I cannot sit in a chair or lie down on my bed. I sleep only in snippets throughout the night, awakening abruptly whenever the bedcovers or blankets, sharper than a razor blade nipping deep within my skin, come in contact with the blisters. When I'm not in bed, I wear a loose-fitting, 100 percent cotton robe to prevent my skin from touching or rubbing up against anything. I may think my money has made me royalty, but I feel like a leper.

* * *

My pain is relentless. It has been a month now. My steady daily routine is as follows: Wake up (or, more accurately, get out of bed). Drag my tired and infirm body to the bathroom. Return to the bedroom. Swallow bitter pills and push aspirins that don't work down my sore and raw throat. Chew Amparin while sitting on the edge of the bed. Try to watch TV or read the paper. Race to the toilet with diarrhea. Gulp down cups of water to avoid dehydration.

I keep a bottle of aspirin on my nightstand, a roll of toilet paper in my left hand and a cup of water in my right. I agonize about wanting Jeanette every day and feel imprisoned in the huge house with a woman I don't want to be around. I'm in too much pain to attend church, talk on the phone or read the get-well cards I receive. The pain is so unbearable. It's messing with my mind. I may resort to taking Valium.

Nothing is working. I return to the neurologist for additional medication. Doctor Trouth tells me I've reached the third and most severe stage, the post-herpetic stage, and gives me a prescription for tranquilizers and Lyrica. She urges me to see a therapist and to participate in group therapy. "Talking about your illness or sharing your pain and problems—your stresses—will help eliminate the pain," she says with her Indian accent.

"Really?" I ask. Until now I've been too busy bellyaching to take her advice. The average man can't stand the idea of gonna to therapy—or the word itself. Neither can I. It frightens me to even consider talk therapy. Just the thought of it makes me feel more flared than I already feel. How can I trust my feelings and thoughts— nightmarish memories of childhood abuse and ridicule, bloody Vietnam—to a stranger? How can I tell someone I'm being abused by my own wife? Do real men go to therapy?

"Shingles starts in your brain, Mr. Beamon, because of extreme stress," warns Doctor Trouth. "Without seeking resolutions to your problems or grieving your losses, recovery can be extremely difficult."

"That's me for sure," I reply.

"When you talk about your problems, the pain can lessen or even stop, which allows healing to take place."

"That's exactly what Doctor Ginsburg said."

I've been out of touch with Jeanette because of my illness. But my guardian angel, Lisa, visits me again in my dreams. She tells me my emotional illnesses are the underlying cause of my shingles and anxiety attacks. She says procrastination makes matters worse. She tells me I need to get help.

Jasper, she says, her ghastly face tear-stained, *you're carrying a cargo load of emotional illnesses: post traumatic stress disorder, avoidance personality disorder, paranoia, dysthymia, generalized anxiety disorder, you name it.*

"Oooh!" I moan as I fall back on my pillow.

I am finally cured after several months. It has taken just that long to get back on my feet. I have never had a more painful illness in my life. I think the reason why it has taken me so long to heal is that I didn't follow up on the recommendation of my doctors.

The story of your life, says Jimmy Mack.

* * *

CHAPTER 14

"Deceive the sky to cross the ocean."

Sun Tzu

My nightmares have not ceased. I dream my stepbrothers are making fun of me again and locking me up in a shed in the backyard. I cry, but no one hears me. I have to sleep there for the night. No one comes to my rescue. I see disintegrating body parts lying on the beach in Vietnam. I wake up shivering and shaking like a malaria patient. Returning to sleep is impossible.

The next morning, I decide to talk to Jeanette in lieu of a therapist. I send her an e-mail as Martha practices on the piano upstairs. I can't help myself.

I've been in the hospital again. Trustee Anderson read Chapter Twenty-Seven. I need to see you ASAP.

...Jasper

I really need her now. I'm gonna out of my mind. I don't know what I'm gonna to do. We have to strategize about how to deal with him.

"Tell him you are pals, ha, ha," says Jimmy Mack.

I e-mail Jeanette again, and when I receive no answer, I call her a few hours later.

"Today I *must* see you; it's urgent."

"Where are you?"

"In my same old familiar place—you know it," she says laughing.

I'm serious and although her teasing feels good, this is no time for playing around.

"I've got to come over!" I repeat worriedly.

"When?"

"Right now?" My teeth are rattling like a loose muffler.

"What's gonna on," she says distressed.

"I'll tell you when I get there."

I speed across the bridge, running two red lights and arrive at her house in twenty minutes. I enter the side entrance to her building behind another tenant, taking the steps two at a time.

I knock on her door, breathless. "It's me—Jasper! Please open the door!" I yell.

I dash into her apartment and run to the table, heaving as if I'm in respiratory failure.

"Sit down, Jasper," she pleads, pulling the chair out from the table, "and tell me what's gonna on."

"Huh!" I gasp. "Trustee Anderson broke into my desk drawer . . . I caught him reading Chapter Twenty-Seven of your manuscript. I tried to e-mail you . . ."

"WHAT!" she cries.

"YES."

"How did he get into your drawer? When did this happen?"

"Musta pried it opened with something. It was a while back—before I got sick and was in the hospital."

"That man is EVIL," says Jeanette.

"Conniving devil," chimes in Jimmy Mack.

"What's he gonna to do?" asks Jeanette.

"Blackmail him, of course," Jimmy Mack says angrily.

"He's been looking for a chance to get me every which a way I turn. Now that he has seen the manuscript, he'll get me for sure."

Jeanette runs to her desk and pulls out a copy of the manuscript, turning to Chapter Twenty-Seven. "Let me read it again. Can he really tell anything from reading this chapter?"

"Yes, he can tell we had a relationship. I was pursuing you and . . . I gave you some money."

"What are you gonna to do?"

"I don't know. I don't know," I say as I slump over the table.

"Calm down," she says. "I'll make you some tea. Give me your coat. Do you want juice? Did you say you were in the hospital?"

"I had an anxiety attack from all of this stress."

"Calm down, calm down." Poor baby.

After giving it some thought, I say, "Jeanette, I'm gonna to deny we are involved. We were only having dinner. I was giving you advice about your business. What do you think of that?"

"You advised her on setting up *her business* alright," says Jimmy Mack.

"It was much more than that," she says.

"I had Shingles, too," I inject for more sympathy.

"Oh, no!"

"For Christ's sake," says Jimmy Mack. "You think he is gonna to fall for that?"

"I'll say nothing ever came of it . . ."

"You didn't want to get involved with me
. . ."

"You'll back me up, won't you, Jeanette?" I ask, holding my breath as I cross my fingers under the table.

"I will."

"I will, too," says Jimmy Mack, air flowing out of him like a pinched balloon.

"Nothing physical happened," I say.

"That's a fact I can testify to," says Jimmy Mack.

"That's halfway true," Jeanette says with a thoughtful look. "I wouldn't let you. We did become emotionally involved."

"Still are," says Jimmy Mack quietly.

"Jasper, I won't publish my book, at least not now."

"I don't think that would be a good idea," suggests Jimmy Mack.

I never did.

"Alright? But I want you to know I am terribly disappointed," she says.

I'm not.

Three hours later, still at Jeanette's, I panic. "I've got to go! Martha is expecting me to eat dinner at this new restaurant. That's her new way of trying to keep track of me."

"I'll think about what I'm gonna to do. Maybe I'll make a documentary," Jeanette says dreamily.

Impassioned at our parting, I say, "I'll call you tomorrow." I'm still hoping to convince her to support me in this crisis.

She nods and smiles as I exit. Her dimples make leaving less painful and my life so much easier to bear.

* * *

CHAPTER 15

"As a child my family's menu
consisted of two choices:
take it or leave it."

Buddy Hackett

ucked in my glove compartment is a brown paper
bag. Loaded with Jeanette's hot tamale, I don't want
Martha to taste, smell, or—Lord knows—see it! I want
to avoid Martha's wrath.

I push my foot down on the accelerator of my Lexus.
Swerving in and out of midday traffic, I make it to the restaurant on time. Smiling, I remember the time Jeanette said that
I drive better than a jockey. Something about "my having
good spatial intelligence."

"Woman knows what to say," teases Jimmy Mack feeling my pleasure at the long-ago compliment.

I see Martha through the front window, glancing at her watch, and pacing back and forth impatiently. Halting before entering the restaurant, I wipe the sweat off my brow with a hanky. I keep it in my pocket for occasions just like this—and for certain other times that I don't care to discuss right now.

"Amen," says Jimmy Mack.

Today my wife has chosen a new Mexican restaurant on I-95, about a mile from the city and two from where we live. Tex-Mex food is all the rage. Washingtonians these days are craving foods ranging from the southern pig and Asian ramen dumplings to Korean tacos like they are delicacies. Give them whoopies for dessert instead of the tired sweet crepes. They can't stand another helping of Brussels sprouts or swallow another Diet Dr Pepper.

I must say that like most rich folks we are "snotty foodies"—shopping at all the upscale places like Whole Foods and buying gourmet food to impress others.

"You better concentrate on the situation at hand. Forget trends," says Jimmy Mack.

Martha is hoping that eating out every day—another thing my money can afford, along with shopping and planning and ordering event food from Whole Foods Market—will put what they call in Carolina "the shine" back into our tornado-stricken marriage. But this terminal relationship has been on life support over thirty years, so I don't think a few meals in new surroundings is gonna to cure it.

The restaurant's colors, black and red, are as hot as Eugenia Leon's passionate, cabaret-like voice singing, "*El Fandango Aqui*" as I enter. But Martha's mood is even hotter than the lyrics coming out of Eugenia's mouth. She glares at me, like a tiger about to rip the heart out of some poor soul, then glances at her watch just as I sit down. I have to admit, I'm frightened.

Nervously, I stumble and pinch my toe. Having this manuscript on me and finding Trustee Anderson reading a chapter puts me on edge.

I decide to sweet-talk her because I'm late, and she is mad. I want to get myself grounded—if I ever was. "How's your day gonna so far?"

"As well as most of my days. Why do you ask?" she replies, smirking.

"Shucks, man," says Jimmy Mack.

"Just trying to show some interest, that's all, Martha."

"Yeah, right."

Already spent by the anxiety of Jeanette and her novel, about now I am running out of patience with her. We eat in silence—at least on my part. Martha carries on a one-sided conversation, berating me for everything from almost being late to the clothes I'm wearing.

"I thought you might dress up for a change. Why *did* you put on that country-looking plaid shirt with those khaki overalls? They don't match."

She thinks she's better than I am. *More cultured,* she likes to say.

"That's why you married her?" "Really."

Both of us were abandoned by our parents (so who's better than whom?). Well, technically my mama was present. But nobody nurtured me when I was growing up except my grandmother (on the few occasions I saw her). I might as well face up to it.

Still, she justifies her superiority over me because her middle-class aunt sent her to the exclusive Palmer Memorial

Institute, where a "good education" included piano and ballet.

"Excuse me, Jack—you talking about The Alice Freeman Palmer Memorial Institute?" asks Jimmy Mack. "That bougie black boarding school."

"Yup, that's the one."

"Marie, Nat King Cole's wife, went there—the one in Sedalia, North Carolina?"

Nodding my head, I tell him, "The founder, Doctor Charlotte Hawkins Brown, was her aunt."

In the end, let's be clear. Martha loves money so she can buy material things, and she would go to any extent to keep me—a rich man—even if it means paying off her rival and threatening to take all of my money in a divorce battle.

"Correction: *rivals*," says Jimmy Mack.

"Hush your mouth!" I reply.

Martha could beat Elizabeth Edwards in a rattlesnake-eating contest. This wouldn't be hard since she grew up where Elizabeth has spent most of her life—maybe it's something in the Carolina soil. Don't get me wrong. I love the Tar Heel State. I'm just talking about a couple of its women.

I can't wait to get home. I want to finish reading the last chapters of Jeanette's novel as soon as I can. I spend the whole dinner daydreaming about Jeanette and about watching the women of Alexander McCall Smith's "Go-Go Handsome Men's Bar" shake their God-given taken talent. But I keep my cool. I don't want to give Martha the slightest idea of what's gonna on.

* * *

I drive my car back to the house, enter through the garage, and go straight to my office. I hide the manuscript in my desk drawer and lock it. In Martha's mind, the word "privacy" is synonymous with "prying," since they both begin with a *p*. She thinks it's her job as my wife to invade anything that belongs to me.

The next morning, while Martha is practicing upstairs on her piano, I decide to start reading the last few chapters. Turning the key in the locked desk drawer, I see (*thank God!*) the bag with the manuscript in it. I exhale like a propane tank seeping gas—like a man acquitted of murder charges. If she knew what I had in here, she would break the lock and set the pages on fire.

I swallow a few sips of coffee and move out to the deck. A large, modern "porch," as my southern mama would call it, overlooking a quarter of an acre of the best-manicured lawn and a man-made pond the size of an Olympic rink, where ducks and geese are gliding along like ice skaters. My grandmother, if she were alive, would enjoy rocking on the porch, smelling, and counting the flowers. And Jeanette would love the view—and the breeze. I can see her now, pulling off her shoes and making herself comfortable. Then I could massage her toes—and anything else she would allow.

I start reading where I left off, at Chapter Twenty-One. It's unbelievably romantic, bringing back delicious memories of a dinner we had at Mie N Yu, a Moroccan-themed restaurant. Unlike before at her apartment, now I read line by line, recapturing a photographic kaleidoscope of that day.

Chapter Twenty-One
"Only be careful and watch yourselves closely."
Deuteronomy 4:9

That Thursday, I decide to be on the safe side. I wear a sober black, floor length skirt with matching accessories so Roscoe will know that I am serious about doing business.

I arrive at the restaurant on time. Inside the door, the entrance is covered with a thinly woven muslin curtain, with fringes at the bottom and gold tassels at the top, blowing seductively in the wind. The minute I cross the threshold, I feel as if I am in a foreign land. I stop momentarily. Maybe I'm at the wrong restaurant. I check the address in my electronic date book. I've got it right.

Hanging from the ceiling in the dimly lit reception area are three beautiful, Moroccan lamps the color of dark wine. My hostess escorts me through an area that looks like a desert marketplace. The tables are covered in colorful mosquito nets, and the seats arranged in a round covered tent are pure lambskin red and gold leather. As we move up the staircase, I see a Buddha sculpture on the wall. I am thinking, 'Roscoe Wilson sure knows how to choose an exotic restaurant.'

At the far end of the room, my hostess leads me to an enclosed area where heavy maroon draperies hang from ceiling to floor. The draperies hide two tiny rooms, each about the size of a French water closet. As I get closer, I realize there is space enough for only two people. 'This is the idea, isn't it?' I think. The lack of space frightens me; I stop a few feet away.

No, I think. He didn't book this suite. How in the world are we gonna to conduct business sitting in such close quarters? I feel like I am entering his French boudoir, where I'm expected to disrobe immediately.

The hostess, with both hands, motions me to come closer. I can't move. She walks over to where I am standing and gingerly pulls me forward with her left hand, but I freeze. I resist her with the force of a disobedient dog being pulled by his master's leash. Still, she pulls. I grind my heels deeper into the carpet. My chest starts to heave up and down as if I am having an asthma attack.

Finally, I relent and step forward. Holding me tightly by the hand, our hostess swings out her other hand and unties the curtain-roped cord like a maestro conducting her orchestra.

"Welcome to the Love Nest." She smiles.

Behind the draperies sits Roscoe, smiling like a Cheshire Cat. He is seated at a table that would best fit two midgets. He motions me to sit beside him.

If I turn to the right, his face will be almost in mine, and if I turn to the left, my body will touch his. If I shift my feet or hands in any direction, I'll bump his knee or some other part of his body. Our bodies are almost entwined. I feel trapped.

Our waitress quickly appears. I think she senses my dismay. She pauses for a moment before speaking and asks if we are ready to order.

"I think we need a few minutes," Roscoe says, shooing her away. "You okay, Katrina?"

"Do I look okay? "

He chuckles. "What do you think?"

Gaining my composure, I ask, "Why did you choose this room?"

"I think this will afford us some privacy," he says as if he's planning a business conference.

"You got that part right." A little too much privacy, with an unwanted dose of intimacy.

"I want to talk to you without distractions."

"I see."

"You know how it is, Katrina," he goes on. "I have to be careful 'cause I'm married."

"How could I forget?"

"I don't want my wife or anyone she knows to see me."

"I don't want anyone to see me either. Of course, you took care of that." I sigh. "We might as well eat and get right down to business because I have to be home at nine p.m. sharp."

That's not quite true. But I want to create urgency and limit the time he'll have to entice me to do anything I don't want to do.

"What do you recommend?" I ask.

He simply replies, "I've never been here before."

I jerk the menu out of his hands, scan it in a flash, and decide on a couscous dish.

"I'll take the American-style chicken."

Does he think I really care what he'll take? I just want to eat and get the heck out of here.

After we are served, we eat in almost total silence until he says, "Katrina, I hope you aren't angry with me about inviting you here." He nervously taps his right foot on the floor. "You do understand, I hope?"

"Yeah, I guess I do. But I don't like hiding behind these curtains. I feel like I am in a mausoleum."

The food is delicious, and in spite of the atmosphere, I relax, and I ask about the referral.

"Katrina, my contact was supposed to call me back today, but he didn't."

"You invited me here for nothing?" This was supposed to be a business meeting, but Roscoe has turned it into a romantic dinner. He promised me a business referral . . . I get that sinking feeling again—the feeling that Roscoe is saving me for himself. I start to feel like a concubine candidate.

"No, that's not how it is."

"How is it, then? I thought you had someone who could hire me, but you don't. That's the only reason I came here. I thought you had a real contact."

"Wait! Hold it a minute. Calm down," he says. "I called him before I left my office, and I couldn't reach him."

"I don't believe you. You planned this, didn't you?"

"I truly want to help. I do."

"Do it, then." I decide that as soon as I finish my dinner, I'm gonna. I don't want dessert, tea, or coffee, and I certainly don't want him. "You misled me."

"No, I didn't."

"Yes, you did!" I shout.

"But I need contracts, do you understand?"

"Did you buy the book?"

"I couldn't find it."

"You couldn't find it! You must be kidding. I don't want to talk about it anymore."

"Ahh, don't be like that. Come on. Do you need anything, Katrina?"

"I just told you what I need. What's wrong with your ears?"

"Why don't I help you out? Give you some money until we can find some contracts?"

"Until we can find some? How long is it gonna to take 'we'?"

"Please let me help you. Katrina?"

"I'm leaving in ten minutes," I say as I wolf down my food.

"Finished already?" he asks.

"What does it look like? Doesn't it look like I've finished?"

Realizing how angry I am, he calls the waitress and asks for the check. The waitress looks puzzled, and I'm sure she wonders if there was a problem with our food.

After she leaves, I stand up and pull my bag off the back of my chair, fling it over my shoulders, and walk down the steps like a Naomi Campbell diva. Roscoe follows right on my heels, a greyhound trying to keep up with the pack.

Every few steps, he apologizes. "I'm sorry, beautiful."

"That's Katrina to you."

When we get to the front door, I pull it open, dash out, and let it swing behind me. It almost hits Roscoe in the chest.

He runs behind me and sticks an envelope in my coat pocket.

"What is this?" I demand.

"Your cab fare. A little something from my secret account."

"Fine. Now, would you please leave me alone? I don't want to punch you in the face."

I take the envelope and shove it down in my pocketbook. Lucky for me, a cab is passing. I hail it and jump in before it comes to a complete stop.

As the taxi pulls up in my driveway, I open the envelope. Roscoe has written a curt note that reads:

Dear Katrina,

This is hard for me to say, but my friend reneged on the referral at the last minute. I knew you would be angry. To tell the truth, I do not know many people in the event-planning industry. But I will try harder the next time.

Let me make it up to you. I would like to be your mentor. I want to help you succeed. Here's a "little something" to show you how sorry I am. Forgive me for not being upfront, but you just don't know how much I care about you.

Roscoe

PS. Oh! Forgive me, but you are the most intriguing woman I have ever met.

I read the note and realize how difficult it must have been for him to write it. As a result, I start to feel a greater respect for him. But I know he can do better. The money is fine, but I want to stand on my own. I ponder this for a moment and then peep in the envelope. To my surprise, there are more than fifty $100 bills and various others in smaller denominations.

He has given me more money than I can safely count in the backseat of a cab—much more than I expected. After fumbling around in the envelope and the initial shock wears out, I find a single $20 bill and hand it to the driver.

"Keep the change," I say.

As soon as I enter my apartment, I kick off my shoes, flop down on my sofa, and began to count the money more carefully this time.

I am flabbergasted. When I finish tallying it up, the total amounts to $5,200. I am shocked. I don't know what to do.

I am so caught up in reliving the experience that I don't hear Martha's red Mercedes drive up in the garage. I snap out of my reverie when she screams my name.

"Jasper!"

My head jerks up faster than a snapping turtle's bite, sending pages flying all over the deck. I knock over my coffee cup, smearing the pages with the last few drips, and lean over to pluck them up quicker than my mama picking feathers off a chicken. Scrambling, I put the pages between the sections of the morning newspaper.

"What you up to, Jasper?" asks Martha.

"Making some notes for the deacons' retreat," I say.

"Close, man, close," Jimmy Mack says.

✳ ✳ ✳

PART II

Emotional Well-Being

"Ninety percent of African American congregations do not believe in therapy. They use the excuse that God can cure all illnesses—not accepting that God gave us therapists and doctors to cure the mind and the emotions."

— Jeanette L. Priceless

"The trouble with life is there are so many beautiful women and so little time."

John Barrymore

I avoid—my usual way of dealing with things, especially with Trustee Anderson whenever I'm at church and wityou know who whenever. Just whenever. So far it has worked. I know he hasn't given up though.

I turn my attention to Jeanette more frequently, e-mailing her after a severe bout of missing her.

> *I haven't heard from you in two days. How are you?*
>
> *Jasper*

All this contact between us soon threatens to turn into something much more, and it looks like I might be putting our relationship right back on the hot track.

Today she's agreed to meet me again. As always, I'm excited to see her because I don't know what she's planning. When she opens the door to her apartment, she is an emperor's vision in a flowing white African robe accented with a gold embroidery neckline and a smile to outsmart a Colgate whitening toothpaste commercial. It gives me the willies to be here, but my passionate desire for Jeanette far outweighs my fear.

"What is life without a little risk and recklessness?" says Jimmy Mack provocatively.

"I'm terrified that Martha will find out. The main thang, man, is I adore Jeanette. Can't stay away. And she never found out about my thirty-year relationship with Rebecca, did she?"

"Okay."

I whistle softly as Jimmy Mack holds his head up. I stride across the room like a cheetah in a Botswana game reserve. As the beastly king, I am at home among her eclectic old-world furniture, her vibrantly colored African American and African art collection, which remind me that I am supposed to go to Africa. She smiles, and her cheeks nearly touch the gold earrings dangling on either side of her face. From below a white head wrap, her eyes beckon like an ocean buoy on a dark and mysterious sea. She spins around, and I can see a few strands of her hair peeking sensually from the nape of her neck.

I'm toast.

"Hello to you."

"And to you."

She hangs my coat in the closet, laughing for no apparent reason I can discern.

"She know you got the hots for her," says Jimmy Mack.

I drop my hat on the heart-shaped table and slide comfortably into what has become "my seat" at her dining-room table. I glance at her toenails, painted crimson red, mocking me from a pair of gold metallic sandals. I feel feverish, like a patient in the early stages of influenza.

"She is rocking it," says Jimmy Mack.

Jeanette is weaving a spell on me. I gaze across the room, trying to break it. My misty eyes notice her huge red couch, a place where I have never before sat nor lain, taunting me each time I lay eyes on it. I sink into it; in my fantasy, I watch as she dances toward me, Tina Turner style, and the wrap falls suddenly off her head. She quickly gathers each end and loops the cloth around her hands, as if she has choreographed this whole incident.

"I'm your fairy godmother," she says, smiling, as she picks up a wand, a star-studded candy-colored toy. She twirls it around in her hand playfully, as if it actually has magical powers. She pushes a tiny knob, and the lights blink like Christmas.

Just the thought of having a woman nurturing me makes me feel strong and oh-so-good inside.

What is she gonna to do next? I wonder. I know that it's fun time, and I'm willing—that's for sure.

She picks up a black-striped tiger puppet and says, "I want to play a game. Put your hand in the puppet."

"Which one?"

"Either one. As your fairy godmother, I can give you incredible power with my wand—power to take charge

and rule your entire universe. Power to withstand your ene-
mies—especially Trustee Charles Anderson."

"Good!" I say self-assuredly.

"As I wave my wand, repeat these words after me: *My
strength will increase tenfold. I will feel my power grow
deep, deep inside of me. I need only believe. I take control of
my situation with Anderson.*"

I repeat her words, my voice booming like Paul
Robeson's.

She pushes a button and the red, blue, and green lights
spark and flicker. "By the power invested in me by the universe and God, I command you." Her face wears a serious
expression. "Now wiggle your tiger fingers, and all your
fears of anything and anyone will dissolve."

I struggle to wriggle my fingers inside this cramped
puppet. I sit up as tall as a rear admiral and smile like I've
won the billion dollar lottery. I want to cry. I want to grab
her by the waist and give her the biggest football huddle-
hug ever displayed by a quarterback... electricity surges
through my body like current through an eight-inch power
cord.

"Your decision-making power will influence the lives
of millions and millions of people, and you will be known
globally as the great decision maker."

I feel I could be president not only of the United States
but the world. I can conquer any situation.

Finally, she waves her wand again over my head. "You
will receive the happiness that you deserve."

"I told you that my son-in-law wants us to go to Africa
this summer?" I ask. "If I go, I'll probably see tigers."

"Sounds exciting," she says, though her tone is unim-
pressed. "You sure are traveling a lot."

"I'm not sure yet if I'll go. But I am gonna on the deacons' retreat this weekend.

"Okay . . . to seal these traits into your spirit and soul for all eternity, I'm giving you extra stars for vulnerability and willingness to play."

"Hold out your hand," she commands. "What is your favorite color? By the way, my favorite color is red—and any derivative or shade of it within the color spectrum," she informs me.

"Mmmmm . . . blue, I think."

"Fine, then. Blue is what you'll get."

Reluctantly I extend my palms toward her. She grasps my left hand and examines it like a nurse searching for a vein. She gently places in my palm one by one several of Mrs. Grossman's blue stick-on stars, a popular brand used by early childhood education teachers, which makes me nostalgic for my sweet kindergarten teacher. I'm so nervous and excited that beads of sweat break out on them like chicken pox. The stars don't stick.

"Where else can I put them?" Now that it seems I can't have the stars, I want them even more.

"I'll put them on your arms," she says.

Anything to please her.

I dutifully unbutton my shirt and carefully roll up my sleeves. Like Mother Mercy, she examines my hairy arm for the perfect spots to place them. She lovingly plants one in the sweaty socket of each elbow.

Gazing up in her eyes, I think, *My lovely.*

"Each star represents your bravery this week. One for each act," she says. Her statement is powerful. Nothing could feel more profound.

God, I wish she were my wife, I think. Overwhelmed, I simply stare at her.

"Wife and lover," says feisty Jimmy Mack.

True, true, true.

"I could get addicted to you, Jeanette," I confess. "You are the epitome of what every fairy godmother should be. You know, since I retired, I've been trying to repair my marriage. But ninety percent of the time, I've been thinking about you."

The atmosphere is as pregnant as a mother carrying quadruplets. She seems not to know what to say. There is nothing to say.

"I have written a children's book about Obama," she says, beaming with pride. "I hope he can turn this economy around. I've got all my money in the bank."

"I'm so very proud of you," I say.

"Creative people just have to be creative."

"Read it to me," I say anxiously.

I listen with the ears of a maestro, intently giving her my undivided attention. When she finishes, my chest swells like a proud papa bear.

"Your writing is flourishing."

"Thanks," she replies, childlike.

I stand, taking her gingerly by the hand, and pull her to the center of the Oriental rug, leading her into a slow dance.

* * *

That weekend I attend the deacons' retreat. We discuss church business as usual. In the evening we have a guest speaker, the Reverend John Motley, III, who speaks on maintaining a strong relationship with your family. Since the most pressing subject on all our minds is the economy, I also invite Assistant Professor of Economics Dr. Ratha of Howard University.

* * *

Obama appointee Timothy F. Geithner has taken over as secretary of the Treasury, causing a great outcry from the public. He is not progressive enough for some people and too liberal for others. He signs a law giving a $780 billion bailout to several major banks in jeopardy. Thank God it was not my bank, *Let the Sunshine In*. Many just went under or merged, like Bears Stearns and Merrill Lynch.

I don't know where my bank got its name, but I do know when I lost that $10 million I invested, right before I slit my wrist, I collapsed into black clouds of utter darkness and reacted like a man I never met.

* * *

"Doctor Armstrong, Doctor Armstrong, report to the psych ward immediately!" a frantic voice repeats over and over again. Swiftly two men converge on me like CIA operatives in an Al Qaeda raid. They lift me up by the armpits, dangling my body like a trapeze artist.

I form the biggest ball of split and hurl it at the technician, who looks like a Samurai. The last thing I remember hearing is: "Okay, take 'im down."

My takedown is swift. The Gestapo couldn't have done it any faster.

Stopping in front of a door to a nondescript room, the technician unlocks it quickly, stands back, and pushes me in. He locks the door behind us.

The takedown crew deposits me in a stark and tiny room with cinder-block walls. They plop me down on a tiny twin-sized mattress covered only with a white sheet. Scanning the room from my position, I stare up at the ceiling. Everywhere I look, I see nothing but bubble white—a pristine room without the heavy medicinal smell.

"This is the quiet room," says the technician. "We've brought you here for your safety."

I feel worse than a kindergarten kid sent to the "time out" room. In a real sense, this is the case.

"Take your clothes off, Mr. Beamon," says the other technician.

"WHAT?"

"Take your clothes off, man!" says the linebacker as he rolls back his shirtsleeves, exposing thick hairy arms the size of Mike Tyson's.

By now I'm too afraid to argue. I hesitate for a second then asked timidly, "All of them?"

"All of them," he repeats.

My anxiety begins to rise again. *I'm not a vicious criminal,* I think. But this is the official protocol for a combative patient like me.

"Now?" I ask.

"Now!"

They hand me a hospital gown. I dress with my back turned to this unwanted audience. I must be taking too much time, because without any warning, they gently lay me down on the mattress. Then they flip me over on my stomach. I struggle. They pull my pants down and off in a split second. I'm as naked as I came into this world. And embarrassed.

The linebacker seizes my left and right legs while the other technicians hold me down by my arms and head.

A nurse enters the room. She folds my clothes neatly and places them on a cot next to the door. Then she scurries over and takes my vital signs. "Mr. Beamon, I am gonna to give you 20 milligrams of Geodon," the nurse says, "to help you calm down." She shoots me up. All my feelings evaporate like morning mist. Within ten minutes, I'm hang gliding. Not since I smoked my first marijuana cigarette in college have I felt so carefree. This is almost as good as I felt when I made my first million dollars.

The linebacker, standing a leg's length away, stares at me, as if still thinking I might escape.

What's wrong with him? I think.

"The question is, what's wrong with you?" says Jimmy Mack.

"I feel gooood!"

* * *

Over coffee with the deacon and the trustee boards (which consist of several rich men like myself), the conversation for the first thirty minutes is about Obama and black men. We are supposed to be reviewing the church's end-of-the-year fiscal status and planning for the next five years.

"Obama reminds me of Gravely," I say, recalling how he stood up for me when I was in the Navy.

"Who is he?" asks a trustee.

"You know, man, the first African American admiral," I say.

"Yeah, I think I heard something about him," says one wealthy deacon.

"He's one of the reasons you've been able to make so much money?" asks another deacon.

"Yeah." He was a mighty good man."

Sarcastically, Charles asks, "He's black, isn't he?"

"Sure he is. But many commanders and folks of that rank rarely acknowledge the presence of some enlisted men, more or less lower-ranking officers. He was a real cool cat," I reiterate. "Gravely spoke to all his Navy ship staff regardless of rank or creed or color," I add proudly. "Always spoke to me even when I was off duty. Helped me to get training I was able to use in my business. Some called him an Uncle Tom, but he was a 'race man' in his own way," I say.

"Like Obama, huh?"

"I'm not sure yet," I say.

"Or like Mayor Fenty," another deacon laughs.

"Whew," Jimmy Mack says, "you can breathe easy—you've got money."

"Just a little. I don't want to lose it," I say. "I already feel guilty for folks who don't have any, and especially when I think about retiring—selling my company up from under all those hard-working employees of mine."

"Why'd you do it, fool?" asks Jimmy Mack.

"Martha made me."

"Say no more," says Jimmy Mack.

"Bush restarted AIG," says Trustee Anderson.

"Yeah, some folks didn't want him to do that, but I'm glad he gave them a shot in the arm. Where would banks get their backup? Now my money is insured. Up to the limit, that is."

"That's only $250,000 for each account holder regardless of how much money you have, Jasper," says Trustee Anderson in a jealous tone.

Do you even have $250,000 to insure, Anderson? I say snidely to myself.

I admire folks like Obama and Admiral Gravely. Both of these men are the first in accomplishing many things that other black men have never done. I'll never forget the first time I beheld Gravely's face.

* * *

Stepping on the deck of the *Taussig*, Commander Gravely is a towering figure at six feet three inches tall. I'm happy to serve under him.

"Tall like you wish you were," Jimmy Mack whispers.

I'm average height, but some folks tease me and call me "little man."

His two-hundred-plus-pound body is as imposing as that of an offensive lineman. If I were a woman or of the other persuasion, I'd whistle *ooh la la*. A hush falls over the deck. As I watch him stride across the room, I recall his many accomplishments, the honors he earned—the Korean Presidential

Unit Citation award and the Meritorious Medal—and not least of all the barriers he has overcome to become the first African American to do so many important things.

With the 40mm gunnery as a powerful backdrop, Samuel L. Gravely's voice booms out like a cannon. The water surrounding the ship shines and glitters reflectively like blue pearls and diamonds. The ship's wheel slices the waves like the giant blades of a hammer saw.

His speech is awe-inspiring, meant to encourage and inspire the crew for the dangerous mission ahead in Vietnam. He sounds like a football coach rallying his team to win the homecoming game. As I hear him talk, I almost get goose pimples.

"We've been called in to support our fellow Navy comrades," he says, a somber expression unfolding across his face. At the end of his speech, surely there is not one member of the crew who wants to disappoint the commander—I know I don't. So perhaps my attachment to him goes beyond his record as a Navy officer.

"Yes, sir!" responds the crowd.

The gravity of his statement makes me realize the seriousness of our mission. I feel like I've been hit in the gut.

I remember my training days when bullying mounts from within my platoon. I awake before Gunnery Sergeant Raleigh blows his whistle and the bells start ringing. I can't sleep well—who knows why? Maybe because I'm not adjusted to sleeping with a room full of men, complete strangers varying in ethnic groups and races. Blacks are in the minority here.

How can I sleep when my rest is interrupted five times a night by the two loud, snoring brutes on either side of my bunk? They are overweight recruits, bullies from Mississippi and Alabama *respectively*. They sound worse than cows mooing on the farm at four in the morning.

I struggle out of bed and run to the head. I want to take a shower before all this Navy livestock rushes in. I don't like men noticing my body. It's not that I'm ashamed, just that I don't feel comfortable taking showers with a lot of strangers—and especially strange Southern white men. I remember how much my stepbrothers ridiculed me; that scar tissue isn't healed yet.

They say size matters, though, and I'm satisfied with my manhood, my Jimmy Mack. God gave him to me. But I don't have to show him to the world. I mull over this weighty matter, dress, and climb back in bed, throwing the covers up over my head.

"Well, if it ain't Jasper," says one of my neighbors, pulling back my blanket. "Hey, boys, he's finished showering already."

Droplets of sweat fall from my armpits like medicine in an IV. I feel like dashing for the nearest exit.

"What you trying to do, man, gain some extra points with the Gunnery Sergeant?" says the big muscular redhead from Mississippi.

His partner in abuse, George, is a slender guy whose accent sounds as if he's just left the pig farm.

"Naw, man, he's worry we'll see that tiny dick of his! Don't all y'all black boys have big ones?" he asks as he reaches out to grab my crotch.

I jump out of bed like a moon bouncer. "Maybe they put something in the food and this here boy's got hissef the runs," laughing as I race away.

After I hear them leave the head, I try to brush off their comments and return to my cot, just as the rise-and-shine lights are blasted in my face.

I know that I've got to do this every day. Get up early, eat like a wolverine, tolerate the yelling and the bullying.

Follow the rules. If I don't, I won't make it through. All this abuse reminds me of home, but I take it in stride. I have to. I shore up myself by dreaming about my future.

But I admire Gravely for his activism on behalf of black seamen. My college recruitment officer schooled me on the racial situation before I joined the Navy. On July 26, 1949, Harry Truman desegregated the military, but discrimination has remained rampant. In the beginning, they were allowed to do little more than domestic or menial labor such as cooking and cleaning the ships. Black soldiers and sailors are denied promotions, salary increases and are treated as less than human.

When I join the Navy, in 1963, racism is still prevalent in civilian life as well as the military. Black organizations like SNCC and leaders like Malcolm X and Dr. King are steadily organizing protests and fighting for our rights. These are tumultuous times, and our leaders are rigorously breaking down racial barriers in all aspects of society. But it is still difficult for African Americans to find gainful employment that matches their skills and education.

The armed forces is one of the few places, besides prison where a young black man can find steady employment, earn benefits somewhat equivalent to his white male counterpart (who receives good pay just for being white), eat three meals a day, and sleep in a decent bed every night. These are the primary reasons I sign up.

The Navy is my first choice because of its elite reputation, selectivity, and its opportunities for promotion to leadership positions within a complex hierarchy. My bachelor of science in engineering from A & T University qualifies me to become a commissioned officer right after OTS, Officer Training School. As an officer, I am promoted to a managerial position where responsibility, respectability and status is bestowed upon me. In addition, Navy training is regarded as equivalent to the best Ivy League education. On the job, I acquire technical skills and further training that enhance my career and help me reach my primary goal of becoming rich.

President John F. Kennedy, Jr., whom I admire greatly, served as a lieutenant in the Navy. He also came from a large, wealthy, and loving family, unlike me, but I'm not discouraged or deterred by this. I can earn my money. What better way to feel loved and accepted than to join a military service in which our president belonged and succeeded so admirably? Furthermore, President Kennedy created the Navy SEALs, the most daring group of service men in the entire military arena.

The Navy is still discriminatory even in the 1960s. By joining, I strike preemptively. It is not a revolutionary step for me. I can control where, how, and possibly how long I live even as I fulfill my military duty. I wholeheartedly agree with Frederick Douglass's view on the African American man's ability to fight in wars, though I am in no hurry to prove it. I joined the Navy because I *don't* want to get killed. I joined because I don't want to risk fighting on the front line where my chances of getting killed are much greater.

During the Civil War the tens of thousands of slaves were permitted to fight only after white soldiers on both sides annihilated black men. Reservations about black men serving in the war came from the highest office. President Abraham Lincoln himself thought that Blacks were unqualified in protecting themselves in a war. Many like him agreed that it was an absurd idea. In 1862, blacks were recruited on a limited and experimental basis. Frederick Douglass, whose son served in the Union Army, wrote and spoke powerfully urging black men to enlist as a means to gain their freedom. As Douglass predicted, black men fought bravely and valiantly in the military.

African Americans are being drafted disproportionately to serve in Vietnam, and are more often given the menial jobs as well. More of them are being sent into combat than any other racial or ethnic group, and more of them are being killed. Our black leaders have begun to pressure the Army about the high casualty rate among African Americans. I don't want to put myself at risk of an early demise.

Several years later, I will learn that Stokely Carmichael accuses the Pentagon (and rightfully so since we were dying by the handful) of using blacks as "cannon fodder."

"You made the right decision," proclaims Jimmy Mack. "Sho 'nuff."

Plus, I want to taste life like it was at my university: one big party after the other. With ship assignments in ports from France to Japan, the Navy can provide me with the ultimate opportunity to enjoy my life again.

It's another prestigious organization, like the Omegas, that can offer me the status and later on the ability to make money. It makes me feel good to associate with the best.

Anyway, I want to get as far away as possible from the Grimes and my past, as far away as the sea and a Navy vessel can take me.

I've heard nothing but good things about Gravely and how well he treats his crew. He's known for his gift of nurturing fatherless men like me. I want him to become my "sea daddy," which I still need even at my age, 'cause Grandmama was the only "parent" who ever doted on me. I still feel the

A MEMOIR OF MY DEMISE AND RISE

deprivation from growing up fatherless. In fact, the day I applied to join the Navy was the very first time I wrote my real daddy's name on any application or form.

* * *

"Beamon, I'm surprised you didn't jump ship," Trustee Anderson says, putting me down again.

"Give me a break—I rescued Navy SEALs, won a prestigious medal, and got honorably discharged."

"Good job, boy," sneers Anderson.

I try desperately to shut out the memories that Trustee Anderson keeps resurrecting. But it's impossible.

"A & T, A & T, Aggie, Aggies, I'm tired of hearing about that school—it's little more than a training ground for hicks," injects Anderson nastily.

"Who's a hick?" I ask, feeling like I could go to blows right away.

"You and all those other farmers who go to that school," Trustee Anderson says, poking fun at me even more.

"Jesse Jackson went there."

"So what?"

"Lighten up, Trustee Anderson," says Deacon Pearson. "After all, Jasper is rich."

"Okay, Beamon, we came here to talk about the church's financial shape not your exploits in the Navy," protests Anderson, with his glasses dangling from his chest like Hercule Poirot's pince-nez.

"Gravely was some man!" agrees another deacon.

"Yeah . . . but we've heard enough," says Anderson. "The Obama administration gave American International Group a shot in the arm, too," he continues, interrupting the recap of my Navy experience.

"A shot alright. That's a major and an expensive surgery to the tune of $780 billion dollars!" says Jimmy Mack.

"No way," I say.

"What are these banks propped on anyway?" says one deacon.

"On the Federal Reserve," says another.

"Someone needs to take control of the New York Stock Exchange and the banking industry. How can they run wild and play with our money like this? They invest in all kinds of shady and worthless deals, proclaiming to their investors that the companies are worth billions of dollars. Their aim is to make as much money as possible for their clients and themselves."

"You know what they call it? 'Collateral debt obligation.' Man, they are just as bad as Enron selling worthless energy. They call it 'assets,' but it's just trash."

"They know. The government and Congress know it," I say.

Shaking his head, "Yeah, many times they do," says Trustee Charles.

It's one of the few times he's ever agreed with me.

"Deregulation started slowly under the Carter administration and came into full force under Reagan," says Trustee Charles.

"He deregulated the banks, Wall Street, and other industries," says one deacon.

"Even the airlines," I join in. "Don't you remember that?"

"Yeah," says Charles.

"You see what's happening. They regulated themselves for real," I say. "They make the rules."

"You're right," they say in unison.

"Reagan favored the supply side economics. He also gave tax incentives and subsidiaries to these guys and even allowed interstate banking!"

"Before he did, banks could only operate in one state. Now the crooked bastards are all over the country," Jimmy Mack whispers quietly to me.

I campaigned for Obama, too, once I saw he was winning. I did a little phone banking, but mainly I contributed money to his campaign. The maximum amount allowed.

"You're right again. They all shouldda done that," snarled Jimmy Mack.

The way things are gonna, I don't know if this country will survive. It's like the Great Depression my mama talked about so much.

"We'll be standing in bread lines like before," says another deacon agonizingly, as if the prospect is unthinkable.

"I give Obama credit. He's doing the best he can," I say.

"Yeah," says Charles unquestionably. "Man, the mess he inherited started decades ago."

"He's trying, if those Republicans will let him, to regulate the financial industry by putting some regulations in place."

We get little accomplished at the meeting. Even when we are discussing other subjects, my mind is wracking over the outcome of what these jokers are calling a recession.

I feel like I'm losing control of my senses. If the government can't insure my money, who will? Maybe I will transfer it to an offshore bank in the Cayman Islands and go live there. But what good would that do? *Their banks are probably in the same situation as ours are in the U.S.,* I mutter to myself.

We adjourn the meeting after two hours. I drive home slowly, my brain burning with the "what ifs" like I'm coming down with the measles.

What if my bank goes under?

Yeah, it's okay to insure my deposit to $250,000—but I've got $40 million, 90 percent of my money is uninsured.

"You know the Federal Reserve isn't gonna to let a bank like *Let the Sunshine In* fail. It'll try to set up a merger if nothing else," says Jimmy Mack.

"What if they can't find a bank to merge with?" I ask.

"They'll buy it out like they did *First Chicago* in the 1980s," says Jimmy Mack, poking me on my legs, "and the Federal Reserve Bank will take over the executive management of the bank until it gets back on its feet."

"What if I can't pay my mortgage?"

"Now, you know you don't have a subprime or an adjustable mortgage or interest-only loan. Even if you did, you could still pay the mortgage."

"Yeah I hope so. That's why I have nightmares and insomnia every night. I hope the banks can stay afloat so I don't lose any of my money and can keep on paying the mortgage. The value of my house doubled from the late 1990s when I bought it, but by 2006 it is worth less than what I paid for it."

"I feel you. Obama is trying to use Keynes's economic policy," says Jimmy Mack. "You know, the economical model that Franklin Roosevelt used. But it is a different time now."

"You got that right," I say.

"Back then the depression was so devastating, Roosevelt could get anything through Congress. Obama's trying his best to put regulations back in place and stimulate the economy, but the Republicans are fighting like a pack of lions to keep deregulation. Whereas Roosevelt could push through what he wanted, including Social Security and other entitlements—which were best for the American economy."

"There is one person I wish I could talk to, confide in. But it is much too late for that, huh?"

"Two fucking years too late," says Jimmy Mack.

"What does that make me?"

"Let me spell it out to you. *Air h-e-a-d*," says Jimmy Mack, weary and more disgusted than I've ever heard him.

* * *

I've still got to handle my situation myself. I can't get into therapy now. People will laugh at me. Ridicule me. Don't I belong to one of the richest churches in the nation, one of those "prosperity theology" kind? God will take care of me.

I call Jeanette before I go to bed.

I stayed at PIW for only 72 hours, the least amount of time possible. Little do I know that procrastination and fear will become my downfall in the near future.

* * *

> "What do we live for, if it is not to make life less difficult for others?"
>
> *George Elliot*

"Why don't you ask someone else?"

"I can't believe you said that," says Jimmy Mack. "You are so selfish—after all the time and energy she spent listening to you whine about your problems, being your confidante, and siding with you against Trustee Anderson. And don't forget not publishing her novel. The gall of some people."

We are sitting at Jeannie's dining room table where all the organizing and editing of her novel so recently came to a halt. She has just asked me to invest in her latest project, which she's been working on in the several weeks since she decided not to publish her book.

"I don't know anyone else," she says plainly.

It is ironic, really. This morning I came here because I want *her* to invest in *me*. I've even dressed for that purpose in a stylish outfit I don't usually wear, even dashing a palm full of Caron on strategic places all over my body. I've got my agenda, and apparently she's got hers.

She was sitting very close to me with her eyes shimmering and her dimpled cheek enthralling. I was thinking, *The Holy Grail is mine*. And then suddenly, she throws me this hand grenade.

She carefully led me to the apex of the afternoon by showing me pictures of renowned filmmaker Charles Burnett. And two articles with selling points on how documentaries have turned into million-dollar investments. She used shrewd business terminology, knowing it would ignite my passion. But it also ignited my suspicion.

"Invest? Invest in what?" I snapped back, flaring up.

"My documentary."

She tells me that she's decided to make a documentary instead of trying to publish her novel. The documentary will be about men "like me" and famous men who desperately need therapy for issues they've had since childhood but who are afraid to get the help they need. Afraid of the perceived stigma they would face in their communities. She has decided not to publish the manuscript now because of Trustee Charles Anderson but to work on a documentary film script instead, and she wants me to fund the project and help contact celebrities to participate in it.

This is when I ask her to find someone else. "That money is for me—for my retirement. For us."

Her face crumbles into a trillion tiny pieces. Despair is a choker around her neck. It's not that I don't want to give her the money. But I'm scared to. It's discombobulating. I do not feel that I deserve the love of this spirited, fun-filled woman—this woman whose company I can never get enough of. I must have the emotionall stability of an orangutan.

I have long accepted that I'm trapped in a marriage to a woman I am too afraid of ever divorcing. Yet it's never occurred to me how selfish and ungrateful I am toward Jeanette.

Jeanette continues, "You ought to ask me how much money I need. Or just offer the amount you think it's worth. Jasper, I had to ride your back, call you, e-mail you, text you for five months to get you to read my manuscript. I've been trying to *help* you. Now it is your turn."

She's mad. I'm in TROUBLE! She's been trying to save my butt, and for that, I should be grateful.

"There you go again. Now, that she has decided not to publish the novel and to collaborate with you on a tale to disguise your relationship from Trustee Anderson, you forget about what she has sacrificed for you," says Jimmy Mack.

I try to explain. "I've consolidated my money with my wife into a joint investment account. It's a lucrative deal: For every million dollars, I accrue $40,000 a year."

"Now don't you sound foolish," Jimmy Mack says.

Jeanette doesn't mumble a word, waiting for me to say more, to give in. But I'm a pig-headed man. I'm only concerned about Martha finding out about my giving her a large sum of money. If I do, I will have to get it from a joint account and hope she doesn't find out about it.

It has been a difficult time. Crisis after crisis. I know deep down just how much Jeanette has given of herself. Much more than I could ever repay.

"You thought I would help you?" I say, softening, sympathizing. Coming to my senses.

Her eyes are watery, and she bites her bottom lip. Suddenly, stomping her feet twice, she pushes her downtrodden body up from the table, saying, "I worked so hard!" She moves a few steps forward and gazes out the window dispiritedly.

Like a man, I want to fix this.

"Well, you caused it didn't you, asshole?" Jimmy Mack says angrily.

"I want to see you succeed, Jeanette," I say.

"That's what you always say, Jasper." She sighs. "I have been incredibly generous with my time, with my emotional resources."

I gaze into her eyes for a millisecond. "How much do you think you need?" I ask affectionately.

She looks up, a glimmer of hope in her eye. "I don't know. Anywhere from $250,000 on up. Some documentaries cost a million dollars. I'd have to let you know."

"I can't give you that large a sum of money," my palms sweating profusely. I walk closer to her, touch her hand lightly hoping she will understand. I look closely into her eyes. "Not now, at least," I stammer. "Gather the financial information, and I will see what I can do. It may take a few days." I'm terribly afraid that Martha will find out since we have joint accounts now. I'm afraid of Martha, but my feelings for Jeanette compel me to show her how much I care. Giving her money is the only way I know how to do that.

I turn my hat around and around in my hands.

SILENCE.

I walk over quietly behind her. "Let me give you a hug," I say, feeling guilty.

* * *

I have nightmares all night long. By the next morning, my fear of Martha finding out has made me change my mind again. I try to come up with other solutions—organizations, government agencies, anything else but me. I call Jeanette the next day. She isn't answering, so I leave a message: "I hope you're feeling better, Jeanette. I've thought of a creative way to get funds for your project."

"You said you were gonna to find out what you could do, man. She needs the money," says Jimmy Mack.

I call again later the same day.

"Jeannie, I know how you can get money for your project!"

"Yeeesssss?" she says, sounding skeptical.

"Check with NIH they have funds for projects like yours."

My suggestion does not appease her. She isn't buying it. "It's very difficult to get money from organizations, much less from an individual," she scoffs. "I don't have a background in filmmaking or psychotherapy."

SILENCE.

"I've never begged you for money, Jasper, and I'm not starting now. I'm gonna to leave it up to God."

"Yeah, do that," I say sarcastically.

Bang! She slams the phone down. Then she calls back immediately.

"You said that you were gonna to help, and I expect you to do it!"

Bang!

I hang up the phone, then turn and trip over Lulu, crashing my head against the edge of Martha's piano.

I expected Jeanette to be upset when I turned her down. But I'm surprised at her fighting indignation, her dogged determination to make me keep my promise. She's a tough one.

What am I gonna to do? I want to help Jeanette. I don't want Martha to find out. I know I need to do something. Can I move enough money into my secret account?

Lulu dashes into the living room and hides under the couch, startling me. This is easier to do these days, and it happens more and more often--a result of my traumatic childhood and exacerbated by my service in Vietnam. The next day I receive the following e-mail:

Dear Jasper:

You are acting very selfish. You are self-centered and unethical. I have been very generous to you. Generosity should beget generosity. I agreed not to tell Trustee Anderson about us. I allowed you to change ANYTHING in my novel that would in the slightest way identify you. And there were many instances of that. You said, "I don't want to get close to this." Well, guess what, Jasper, you should have thought about that some time ago. You already are! And now you need to run toward it not away from it.

If you were not gonna to invest in my project, why did you tell me to gather the financial information? You say you want to see me succeed—well, put your money where your mouth is. This is not the first time you've changed your mind. Why do you have to behave so dishonestly? Why do you always have to take the easy way out?

I prodded you for months to get on board. This is your project, too—your baby, too. You should be asking me what you can do for me and helping me any way that you can!

If I do not hear from you by Thursday at noon, I am gonna to show you that I can learn to be as selfish as you are.

Jeanette

I e-mail her back.

Dear Jeannie,

What are you gonna to do to me? I've postponed my trip to New York. I am gonna to find a producer for your documentary. Please try to understand! I am very sorry that I have poorly communicated with you. I said I would see what I can do, but it will take more than a few days to sort that out.

I do ask you to p-l-e-a-s-e send me the financial information. It will give me a better understanding of what your needs are, and in a few days, I'll be able to tell you exactly what I can and will do.

Without Martha's knowledge, I pray.

It has never been my intention to be selfish, and I am so sorry if that's what I am communicating to you. I think you know that I do make good on my promises. And I promise you that I will do anything, and I do mean anything, to help you!

... Jasper

"She told you. She told you. She told you not to 'f' with her. You led her on, promised to get help, broke dates, lied, promised that you would work things out between you two," says Jimmy Mack.

"Jeanette doesn't adhere to the 'pay to play' theory, so prevalent in PG County but she does feel you owe her. Owe her a great deal, as a matter of fact. Paying her with money is acceptable—to her, it's just fine. Particularly considering the amount of months and years she was your confidante and lay therapist and that you were trying to "play" her. You live in Parental Guidance County— you're familiar with this concept. Above all, she agreed to protect you from Trustee Anderson," Jimmy Mack preaches.

Cupping hands over my ears, I scream, "Stop it! Stop it! Please. I can't stand it." I don't want to dredge up—all that stuff up again!

"It's payback time." Jimmy Mack says laughing like a hyena.

Hi, Jasper.

I'm not gonna to do anything—calm down. It concerns me when you are very upset like this. We can work this out together. I am sending you the financial information and the script in a separate e-mail.

Jeanette/Howard Girl

Whew! Thank God. I've returned from the dead. I write back:

Hi, Jeannie.

My voice is hoarse, like I've been screaming all night. Thanks for your concern. I was admitted to the hospital for shingles and an anxiety attack—racing of the heart due to stress and tension. You remember? So, I am working hard to relax. Jeanette, it's not easy—I try not to get too stressed out over things, but sometimes with all the things gonna on in my life—our past relationship and your upcoming project—it is difficult. I feel like giving up. But I do believe, as you say, that we can work this out together. I desperately want to.

I do have a great lead on a person who I believe will be able to produce the documentary for you at a very reasonable price. I will get that information to you once I get a call back.

...Jasper

Jeannie e-mails me back.

I am so sorry! I know that your life is causing you a lot of stress. I have been worried about you for a long time—I hope you know that. I am glad that you are working on relaxing and calming yourself. And I hope you know that this is what I have been trying to support you to do as well. Please keep trying—and if there is anything I can do, please let me know. And know that I pray for you, too.

Part of releasing tension is talking about the emotions that are making you stressful or the deep underlying issues. This can be frightening, I know. It takes courage and strength. You have both. If you want, we can call back or talk about this whenever you want. Or call me anytime for reassurance.

When I said that I was gonna to learn to be selfish, too, I didn't mean that I would do anything to hurt you. It really upsets me when you get upset, but I needed to express my hurt and pain.

I look forward to getting the contact information. When you come, I will give you a big hug. Okay?

Jeanette

Warmed and relieved by her compassion, I write back one last time.

Thank you for your support and understanding. I appreciate it to the utmost. I know I have changed. I also know I have much more work to do.

...Jasper

My teeth are chattering like an Alaskan polar bear's—I am afraid that Jeanette will tell Martha about the book. Maybe she will find out about all this money I'm giving her, too. I want to be honest about my emotional state of mind: I'm slowly becoming a class-one psychotic.

* * *

CHAPTER 18

"Intuition is the clear conception of the whole at once."

Johann Kaspara Lavator

"We need to talk about the stuff I found in your desk drawer," says the cunning Charles Anderson.

My heart drops to my knees. My mouth is dry as desert sand.

"Deacon, did you forget?" asks Trustee Anderson sounding like the sleazy lizard he is. "Something a friend of yours wrote?"

I repeat my mantra several times before I can reply. *Be calm. Be calm. Be calm.* "No," I reply, so quietly my voice sounds like I've got laryngitis.

"Yes, you heard me. You need to do something about it very soon!" he says.

"I will. Give me some time, please."

"I have already," says Trustee Charles Anderson. "You remember, fool."

"My life is an open book," I say—the same line I gave Jeanette when she told me she had written a book.

"It's gonna be when I finish with you."

"Jeanette and I are just friends. I was trying to help the young lady get her business started."

"It didn't read like that to me." You know what the Bible says, Jasper. 'Whosoever looketh on a woman to lust after her hath committed adultery with her already in his heart."

"Nothing happened between us," I insist.

"Ha, ha, ha," laughs Jimmy Mack.

"Why did you give her five thousand dollars?" asks Trustee Anderson.

"Just a donation—seed money to get her business off the ground."

"You got her off the ground alright," he replies viciously.

"I'm on my way to New York. I've got to run. I'll call you when I get back," I say.

"You make sure you do that."

"*What am I gonna to do?*" I scream to Jimmy Mack. I knew it. I knew it. I knew he was gonna to try to blackmail me.

Graduations are an important ritual in the life of any family. But at a time like this, I can't go to New York. Let Martha go by herself. I need this time to find a filmmaker for Jeanette's documentary and figure out how much money I'm gonna to give her. And decide how I'm gonna to handle Trustee Charles Anderson.

"*A* for *airhead*," says Jimmy Mack. "So you were lying to Trustee Anderson?"

"Yes." With Martha out of town, I can call around without her acting like a detective. "Let's hope he believes I'm gonna out of town."

"Snoop dog," crackles Jimmy Mack.

I hyperventilate like I'm having another attack. I promised my doctor, Jeanette, and myself that I would control my anxiety, but I can't. I am so nervous that after I hang up the phone with Trustee Anderson, I mistakenly dial Jeanette's number.

"It's okay," she says. "Take it easy." Her voice is soothing, like a kitten's purr. "It's okay, Koko," a nickname she calls me when I'm in utter anguish.

She's being extra gentle. Is she concerned that I will have another anxiety attack or that I will renege on helping her with her project? I feel closer to her than ever before.

"Jeanette likes to tease, but she don't play," says Jimmy Mack. "Just show her the money."

"Shut up, man," I reply. But I'm rattled.

"Did you find someone to help me?" she asks.

I tell her I've contacted a group of producers who did a documentary for Martha, a documentary about Christmas music.

"Religious Christmas music?" asks Jimmy Mack.

"Yeah, Jimmy Mack," I reply.

"I am waiting to hear from them now," I say to Jeanette.

I daydream about my runaway scheme, but even dreaming about it makes my heart pound. I toy with the idea of taking a Boeing 747 to anywhere my heart will lead me. And then I think of Jeannie and the dilemma I am in with her.

I've achieved monumental success in my life. But I don't feel, as Jeanette likes to say, grounded. Most of the time I don't even see myself as successful. I thought once I made a million dollars, I would feel good. But I feel like an alcoholic's empty whiskey bottle. I wish someone would tell me what it feels like to be satisfied. To be happy.

"You settle," says Jimmy Mack.

"But I feel unfulfilled. Lifeless."

"It's your own fault."

"Never mind," I say. "Let's not talk about it another time."

The next morning, one of the producers calls me back. "Hi, Mr. Beamon—it's Audrey."

"Hi, Audrey," I say. "Thanks for getting back to me." I rattle off my request as professionally as I can manage, trying to keep my affection for Jeanette and my anxiety out of my voice as I talk about Jeanette's film. "A colleague of mine is looking for a filmmaker to do a documentary for her, and I thought about the professional job you did for Martha." I finally stop to take a deep breath and notice I've been pacing the room and digging my navy blue shoes deeper and deeper into the wooly carpet, hoping to calm myself.

"Colleague, huh?" says Jimmy Mack.

"She's interested in doing something on mental health," I tell Audrey anxiously. "I don't know all the details. I will give you her number, and you can call her. Is that okay?"

"Sure, Mr. Beamon. Thank you for the referral. I'll let you know what happens."

I call Jeanette back and tell her Audrey is gonna to call her.

"Audrey is good," I say, hoping Jeanette will take my recommendation. Then I will have solved one of my problems at least. "The film she made for Martha even won an award."

"Oh! She sounds good," says Jeanette. It doesn't interest her that I am suggesting she use the same film producer that my wife used.

"Stupid! Stupid!" shouts Jimmy Mack. "This could come back to haunt you."

"She's just interested in my healing," I correct Jimmy Mack, "and getting her work done."

"If I was in her head, I'm sure I would hear her brain say, *Poor thing*."

"I made the Guinness Book of Records," I say to Jimmy Mack.

"For what?" asks Jimmy Mack.

"For being the scaredest, stupidest man on the planet." My heart is piddle-paddling like dolphins—I've solved one of my dilemmas. I've arranged to help Jeanette, and I hope she can show me how much she appreciates it.

* * *

CHAPTER 19

"When I know who I am, I will be free."

Ralph Ellison

I see my obituary. I see a playa! A weak and frightened man. A reckless and controlling man. An insecure and unhappy man. An abused man in denial and pretending that a thirty-plus-year marriage represents stability and respectability. A shallow, status-seeking, inauthentic, cheating, lying man always on the skid from his troubles and irresponsible behavior. I see CEO Jekyll and Deacon Hyde. Meeeee!

JASPER BEAMON, 69

Rags-to-Riches Businessman Mr. Jasper F. Beamon, a prominent business owner who built his wealth in fewer than fifteen years after growing up impoverished, died of a heart attack at the age of 69.

Reared on a sharecropper farm in North Carolina, Mr. Beamon escaped poverty through education and hard work. He matriculated to the Agricultural and Technical University in Greensboro, North Carolina with the likes of icon Reverend Jesse "Keep Hope Alive" Jackson.

Mr. Beamon rose to the heights of the business world, amassing a fortune through government contracts for his engineering firm. He often appeared in prominent journals, such as USB Engineers Information and Technology *and* American Society of Engineers, *as well as popular business and cultural magazines such as* Black Enterprise *and* Ebony. *Mr. Beamon was distinguished in his career and is listed in the historical encyclopedia of* Who's Who in Black America. *He received numerous professional awards including the Black Engineer Award as the hardest working man in America (other than James Brown).*

With his money, Mr. Beamon accumulated the trappings of success, with houses in separate states, including a $3 million-plus beach home in Carolina. But he was an abused spouse who lived an inauthentic life of misery and shame.

He is survived by his faithful dog, Ludicrous, nicknamed Lulu; his insanely jealous and greedy wife, Martha; his two money-grubbing children, Rodney and Melanie; no grandchildren, but one in his daughter's oven; three siblings; and various and sundry relatives and friends.

Lord, what's gonna happen to my money?

He is also gone-but-not-forgotten by his longtime mistress of thirty-plus years, Rebecca. Leading a double life, Mr. Beamon was too afraid and too slouchy to seek therapeutic help.

"I feel like Gary Condit—I'm never gonna to be redeemed."

These are the words I blurt out as soon as Jeanette picks up her telephone. I have read her script. Reading about symptoms of men in abusive relationships, the realization that I'm talking about myself hits me like a shock wave.

I am that guy? Oh my God!

"Partner is extremely jealous. Prevents you from maintaining contacts with family members and friends . . ."

That's me. When I die, if people find out about my double life, my obituary will look like this, confirming everything Trustee Anderson says about me.

I got up this morning with the best intentions of helping Jeanette solicit funds for her project. She wants to help people overcome the stigma against seeking therapy. But then I read the script.

It had not occurred to me until now that *I* need to overcome *my* fear—or whatever it is that's keeping me from getting the help I desperately need.

I'm having an "AH-HA" moment, as Oprah would say.

I brew my first cup of coffee, mixing it with too much cream and too much sugar and stirring it with too much guilt and fear. I impatiently wait for Martha to leave the house.

As soon as she gets in her car, I peek at her behind the living room draperies. Before she starts rolling down the driveway, heading towards rehearsal at the Kennedy Center,

I grab my cell phone and call Jeanette. It's early—only around nine fifteen.

"Hello," she answers as if she is expecting this call.

I begin with the news of my impending social demise. I am about to let it all out when the house phone rings.

"Do you need to answer that?"

"Hold on." I pick up the house phone. It is one of Martha's friends. Trying with all my might not to scream, I say, "She just drove off in her car. Catch her on her cell."

I hang up quickly and return to my conversation with Jeannie.

"I am reading your script. I'm upset! I see myself. I feel like the character in your book."

"You *are* the character."

"I see myself."

"Yes."

"I'm convicted. This script of yours condemns me, as sure as if I were a felony suspect. A person in an abusive relationship. I feel like vomiting. I don't want to be like this. *This is not me.*" *I don't want to be like this. This phony me.*

As soon as my words fly out of my mouth, I want to yank them back and crawl with them into my tortoise shell. I'm frightened.

Jeannie's compassion is palpable. Still, I bet this is exactly what she wanted to happen.

"Change will require a lot of emotional work on your part," she says.

"I'm so afraid."

"Cheer up—you're in good company. Anthony Hamilton is right."

"Anthony who?"

"Anthony Hamilton. Thirty-seven years old. Grammy-winning R&B singer."

"Right? About what?"

"That even though men want intimacy and happiness, they run from it."

"OH!" I babble on. "This is a complex situation, Jeanette. I have to make calls without telling my wife. I'm afraid for my reputation. Afraid that someone will find out that I contacted Herschel Walker. I'm afraid of Martha."

"I knew it. I *knew* it."

"Knew what?"

"This is expected. You're having a psychological breakthrough. Thank God!"

I am filled with angst. "I knew you were gonna to get angry," I say.

"I'm not angry."

"I feel like throwing up."

"That's good—that's normal," she comforts me. "You just worked through what must have been a very frightening revelation. This is healing."

But it doesn't feel marvelous. Anguish is all I can feel. I say, "I don't want to be this person. I need to talk to you!"

"You *are* talking to me. Keep gonna."

"I can't keep making all these calls." I feel . . . guilt. I didn't discuss this with my wife.

"I knew it. You were gonna' change your mind," she says.

"I knew you would get angry," I say.

"I'm not angry," she says again. "I need you to keep your promise and heal yourself."

I might as well get this out, too, I think. "I feel guilt because I want you so much, Jeannie!"

"Don't feel guilt. God looked beyond your faults and saw your needs. We're good for each other. There's no shame or guilt connected with my feelings. I have worked them out."

"God's *okay* with it?" I ask. This is contrary to what I have been taught by my maternal grandparents and society's indoctrination. I shake my head, "God's *okay* with it?" I ask again. "You're not serious," I whisper. "I don't feel like it is. Why is my stomach flipping and flopping and my mind racing like its running around a track field. I am restless every night; it takes me an hour to go to sleep, and even after that, I awaken in a couple of hours." *I've got three women who I've been involved with. I feel doubly troubled.*

Jeanette, introspective as always, says, "Like my mother would say, you need to work out your own soul salvation. Deal with your guilt and shame."

"I'm trying, Jeanette. I'm trying. I've never kissed you! I've never touched you!" Still, I—I—I feel guilty.

"God, what in the world is wrong with you?" says Jimmy Mack. "You keep confusing everything. You talk about one thing and then another; first it's the script, then you skip to your guilt, then to wanting Jeanette."

Jeannie continues, "You're doing an extraordinary job, Jasper. It takes a strong and courageous man to do what you're doing. You're phenomenal. Your vulnerability is endearing. Our relationship is pure and innocent. When your fairy godmother sees you on Friday, she is gonna to give you seven—count them, now—one, two, three, four, five, six, seven stars."

"Thank you, Jeannie." I feel understood and relieved.

"Honey, honey," Jimmy Mack smacks.

I talk to Jeannie for more than forty-five minutes. She calms me down. I really am proud of my breakthrough. Her passionate writing—her book, her documentary script—has revealed my situation and emotional state of mind *exactly*.

"What are you gonna to do with it? That is the question," asks Jimmy Mack. "You know your pattern."

I've been living like this all my married life, like a gutless pig and a phony rich man—lying, cheating, and presenting myself as an upstanding citizen as I serve on business and college boards and on my church's deacon board. Until I read this script, it's never occurred to me just how sick I am. I always say I'm gonna get help, but I always chicken out.

"Man, you slack," says Jimmy Mack shaking his head furiously.

* * *

CHAPTER 20

"Why should the devil have all the fun?"

Daddy Grace

The next time I come to her apartment for our "review" session, Jeanette is wearing a pretty, white-and-pink, tie-dyed wrap skirt. Her silhouette is a heavenly configuration of my overactive imagination. Her T-shirt is white and as form fitting as the bra whose outline I wish I could see.

I came looking for it. I found it. I smile and thank the gods for reminding me to dash some sweet smelling after-shave on my face. I'm a cornucopia of passion and desire. I drop my hat on the table and sip my cup of tea as usual. Today it's hotter than ever and honey-sweet.

We discuss various topics, like the president and politics, but my mind ain't on it. I'm ready to get down to more important business.

"Martha makes me erectile dysfunctional," Jimmy Mack says.

"You can't even stand up straight," I chime in. "I told Jeanette about this, too. When I am with Jeanette, I am up like a flagpole the minute I hear her voice. The only way I can have sex with Martha is to have phone sex with Rebecca. You know that as well as I do."

"Hey man," quips Jimmy Mack, "I can't work it."

"Sometimes . . . and sometimes I have to put a brown paper bag over my head."

"You dirty dog. You pretend she's Jeanette."

"Yes," I say, squeaking like a mouse.

"How was your trip?" Jeanette asks.

"Fine," I say, uninterested.

I've just returned from the annual Omega Psi Phi conclave. I have been a brother since the sixties and have sent the organization money for the past twenty years. But I never found the time to attend the national meeting or any local events. Even though after graduation I never see my fraternity brothers for thirty-odd years, we are closer than I am to Martha.

"You've been concentrating on other things, on making money," says Jimmy Mack.

"You know it."

Jeanette loves to flirt, but she hasn't recently. I am operating on a hope and a prayer. Hoping she is as ready to have sex as she is to make her documentary. I snap out of my sexual fantasy, however, because she is asking whether Obama's father is Kenyan.

"I think so," I say.

"Here it is in the *New York Times*."

I glance at the article she's pointing to. "Yes, that's right."

She puts down the paper suddenly and heads toward the kitchen. "Jasper, I've gotta eat something."

I follow her with my eyes. I'm starving, too—but not for food.

The sunlight bursts through her kitchen window, filtering light through her skirt. *Oh! My gracious!* I can see her thighs.

"Jeanette, you better watch yourself. I can see through your skirt."

"Honestly, Jasper, Jeanette could be wearing a potato sack and you would get excited," says Jimmy Mack.

"A choir robe," I confess. Jimmy Mack, my Mandingo Man, is flexing his muscle. I grunt, straining to hold back my overwhelming passion.

"How did you like Birmingham, Alabama?" she asks.

"Despite its horrific history, the merchants were friendly. There were welcoming signs all over downtown. Stores and restaurants gave us deep discounts. We were treated well. Lots of sights and beautiful southern women, although I didn't pay much attention to them," I say jokingly.

Our line brother invited us out on the town like the good ole college days—I told him I was too old for chasing women.

"Sure?" Jimmy Mack smiles back.

Omega Phi Psi made college heaven for me. Omega men, as we are referred to, were the elite and the most macho men on campus. We were allowed to carry out all kinds of pranks and ridiculous behavior with impunity, which impressed everyone from the administration to our classmates—and especially the women, who were in abundance, clamoring at our beck and call. Partying was a mainstay of the fraternity, and it opened me up—brought out my reckless side and, man, once I discovered it, how much I enjoyed it! I've never been the same since.

There were two courts: "lap bunnies" and the "princesses." The former were young women who slurped up their duties: cleaning, washing clothes, doing our homework, and cooking as if they were licking a snowball. They eagerly did their duties with honor and passion.

I watch Jeanette dicing tomatoes on a plastic cutting board, chopping, slicing and juice flying everywhere—it revs up my desire.

"Beam me up, Jim!" I plead with Jimmy Mack. *I feel like a Star Trekker.*

"What did you do while you were there?" she asks.

Barely audible, I say, "We reported on social projects."

She rips lettuce leaves apart into several small pieces. "Do you want some? I can make two veggie burgers as easily as I can make one."

"No."

One devoted bunny took meticulous class notes for me, which didn't happen often. Another, an engineering student, volunteered to take my midterm and final exams. The most exciting bunnies performed private "lap dances," something I wish Jeanette would do right now!

She rejoins me at the table with her plate. "Sure you don't want some?"

The "princesses" supervised the lap bunnies. They were usually very attractive and attentive, too. As supervisors they did anything the bunnies didn't want to do. Needless to say, sex, in its many pleasurable positions and varieties, was plentiful. And as the expression goes, "A good time was had by all"—at least all the men.

That's how I got my line name, which I am proud to carry. It is a variation of my first name (Jasper), plus Mack because I "maxed out on sex," which I'm hoping to do again very soon.

Looking at Jeanette hungrily, I say, "No thanks."

Juice squirts on her T-shirt and drips down her hand onto the table as she bites into her sandwich. "Hmmmm, delicious," she says as the veggie juice sprouts all over her fingers. "You sure?"

Fighting an impulse to suck her fingertips and sink a bite into her neck, I manage to squeak out, "No, thanks."

I watch as she munches and crunches all the ingredients in her mouth. The elongation of her neck tantalizes me. It's as long as a giraffe's and as graceful and majestic as a gazelle's. I want to suck her skin between my teeth.

She finishes the last bite and swipes her lips seductively. She looks up and we lock eyes. I can't hold back no more.

"How about a hug?"

"Okay."

I wrap my arms fully around her waist and squeeze her tight. She smiles. I brush my lips across her neck for a moment and then dig my teeth into her lymph nodes, biting her flesh like a scrawny, mangy dog eating the last morsel of meat on a juicy bone.

She pulls away. "Please, Jasper! Don't suck my neck."

"Oh, you sound so wild!" But I don't pull away. "What are you thinking right now?" I ask as her cell phone rings. I breathe harder.

She jerks her head to the side. "Please, stop," she says, looking right at me. She fumbles for the cell phone but doesn't find it before the ring dies away.

I'm dying to stick my tongue through the gap between her two front teeth.

She eases herself out of my embrace and moves around the opposite side of the table. Her landline rings. She talks for ten minutes. Ten *long* minutes. Bile and guilt rise in my throat.

I shouldn't be doing this, I admonish myself.

When she comes back, I say, "I'm glad that you stopped me, Jeanette. I want to keep things on a business level. But you are responsible for my being so excited."

"Cut the crap," whispers Jimmy Mack.

"I see," she says, looking at me with suspicion. She knows I'm lying.

I get up and walk around the table to be close to her again. Close enough to smell her nature.

"What are you thinking?" I ask, still hoping.

"Nothing."

Jimmy Mack is hard as Christmas candy.

"I adore you," I say.

But she's stronger than I am. She isn't gonna to give it up just like that. I step a few feet toward the door.

"I think I better leave now."

"Testing, testing," says Jimmy Mack.

SILENCE.

"That trick didn't work either," concludes Jimmy Mack.

I walk to the door as she backs up against the wall.

"Your shirt is cute. I like the designs," she says slyly while stepping backwards, putting as much space between me as her wall will allow.

Why is she talking about my shirt at a time like this?

"Thanks," I say.

She bats those "come hither" eyes, and being the "mouth-breeder" that I am, I have an urge to flip her skirt up, yank her panties down, and lick the black fires on baby girl's coochie.

"I'm a-gonna' now," I say, frightened by what I might do if I stay and agitated by what I can't have.

I lose my footing. I put one hand on the wall behind her head.

Lawd have mercy, I say to myself.

I talk like a dog. "You better watch yourself."

She ignores me.

"You're an Omega man," declares Jimmy Mack.

"Where did you get it?" she asks.

"Get what?"

"The shirt."

"I don't remember."

She eases her feet away from the wall. I stir. I wait. I pray for a come-on . . . but no such luck. Disappointed, I hang my head and walk out the door.

* * *

CHAPTER 21

"I have a way of life inside me and I wanted it with a want that was twisting me."

Zora Neale Hurston

Sunday, when the morning radiance bounces off the Romare Bearden painting in my room, I do what I always do. I weasel out. I weasel out of getting therapy and of making a sound commitment to Jeanette.

"Hound dog can't change his swagger?" asks Jimmy Mack.

Driving toward Jeanette's apartment, I practice my closing arguments like a trial lawyer. I've been tossing and turning all night long. I awoke this morning in a feverish sweat, wanting her badly and searching for solutions to this emotional quagmire. I've compared her to Rebecca, but the differences between the two women are so striking that I laugh at myself.

"What if I consummated my relationship with her?" I question Jimmy Mack.

"If she lets you," Jimmy Mack reminds me. "How's that gonna help things?"

I don't want to break things off with Jeannie. But I know that if I proceed with this involvement, I will eventually divorce Martha—and lose my money.

Getting out of the car, I still debate which breakup strategy to use. I settle on pretending I'm a teenager: get angry, blow up, and get it over with. The problem with that is I'm a grown man, almost seventy years old. Why not use my tried-and-true words? *I didn't mean to start a romantic relationship with you, Jeannie. I just want to see you succeed.*

I try to camouflage my nervousness by strutting like Obama. But a Dalmatian can't change the color of his spots. I tap on the door, nervous and excited. Jeannie opens it, and with her brilliant and infectious smile, my resistance fizzles like warm soda pop. She's a sunflower, shining and bursting with energy. She's dressed in a T-shirt and jeans—both are fitting in all the right places. And for the places I can't see, Jimmy Mack fills in the gaps.

"Yeah, man," whistles Jimmy Mack.

She takes my coat, and my hands begin to tremble and sweat. "No hat today?" she teases me.

"No hat." My heart is thumping, like B. B. plucking Lucille. I feel like a dog in heat.

"You devil you," says Jimmy Mack.

"I want her, but to tell the truth, I'm afraid Jeanette might devour me."

"I've heard enough," says Jimmy Mack.

In exasperation, I say, "The 'Fire Dancer' might torch me in her Inferno."

"I can't stand your love, I can't stand it!" sings Jimmy Mack in a bad imitation of the soul man himself, James Brown.

Oblivious to this exchange, Jeannie leads me to the dining-room table. She leans over my side of the table to spread six large envelopes before me, and her breast brushes my arm gently. The room's temperature shoots up 150 degrees.

"You've never seen my pictures," she says excitedly. She pulls out an envelope from a red woven African basket.

"No, what pictures?" I say cheerfully. *I didn't know she could take pictures*, I think, beaming like a proud papa.

"From my trip to Africa," she says grand standing.

Financed by yours truly, I think—a Christmas gift to her.

Her pictorial journey begins with shots at JFK Airport and moves on to her arrival in Casablanca. Most of the photographs are taken in Senegal. Some are whimsical snapshots of her standing in a serpentine line with a group of African travelers making the pilgrimage back home for the Christmas holiday. There are packages and boxes everywhere. The waiting area looks like the cargo compartment of a 757. Jeannie, of course, is clowning around.

Others are colorful pictures of locals: village women receiving a labor-saving grinding machine, young women sewing and crocheting at a youth development center—photographs of National Geographic magazine quality. Jeanette is particularly proud of a wedding picture, a woman dancing the *Saba*, the Senegalese national dance.

"Do you like them?" she asks, fishing for my approval.

"Breathtaking." I am talking about more than the photographs.

Scriptures from the Bible pierce my ears like a siren: *Lust not after her beauty in thy heart; neither let her take thee with her eyelids.*

I try again. "Good pictures. How long have you been a photographer?"

"Stop joking, Jasper. You know I'm no photographer. I just took them with the Canon 450 PowerShot you gave me."

Reviewing them closely, I truly am astounded by the quality of her pictures, particularly one of a rooftop garden and a house with gold-trimmed windows.

"Who developed these?" I ask.

"Ritz Camera Shop . . . they use Kodak products."

"The colors are spectacular."

"Thank you," she smiles. "Look at my prized one." She shows me a picture. A picture worthy of an award or a contract with *Playboy* magazine.

"Can you see it?" she asks.

My eyesight has grown increasingly worse in the last two years. I strain, but what I see is delectable. I can't believe my eyes.

"Look closer. This is a wedding. I was lucky enough to get invited while attending a meeting of a women's business cooperative," she explains.

Jeanette begins to dance, just like I've been afraid she would. A couple of leg movements and I am mesmerized. "Then, the Senegalese dancer," explains Jeanette, "looked toward the sky, just like I'm doing, as if she's sending praise straight to Heaven." A wave of passion and guilt hit me like a cyclone. The dancer apparently performed so acrobatically that her dress flew open revealing that she is not wearing any panties. She moves so quickly . . .

"I am proud that I was able to capture this moment. She's not wearing any underwear," says Jeanette.

"Underwear?" I ask.

"No panties." Don't get me wrong this is a photographic phenomenon, I don't mean to brag, but it belongs in the Museum of Women in the Arts.

I stumble out of the chair, photo in hand, my reckless mind racing to view something sexy, and walk quickly over to the three rectangular windows that face the park. The sunlight is shining prominently through them. I need to get a full view. What I see is nothing less than one of the Seven Wonders of the World. Now that's a Kodak moment!

OO LA LA.

It's a photo of a beautiful woman wearing traditional wedding clothes and performing the Saba in an exuberant and exultant salute to the art of dancing.

The siren erupts again: *But I say unto you, that whosoever looketh on a woman to lust after her hath committed adultery with her already in his heart.*

My mind torments me again. I've made a covenant with my eyes not to look lustfully at a girl. I mean, a woman.

"Didn't work—I'm sinning," I confess to Jimmy Mack. *In a divorce, I could lose a lot of money.*

"For Christ's sake, they're only pictures!" he replies. "Loosen up, man. If you don't lust after women, who you gonna lust after?"

"I'm gonna to *hell!*"

"The devil has got a hold on you," laughs Jimmy Mack.

Thinking God could decide right this second that I should drop dead of a heart attack, I gaze at the picture. I find myself staring until I am embarrassed. Catching one last peek, I slide it gently into the envelope. I look at the others, but my money is on the dancer. Excited isn't the word. The dancer's artistic talents and her body are—what's that expression—fly. *It is a feat for Jeanette, an amateur photographer. I know how difficult it is to photograph a figure in motion.*

"Front field in motion," jokes Jimmy Mack.

When I snap out of my trance, Jeanette is holding a small gift box, saying, "I've been waiting to give this to you."

I am under strict orders from Martha not to accept gifts from anyone, but when Jeanette carefully opens the box and places a silver bracelet on the table, I pick it up.

"I got this for you in Dakar."

"You did?"

"Look at it."

I turn it over, and my hand coils back like it has touched a Cobra. It is engraved, with a bell on each end and my name inscribed in bold letters in the center: Jasper.

"It's for you."

I stare at it for a few seconds. Jeanette senses my fear.

"I'll keep it for you until you're able to wear it."

I am dumbfounded. I know that Martha will set the house ablaze if she sees me with this bracelet.

* * *

I have to break up with Jeannie. Something I really don't want to do. I rumble holding back tears on the verge of flowing full stream. I hesitate and try to compose myself.

I clear my throat, "Jeanette, Jeanette. I'm sorry I started this relationship with you."

"What?" she asks confounded. "What are you talking about?"

"Please forgive me," I say regrettably.

"Forgive you for what?" she asks as if I have lost my mind.

"I have to break up with you."

"What do you mean, you have to break up with me? Why?"

I am sounding so ridiculous Jimmy Mack wonders if I'm gonna crazy.

"What's wrong with you?" he asks.

"Stay out of this," I tell him.

"I have to break it off with you," I repeat, raising my voice as I lower my head, hoping she will not see the neon pain painted across my face.

"You're not making any sense."

My shoulders drop like a concrete slab hitting a pavement. I mutter, "It doesn't make sense to me either, but it's what I have to do." I am grappling with the enormity of it, too.

"This sounds like something I've heard before," she says, fired up. "A hundred times already. BORING," she says disgustedly.

"You didn't say that when I broke up with you the first time. You were very upset."

"I am a different person now, buster. I don't have time for this," she says harshly. "I don't even want to talk about it."

Weakly, I say, "I do." I'm surprised by the mean-spirited way she is talking to me.

"What do you expect?" asks Jimmy Mack.

"What happened to your miraculous breakthrough?" she asks sarcastically. "You know, seeing yourself for what you are, implying you were gonna to see Doctor Moore, and all that other stuff?"

Oh my God, she has changed.

Shifting my body away from hers, I begin to cry, hoping she doesn't see tears dripping down my cheeks. She's right. I insinuated. I was gonna back to see Doctor Moore.

"Chicken liver," smirks Jimmy Mack.

I thought about doing it when I read her script. I really did. I feel awful. My goal is to get rid of this crippling guilt. Guilt about wanting Jeanette. About cheating in my heart. Cheating on Martha. Giving Jeannie money—even my other affairs over the years. But I don't tell her this. I switch to another subject again.

"There are very few couples like us. We don't want to have sex, right?"

She raises her eyebrows and looks at me as if I have lost my marbles. I quickly revise my story.

"That's not true," I confess shamefully. *Only God and I know how badly I want you.*

"Now she *knows* you are crazy," says Jimmy Mack.

I am heartbroken.

✳ ✳ ✳

CHAPTER 22

"Breaking up is hard to do."

Neil Sedaka

I feel disoriented—this is not gonna well at all. Not like I planned. I didn't think I would be this upset about breaking up with Jeanette or that she would take it so calmly.

I try a new strategy. I start to recite my illnesses. For what reason, I'm not entirely sure. Maybe I want her sympathy.

"I have high cholesterol. Probably from eating too many cheeseburgers."

"You're talking in circles," says Jeanette. "How high is it?" she asks, sounding sick to her stomach.

"Two hundred thirty-five. I have a heart murmur, too . . ."

Throughout my painful litany, Jeanette hardly responds to me at all. And when she does, it is with utter disgust.

I suppose she has had enough of me. I'm not making any sense—and I haven't for a long time. I meander from topic to topic. I feel like I'm coming apart.

"I can't do this anymore," I say quietly. The words cause me pain.

Sucking her teeth, Jeanette asks, "Which subject are you on now?"

"That didn't work," says Jimmy Mack. "Try again."

"I can't be emotionally involved with two women at one time." I wish I could yank those words out of the air and quash them like a roach.

"How can you be emotionally involved with someone you only think about ten percent of the time?" she asks her face a stupefied mask. "You're just afraid of losing your money."

"I'm not afraid," I say meekly. "I was a CEO!"

"Okay, Jesse Jackson. You are somebody."

Jeanette throws her hands up in the air. "I give up," she says.

"Are you cracking up?" ask Jimmy Mack. "Still in denial, huh?"

"Yeah, I guess you're right," I say to him.

I hesitate.

"You sound like an imbecile," says Jimmy Mack.

I do.

I am more conflicted than the uprising in the Gaza Strip. I hear the bullets swish by my left ear and then my right, faster than the speed of sound. As I run from them, I look over my shoulder. I see smoke billowing from bombed buildings and cars, and children being mourned in the arms of their wailing parents. My feet are paralyzed, but they carry me like an Olympian. Inside I feel like I am waging a battle between the real me and my fake exterior.

There are warring factions gonna in my mind and heart. My heart says: *Stay with Jeanette. Make a commitment to Jeanette. Divorce Martha.* My bank accounts says: *Stay with Martha.*

"I don't want to do this. I don't want to do this. I don't want to break up with you. Please tell me what to do, Jeannie."

"I can't tell you what to do, Jasper! I've helped you enough: praying for you, finding therapists for you for more than five years. What does it say about you? You think about me ninety percent of the time, but you spend your life with someone you're obviously not in love with?"

"You blew it," Jimmy Mack says to me.

I grunt like a groundhog, drop my head. "I don't want to do this."

"How many times are you gonna say that?" says Jimmy Mack. "Don't, then."

"I don't want to do this. But I am. The results are the same, right?"

She stares at me as if I am under some type of spell, and she doesn't care anymore about bringing me out of it. I look at her and can't believe my eyes.

"I'm a big girl now," Jeanette starts singing the song of the same name.

"Every day I want to cry; every day I want to die." I pause, looking for clarity. I feel as though I don't know who I am or how to express the torturous feeling that is ripping my heart apart. "I am depressed a lot. Depression will kill you."

Abruptly, Jeanette jumps up. Her swift movement startles me.

What's she gonna to do?

"What's wrong?" I ask.

"I have to dance, Jasper. That's my song," she says. She refuses to listen to my venting any longer, and instead starts singing along with the music coming from a small radio.

Oh God! She's a fire dancer—on and off the dance floor. She's the essence of a strong woman—like Fela sings, "She be lady, oh!" Just like the title of her book, *Fire Dancer*.

"I'm tired of living in your spotlight," she sings. The lyrics are to Jennifer Hudson's song. I start to sing along with her. Honestly, it is an exciting jubilation.

She flops down at the table, and I take this as an invitation to start ranting again.

"High blood pressure runs in my family," I continue desperately. "I told you that my brother had another stroke, didn't I?"

She nods her head and walks into the kitchen.

"Why are you telling her all this?" Jimmy Mack whispers. "Do you really think she cares about your health after the way you've acted?"

She strolls back across the living room, aloof as a tiger. Flirtatiously, she raps a bottle of red finger nail polish against the hardwood floor. Watching her gingerly stroke every toenail, I am tantalized.

"I can't help you," I say.

"You can't help me?" she says, petrified. "Help me do what? You're changing the subject again."

"I can't help you with your project." Part of me hopes she will get angry because of this. Make her fight back. Resist what I so obviously don't want to do.

"My documentary . . . is that what you're talking about?" she asks.

"But I moved the money. I can't make phone calls, but I can give you some money to help you get your project off the ground."

"Make up your mind, man. That's what you always do— you just be savin' her," says Jimmy Mack.

"What?" Her face is an expression of delight and acceptance.

Tenderly I say, "Giving you money is helping," pleading for understanding.

"Fine," she says coldheartedly, but I see pain flicker in her eyes.

SILENCE.

"I moved the money," I repeat.

She is acting like money is her least concern. She ignores me, opening a manila folder, and begins to reads from a list. A list of souvenirs she wants me to bring from Africa.

"A diamond."

I raise an eyebrow. "She is hurt, I know," I say to Jimmy Mack. "I am breaking up with her and gonna to Africa with Martha. I get the feeling she is demanding things—messing with me, to collect what she feels in her mind is her due."

"Her survival instincts are kicking in," proclaimed Jimmy Mack, explaining her reactions. "You're taking care not to lose your money, right? You're leaving her behind and gonna to Africa, right? What do you think? She's angry, and you have the nerve to break up with her all at the same time. No wonder she's demanding you bring her the whole continent. She knows the way you communicate your love for her is by giving her money. She knows asking for money is the strongest way to strike back at you."

"She knows me better than anyone else."

"That's what you always say. Hasn't changed you."

She continues. "A female mahogany bust. An original African painting. Some African costume jewelry and African clothes."

"Dumbie," don't you realize she wanted to take you to Africa. That's her maternal instinct and jealousy taking over. After all she was ...what do they call it? An RPCV.

"A What'?"

"A Returned Peace Corps Volunteer."

"And on top of that, she's been to Africa seven times."

"She wanted you to travel *with her* to Africa," says Jimmy Mack. "You got yourself in a world of trouble. You break up with her, and she's gonna collect what she feels is her due."

"All of that?" *Is she messing with my head?*

"As much as you can," she says, as if she is entitled to have anything her heart desires.

"Okay. I'm gonna now."

I am hoping that this statement will cause her to feel remorseful, but it has no effect on her at all. She merely gets up from the table and escorts me toward the door. I stop halfway.

"Do you want the money now or when I get back from Africa?"

"Now."

"Do you want some more money?" I ask, hoping to stall off my own heartbreak.

She shakes her head affirmatively.

"Do you want to hug?"

She looks at me as if I'm a moron.

"Too difficult?" I ask.

She just shakes her head from side to side.

"Too difficult for you, Jack," says Jimmy Mack.

I want to reassure her of my intentions to get better.

"I am still gonna to keep healing, keep working on it myself."

"Get professional help?"

In my mind, I visualize the dollar bills—millions of them—flying out of my bank vault. No. I'll have to divorce my wife if I do. If I get therapy, I'll get a divorce and lose half of my money to Martha.

"You're gonna to wait until it's too late, until you have a crisis," she says.

I walk slowly toward the door. I stop again. I take her hands gently in mine and smell her aroma. Holding back the tears stuck in my throat, thinking how much I miss her right now And, oh, how much I will miss her in the days to come! I made this break, but I'm still gonna miss her forever.

"Jeanette, Jeanette," I mourn.

SILENCE.

I grab her hands, swinging them from side to side like a preschool teacher singing and playing a nursery rhyme. I feel worst than Shakespeare parting is torture... I wish I could say goodbye until eternity. A lump the size of a golf ball lodges in my esophagus. Fighting back tears, I stop and I go to the door in despair. I stop again waiting for her to follow me, as is our ritual. Hoping she will make me change my mind. Like a preschool teacher singing and playing a nursery rhyme.

Not this time.

I drag one foot forward and open the door gradually, like a soldier deploying to Afghanistan knowing he will never return.

"What do you want her to say? *Baby, please don't go?* She's had enough of you, James Brown," says Jimmy Mack.

I hear the chunks of hard dry dirt hitting the top of my coffin. I wait. I wave good-bye. She looks expressionless.

I hurry to the elevators, trying to escape my pain.

* * *

I drive to *Let the Sunshine In Bank* for the certified check. I have always given Jeanette money, but it came from my secret account at the *Navy Federal Credit Union.* I am terrified this time because it's the largest sum I have ever given her and some of it has to come from the joint account that I hold with Martha at *Let the Sunshine In Bank.*

I am always willing and ready to give Jeanette the money she needs and more, regardless of what happens. I may be afraid, and although there is risk involved, this the only way I can show her how much I love her.

Leaving the bank, I push hard on the accelerator, rushing to the FedEx office so I can send it right away. Then I call her again just to hear her voice, hoping she will persuade me to come back.

"I've sent the money."

"Thank you, Jasper."

She sounds sad, but I'm not sure whether it's disgust or disappointment.

I can't even stomach myself.

* * *

PART III

Money

After examining data from thirty-seven countries over twenty-two years, researchers found no link between greater happiness and more money—absolutely no relationship between income and happiness.

— Proceedings of the National Academy of Sciences

CHAPTER 23

"Don't worry, be happy."

Bobby McFerrin

Monday comes and goes. I am nervous as hell because I haven't heard from her. I've never given her this much money before. *Did she receive it?* I wonder. *Is everything okay?*

The next day I e-mail her through the blinding, unmerciful pain of a migraine headache. I can barely see the keys on my computer, but I manage to tap out:

Jeanette, did you get the FedEx?

. . . Jasper

Nothing romantic or lengthy—I'm nervous, and I'm too cautious anyway. Martha is calling me to eat breakfast. My head is hammering. I place a cold pack from the refrigerator on my temple. The pain is ruthless. I'm worried it will drive me to do something violent, something insane.

I ponder the idea of running to the pharmacy and having my blood pressure taken at one of these machines. Instead I pop a couple of Tylenol and swish them down with a tepid glass of lemonade.

Finally, she e-mails me back.

> *I picked up the FedEx this morning. I got busy. Thanks again. Have a good trip.*
>
> *Jeanette*

I am immensely relieved that she has received the money. I was worried that it had been stolen, lost in the mail, or—a greater calamity—intercepted by Martha.

I e-mail back right away.

> *I'm glad that you got the package okay, and I pray you have much success in accomplishing whatever goals are most meaningful to you. Please pray that I may continue growing in strength mentally, physically, and spiritually.*
>
> *… Jasper*

I'm completely unprepared for Jeanette's next e-mail.

> *I just received your e-mail this morning. I would like to pray for you, but it is difficult when I feel angry and betrayed. I*

am writing this e-mail because you are traveling a long ways, and I don't like to keep things inside of me for long periods of time. So, I am persuaded to write this now: I am not a prostitute. I am not responsible for your getting excited.

You said that I am "wild." I thought you were the one person who understood me. I am wild in a positive way and a Christian way, and I have no shame or guilt about anything that I do or have done. I try to practice my religion every day.

It is Jeanette's right to express herself anyway she wants. In therapy, I dealt with having a relationship with you, and I explained to you that my therapist and I saw it as a positive thing. Remember, everything perfect comes from God. If I were not a Christian, I would definitely handle our situation differently. Whenever I do anything that is difficult, I consult God, my therapist, and my friends, and I meditate. What you don't understand is that you were feeling horny. And you projected your feelings on me.

I wear my clothes in an appropriate manner that does not entitle anyone, not even you, to assault me or to make derogatory comments. I am referring to your statements: "You better watch it, because I could see through your skirt." and "You are wild!"

I am not responsible for your sexual response. This comment is the reason that I don't engage in sex with you. I make love in a committed relationship with someone who respects and understands me. Just think how I would feel if I had gone to bed with you? What would you have said then?

I am a human being with feelings, not a ping-pong ball, in case you didn't notice. I disapprove of what you said and do not allow anyone to speak to me the way you did. Did you think this about me when I was helping you with your emotional crisis? I do not deserve to have anyone speak to me this way. I don't deserve this type of treatment! I am not a *street urchin. What you said is disrespectful and shows a gross neglect for my feelings and the way I have respected you and kept you in the highest regard. There is always an appropriate way of saying things, and it is our responsibility to find it.*

Consistency

My actions have always been consistent with my beliefs. I have practiced what I preach, even though I have reasons not to, and I have protected you in the process. I have gone beyond the call of duty and done unheralded, unheard of, herculean, and unprecedented things to honor my word and to help you like no other, when I didn't have to do so.

Trust

I trusted you, and you have betrayed my trust. You say one thing and then do another. Trust begets trust. My friends tell me that I am being too nice to you—perhaps I am. My boundaries and feelings have been invaded, and I don't feel good about this at all.

Sexuality

I didn't mean that you, Jasper F. Beamon, were suffering from erectile dysfunction sixteen months ago. It was a question I asked about a character in a novel. I have never thought that you were, although you have complained about having this problem. In fact, I have no way of knowing. In fact, I have seen and felt that you were a virile, zestful, spirited man with the energy of a man much younger than yourself. Since I have never had sex with you, I can only go by what you tell me about your sexual problems. However, it does appear that you have a lot of unresolved sexual issues. I am not qualified to determine whether you are sexually dysfunctional or not. That is another problem that you definitely need to work out in therapy.

Jeanette

I am devasted. It's gut-wrenching to face the fact that once again, I have acted less than honorably with her. I send out an e-mail as quickly as my composure will allow.

Dear Jeanette,

I am so sorry that I have upset you. I never meant to convey that you are "wild" in a derogatory manner, which I absolutely know that you are not. My saying you are "wild" was only meant in a playful manner, meaning that you are a very expressive person. But I never meant to convey that you are wild in a sexual manner, which I know that you are not. If I implied that in any way, I sincerely apologize. I know that you have strong moral values and that you are a Christian. I respect and admire that in you.

... Jasper

Exhausted from wrenching my soul online, I collapse at my desk.

"How could I have done that?" I ask Lulu as she circles around my desk. "Lulu, baby, I keep slipping up, like an ice skater on a frozen pond."

I can't keep it out of my mind. I hit her number on speed dial, scared that she won't answer her phone. She does.

"Jeannie?"

"Yes?

"I'm sorry."

SILENCE.

Full of remorse, I repeat myself. "I'm sorry, I said."

"Sorry is a sorry word," comes the response.

"Yes, I know. But I'm sorry that I upset you. I didn't mean to talk to you like that."

"I don't want to talk about it."

"I need to talk about it.."

"You just want to vent."

"No, I need to talk to you, just like you needed to talk to me before I go to Africa. I've already sent you an e-mail to apologize, but I needed to talk to you, too."

"I'm on the bus. I'm uncomfortable discussing my personal business in public. Can't we talk later?"

"Get off the bus, please."

"Okay, I'll jump off at the next stop."

There's a long pause.

I begin to plead, begging her as if I were James Brown himself.

"Baby, please—please, don't think badly of me. I am so sorry. I didn't mean to hurt you." My words play back to me in my head, and I am astounded. I never would've believed that I could say such things. "I know you're a Christian. I didn't mean to imply that you're wild in that way. I was only joking. It's just that . . . you are very dramatic."

"Oh yeah?" she says.

"I mean, you're playful. That's all I . . ."

"Playful?" she spits out.

"Not sexually, baby, but . . . you know, playful."

"Mm-hmm."

"I mean, you are expressive."

SILENCE.

"I feel terrible, Jeanette. I didn't mean to hurt you. I feel like crying. I don't want go to Africa. I'll cancel my trip. I don't feel like it now. I can't leave you this way."

"Go," she says. "Go . . . and have a good time."

"But I'm gonna to think about you all the time! About what I said! I . . ."

"I know you will, Jasper." She sighs. "But do you know, I could tell that something was up when you walked through my door? It's a pattern with you: Get close. Get scared. Break up."

"You know me so well, Jeanette."

"Just by the way you walk."

"I know. Jeannie, I feel so bad. I don't want to go on this trip," I whine. "I am torn. I feel like . . . I might wind up crazy. I need to talk to you about it. Now. I . . . I don't want to go to Africa."

"Jasper, listen to me. I didn't want to talk to you about this before you went on your trip—I don't want to spoil it for you. But I knew that it would hurt me until I talked it over. Let it out. Said what I needed to say. Resolved it."

"I won't be able to sleep," I say.

"Go. Have a good time. You've never been to Africa before. It's the home of our ancestors—a spiritual place where lives can be changed permanently if we are willing to do the hard work that is necessary. It can give you a sense of identity."

"I am really suffering here. I want to do the right thing by you. I know I will never heal until I do. I want to discuss all of this with you when I return. I think I have to. It's the only path to . . . true healing."

"That sounds fine, Jasper. That sounds real good."

"When I get back, I'm gonna to take you up on . . . on your recommendation to go into therapy. You know, you've recommended it so many times, and so have both Doctor Moore and Doctor Ginsburg. I was gonna to do it . . . I promise."

I feel like doing anything—anything to help me feel better, to relieve my guilt. I shouldn't have said what I did. I feel like a pimp. I apologize, but that's not enough. I still feel stupid. I let my lust get the best of me.

"Getting therapy?" she asks.

"Yes."

"Maybe I need to go back to PIW, to the Institute," I say, breathing heavily into the phone.

"That's an excellent start." She sounds relieved. "There's a book I can recommend to you, by Terrie Williams. It's called *Black Pain*."

"I'll try to get it before I leave," I say.

"*Do* get it. Get it at a bookstore at the airport."

"I will." But even as the words flash back to me, I am whining again. "Jeanette, I feel so bad, I won't be able to stop thinking about it."

"Just try not to. Enjoy yourself. Take a lot of pictures on your safari. And while you enjoy all the animals, think about it subconsciously, okay?"

"I will think about it *all the time*. I just know it."

She is patient with me. "How long will you be gone?"

"Two weeks."

"Miss me?"

"You know I will. I'll call you when I get back."

"Okay."

* * *

CHAPTER 24

"There are only two emotions in a plane: boredom and terror."

Orson Welles

We fly KLM Airlines from JFK to Amsterdam. I sit next to the window. As the Boeing 769 gains altitude, my ears pop painfully. I breathe in the cabin oxygen and exhale to relieve the pressure in my chest. I gaze out and see the clouds float by like dreams in my dreams. I feel like a solo goose soaring through the sky at 500 miles per hour.

I'm traveling with my family—Martha, Melanie, and Matthew. So why do I feel lonely? I eat. I drink. I talk. But I am alone.

How can I feel lonely in a plane full to capacity? I'm gonna home—to Mother Africa. How can I feel lonely when I am finally en route to see her?

I fall asleep and have a nightmare. My biological father is walking steadily away from me. I wave, I smile, I cry out his name, but he keeps walking. Walking away from me! I ride my tricycle as fast as my little legs will carry me. But he keeps walking, and slowly he turns into a ghost and vanishes in the sky.

I am awake.

After a four-hour layover, we fly on to Johannesburg and land at Oliver Tambo Airport.

Africa. I am in South Africa.

Everywhere around me, all I see are black people: directing air traffic, unloading freight cargo, parking planes. I hear my African brothers speaking a language I do not understand—and yet it is one I feel I know, if only in the rhythm of its accents.

As I climb down the steps, I feel like a butterfly metamorphosing into a Zulu warrior. In America, as a black man, I wear racial tension like a second suit. Here, it's melting away. I feel peaceful as I realize I will experience none of those everyday slights—white women grabbing their purses in elevators or standing so they don't have to sit next to me on a bus. Security guards won't be dogging my heels like bloodthirsty surveillance hounds as soon as I enter a store.

"Have you ever seen anything like this before?" I ask my son-in-law.

"No."

"Say it loud!" says Jimmy Mack.

"Me either," I say. "Not even in the Navy."

My feet touch the hot tarmac. The feeling is familiar, though it is one that I have not often experienced—a feeling of love. Only one thing comes close to this... the feeling I get when I hug Jeanette, when I let my guard down long enough to smell her sweet gardenia.

My spirit is soaring, mingling with the spirit of Africa. It clings to me like mist clings to the air. My loneliness has dissipated.

A small bus shuttles us to the hotel, a building in eighteenth-century Italian replica style, located on Nelson Mandela Square. The square is surrounded by an upscale shopping mall and good restaurants, all in the most thriving business district of downtown Johannesburg. It reminds me of New York City.

The hotel is rated five stars by Zagat, and I am pleased by its Italian architecture and huge columns inlaid with classical Romanesque figures. We step into the lobby, and it is as if we have stepped back in time to a city square in Europe two thousand years ago. The hotel has all the amenities that a person could ever dream of.

We register with an Italian hostess and are taken by a baggage handler in period dress to our executive suite, which is the most opulent that I have ever seen. The palatial furniture is carved from massive pieces of oak and walnut. A doctor and a dentist are available for emergencies. We have a private bathroom with a French bidet and an eat-in kitchen that would excite an Italian grandmother. There is, of course, broadband Internet service, a conference room, and twenty-four-hour room service. But also at our disposal are a twenty-four-hour private butler and chauffeur, as well as a private swimming pool. For our suite.

These creature comforts come at the high price of $3,300 American dollars per night. It is well worth the cost.

After traveling for twenty hours, I'm as exhausted as a Navy recruit after the first day of basic training. I take a dip anyway, to relax my muscles. The brief swim helps me fall asleep, which I do the second my head touches the pillow—one hundred percent cotton with down feathers, of course. I sleep for the next five hours. This is a first for me, since frequent nightmares generally keep me awake. In my dreams, it is September 7, 1963.

* * *

Having arrived at OT school in Newport, Rhode Island, I receive an orientation shock that brings back memories of my months pledging Omega Psi Phi. It's pre-dawn, 05:30 hours. I hear a commotion I hope is only a bad dream. Bells are ringing, doors are slamming, and voices are booming. It sounds as though John Dillinger and one hundred convicts are breaking out of the Michigan State Pen.

Ring! Ring! Ring!

"Reveille! Reveille!"

"All hands on deck!"

"All hands dress up!"

A litany of loud, obnoxious commands spouts from the foul mouth of our recruit division commander, the Cassius Clay of physical education training, Gunnery Sergeant Richard F. Raleigh. To us, he is just "Gunnery Sergeant;" as recruits without title or experience, we have not yet earned the privilege to call him by his name. This privilege is conferred after graduation, if we make it until then.

This whole scenario feels familiar.

"Man the hatches!" the Gunnery Sergeant says. "Get your asses out of bed, and do it with all expedience! This ain't no place for mama's boys or sissies. You got ten minutes!"

After this cheerful welcome, I grab my towel, run to the head and jump into the last available stall. I swipe the sleep from my eyes with my left hand and lather my body with the right. I'm showered in two minutes. I can still hear Gunnery Sergeant Raleigh yelling.

"Does he think we're deaf?" I ask no one in particular. No one answers me anyway.

We're in a hurry to flow with his orders without trampling and stampeding one another like cattle. We sound and look like men in a Pamplona bull run. The loud and offensive shouting, howling and screaming noises I've been exposed to in my years—from Pete, from my stepbrothers, from my mother, and from the Omega Psi Phi brothers—have, sadly, not made me immune to this treatment. His voice is enough to frighten the innards out of a buzzard and the chitlins out of a hog. I am disoriented. As if sleeping in a haul with sixty men isn't terrifying enough, now I have to endure this, too? "Get your PT gear on! Make your beds!"

What the heck? Gear or uniform, it's all the same to me! Shucks, there's a uniform for everything. Running shoes, blue shorts, knee-high socks, white T-shirts—these are standard uniform issue. PT regiment. Nothing but a bunch of athletic clothes, just like my high school track and field uniform. Still I'm proud to wear it all, even though my legs look like a turkey strutting. The rest of my body is fit—I could give Charles Atlas some competition.

"Zero-six hundred hours! In front of the mess hall!"

I survive the storm. I run and make my bed, then hightail it to the mess hall.

* * *

I awaken at five p.m., and we dine in "worldly style" on "global food." The hotel's exclusive restaurant lives up to its reputation. On the menu are prawns from Mozambique, salmon from Norway, lobsters and mussels from South Africa's southernmost coast, and Cape Town wines. I eat hungrily like all the other American and European tourists.

The next morning we are whisked away on a tour of the city. I feel the beat of Johannesburg—a pulsating rhythm that reflects the exciting and ethnically diverse residents such as the Ndebele, Zulu and Nguoi populations. With a large bustling, modern business district and eight million inhabitants, Jo'burg still feels to me like New York city. But she moves at a starkly different pace, swaying to the music of African drums and jazz trumpets, the blasting tones of saxophones, haunting traditional music, and car horns honking nonstop, the stop and go of the brightly colored "car rapide," plus a hybrid of hip hop music called Kwaito. She is a quintessentially African city, with merchants hawking wares and women selling food: brilliantly colored greens, beans, burnt-colored ripe mangoes, and golden sweet potatoes. Yet, all is surrounded by modern everything: buildings, cars, restaurants, and people in modern Western dress. So many reminders of traditional Africa, mingling on every corner and at every bus stop with hints of Europe, America, and the world. I am overwhelmed by the stark contrasts and the familiar similarities. I feel breathless from the tempo and pace of this metropolis.

That evening we are invited to a village welcoming ceremony, which is customary for all guests staying in the hotel. The ceremonial dance is a way of showing respect and gratitude for those guests visiting and doing business in South Africa—Johannesburg's business elite. Drummers beat out the rhythm to a powerful dance made popular during the height of apartheid—the *toyi-toyi*, in honor of the father of South Africa, Nelson Mandela. It pays homage to God, to warriors past, and to the brave soldiers of apartheid. The dance reminds me of a combination of liturgical and secular performance done by sisters in church and at house parties. I admire the richly colored cotton of the African costumes, with the word *Welcome* imprinted in the cloth. Perhaps, in some tiny place in my heart, I even feel that the ceremony is for me only.

In the second dance, the dancers and drummers ripple through the performance like acrobats. It is similar to a popular South African dance that migrated to the United States several years ago: the break dance. The name refers to all the possible ways of breaking a body part while dancing. It is a gravity and death defying dance that twists the body into unimaginable contours. I know I am home when I watch a group step—an elaborate dance, highly popular and competitively performed by sororities and fraternities on historically Black colleges and universities throughout the United States and more recently on white campuses too.

Stepping, a forerunner of the "gumboot" dance was created by coal miners in South Africa when overseers refused to drain the cold and contaminated water from the mines.

Instead, they gave the miners boots. The miners forbidden to talk with each other, and in many cases, unable to communicate because of the various ethnic languages, created the dance as a way of talking and entertaining each other.

They used their boots as instruments, hoofing, and stomping to developed intricate steps, sounds and patterns. Watching the performance, I am reminded of the "night-witching" techniques of the chief beater, as well as the joys of dancing the night I went ovah on the Omega Psi Phi line. It brings back the memory of endless days and nights marching at officer's training school when I was in the Navy.

Three ten-foot-tall stilt dancers walk through the crowd, displaying amazing agility and balance. I feel the fire and the connection to my ancestors as I watch the propelling feet, the women's hips swaying, and the rapid-fire pounding on the drums of my brothers.

Next is the Zulu virgin maiden dance, a cultural dance performed for the purpose of picking a wife. In some large villages up to15,000 Zulus attend such events for the purpose of finding a bride.

"Suppose you could've chosen your bride like this," teases Jimmy Mack.

"Mightat made a better choice."

* * *

CHAPTER 25

"Too often travel, instead of broadening the mind, merely lengthens the conversation."

Elizabeth Drew

Our tour of South Africa lasts nine days. Our private guide has chosen the places she thinks African Americans would find momentous—museums providing information on how apartheid was crushed and historical sites where we might meet and visit a few of those brave warriors and places who destroyed its evil forces. I am glad to learn that the Apartheid Museum and Soweto township are two of the sites on our itinerary. I want to feel what it was like to survive in that world, to inhabit that oppression. Our journey will include a stop at Nelson Mandela's house. And Martha and Melanie will shop, of course, in Nelson Mandela Square.

Our leader, Stella Dubazana, is a registered nurse. She is also a long-time resident of Soweto and knowledgeable. I am keenly aware of many things about this city: its historical past, its high crime rate. Murder and rape occur at an alarming pace, matched by American cities such as New York and Detroit. Arriving in Soweto, a township of more than five million people, I am a bit leery of what I will encounter. There's been so much bad news about this town—I'm uncertain what I will see.

The shantytown reminds me of the ghetto towns and rural areas where I grew up in North Carolina. We visit a local family, the Ndovlulus, who have two sons and a daughter. The daughter, a real Winnie Mandela in the making, protested in the Soweto youth uprising.

After our introduction, we are invited inside their two-room home. The house is a little larger than a wooden shack but strikingly decorated in the bold primary colors of the Ndebele ethnic group—blue and yellow. In spite of its brightness, however, the house exudes a feeling of hopelessness and despair, much like the dismal shacks I lived in and those inhabited still by blacks in the Mississippi Delta and in several other southern states. Like my grandparents' shotgun house where I spent time when we weren't rambling around the county slumming in other folk's homes. With us children it was more crowded than a hospital's emergency room on a holiday weekend.

The Ndovlulus, like their southern counterparts, make "something out of nothing."

The interior, although scarcely furnished, is immaculate. It is reminiscent of the Spartan but neatly kept homes in the South. Every cherished item, including pictures of black political icons, antiapartheid champions, and religious figures, such as Mandela and Desmond Tutu, are displayed prominently on the walls and on the limited dresser space, as if they are highly priced photographs taken by Gordon Parks. In my mind's eye, I see the display of pictures on Grandmama's walls and the walls of many oppressed African Americans: Malcolm X, Doctor Martin Luther King, Jr. And now Barack Obama.

The family of five share this meager space. An attached kitchen is so tiny, it resembles a park campsite. On the left side of the room is a makeshift stove that would make a fire plate look like a range oven. A small, rickety wooden table covered with a threadbare cloth rests on three legs, propped against a wall. Nailed to the wall are a large cast-iron pot and various cooking utensils.

I feel puny.

Although the home and its furnishings are scanty, the delicious aroma of the meal being prepared and the background jazz music are the saving grace for this family, much as these things have been for African Americans since slavery. Standing in the poorly lit living room, I catch a glance of a golden setting sun as I study the tiny, drab room. I wish to say a word of encouragement, to give them hope, to tell them my improbable but true rags-to-riches story. I want to shout, "Keep Hope Alive," the slogan made famous by my brother Jesse Jackson. But the pulsating music dispels all my wariness and fires my soul. The feelings of pity in the pit of my stomach evaporate. But still I hesitate.

We go to a *shebeen*, a nightclub, what my mama would have described as a "hole in the wall." It's a juke joint— a "good time" place like where African Americans of the past went to drink, dance, and "cut the fool." So do some of my brothers today. A place to party your troubles away. And wash your sorrows down.

Soweto! Greensboro, North Carolina!

The next day we visit the Apartheid Museum. All visitors must enter the museum through turnstiles according to their skin pigmentation. For my family, the variation in our skin color forces each of us to walk through a different entrance. It is a stark reminder of apartheid, slavery, and the segregated institutions and public places in America before Emancipation and Civil Rights. I feel a chill as I enter the museum. Memories of the segregated lunch counters I helped integrate in Carolina and of the foul-smelling bus bathrooms flash before me and evaporate quickly.

* * *

In February of my freshman year at the Agricultural and Technical University, the Civil Rights movement is gearing up in full force. Students all over the country are demonstrating and sitting-in like their souls are on fire, encouraged by such courageous people as Ronald Walters and his cousin Carol Parks. Ron Walters was born in 1938 and grew up in a household of notable parents, his father, Gilmar Butler, was a Buffalo Soldier, a Tuskegee airman, and a professional musician. His mother, Maxine, was a Kansas State civil rights investigator. His parents taught him to appreciate his uniqueness as a black citizen in the landscape of America's history, which later fueled Ron's passion to achieve justice for blacks through his work as an academician and a life-long civil rights advocate.

In July 1958, these two held one of the first sit-ins of the Civil Rights era at Dockum drugstore in Wichita, Kansas. Parks and Walters demonstrated for six consecutive weeks until the white owner granted blacks the right to eat at his lunch counter. Underreported in the press, the model they used led to the most famously recorded sit-in in the history of the Civil Rights Movement: the Greensboro Four.

Four African American students matriculating at my university—Ezell Blair, Jr., Franklin McCain, Joseph McNeil, and David Richmond—staged a sit-in at the Woolworth lunch counter in Greensboro, North Carolina.

A couple of years later, I participate in a sit-in myself.

* * *

The museum's theme is displayed in historical exhibits that show the chronological order of events leading away from apartheid and toward freedom. Unimaginable photographs of abuse, attacks, and murders suffered by political protesters, prisoners, and even innocent bystanders.

Documents are everywhere. Videos and films run non-stop. I experience the full impact of the horrors inflicted by the former white regime.

I feel as though I've entered a horror house. It reminds me of the Holocaust Memorial Museum in Washington, and I think, *Violence is endless.* I want to glue my eyes shut until I exit the museum. In the "Hangman's Room," I cup my hands over my mouth, feeling my lunch floating up my throat. I tremble, dumbfounded at the 121 knotted nooses that represent the political prisoners executed during the apartheid era. I shake uncontrollably and shut my eyes as graphic images of black men appear before me wiggling—then swaying from trees. Lynched in America's southern states for political and economic reasons. Many for their beautiful black skin. NIGGER!

My journey ends with a monumental victory: the democratic election of Nelson Mandela.

* * *

One morning in mid-March, we divide into groups of fifteen students to take turns sitting in at a local restaurant. I'm on the front line. I feel like I'm on the enemy's line. We enter the restaurant and spread out, sitting down defiantly on the stools at the counter, moving cautiously, with understated defiance.

I'm scared, but I can't cop out on my family, my fellow protestors. *I'm too ashamed,* I say to myself, gritting my teeth.

The waitstaff look more worried than angry. They are silent but belligerent. One red-faced man reminds me of a flashing police siren.

"What do you kids want?" he says. "This here is my store, and I don't want you in it."

Immediately his southern voice, yellow teeth, and white skin enrage me. I see Melvin, the tobacco auctioneer, cheating my stepfather, robbing him of thousands of dollars he should have received for his bumper tobacco crop.

"I want a burger," I demand of the redneck.

A white woman wearing a bouffant hairstyle says, "We don't serve no *Negroes* here!"

"We gonna sit here until you do," one of my classmates says boldly.

The public relations volunteer, a female classmate with a close-cropped Cicely Tyson Afro, has already alerted the media, including a radical but much-read local newspaper.

Seconds later, another member of the group demands service, too.

"I want a milkshake ma'am," says Dwight, a fair-complexioned brother, a little too politely for my taste.

"Miss, I'm waiting for my hamburger," I say.

Rage surges through my body, as I utter each word. The feeling is new to me, as foreign as a thousand-dollar bill. It could, in a mob-like setting, become dangerously contagious.

We take turns sitting in. This goes until the six p.m. news comes on the diner's black and white television when one exhausted, beaten-down waitress sees Dr. King endorsing our sit-ins. She stuffs her hair net in her apron and reluctantly goes to the kitchen.

"I'll give you a milkshake," she says. "But you gotta drink it and get out of here."

"Ma'am, we're human beings," he responds. "Just like you."

"We have the right to eat here," declares our leader, an outspoken boy-man sporting a huge, curly Afro.

"We ain't gonna' nowhere," another student says.

The waitress returns, carrying a milkshake and the juiciest burger I'd ever seen. She plops the shake down on the counter spilling it over her hands and shoves the burger towards me.

"Yes!" The word thunders triumphantly throughout the store.

A TV camera captures the historical moment and broadcasts it around the world.

* * *

I leave behind the heart-wrenching visuals but find they are glued to my mind like gum on a concrete sidewalk.

We take a quick tour of the Mandela House, which is a much-needed respite from the horrific scenes in the Apartheid Museum. This family home is a small brick cottage full of interesting memorabilia from the lives of Nelson and Winnie prior to his political incarceration.

The next day Martha and Melanie shop at the posh Sandton Market while Mathew and I take the day off to rest, except for a cursory tour of Johannesburg's "Wall Street." With all the extra time, I find myself playing wet nurse to my own troubling thoughts of Jeanette and my promise to get help.

At dusk, we ride over the Nelson Mandela Bridge; from a distance, the lights look like old-fashioned icy blue Christmas bulbs. We top off the night with dinner at Linger Longer Restaurant and find that it has chosen the right name. The dishes are as succulent as pulled barbecued pork soaked in Grandmama's secret hot sauce. The celebrity sightseeing is A List. I almost expect to see the father of Africa,

Mr. Nelson Mandela, in the flesh. I admire him a lot. The difference between the two of us is Mandela chose liberation and I chose money. In theory, I probably would have made the same choice too, but in reality, I'm not sure I can.

"If I could only dillydally here with you know who!" I say ever-so-longingly to my buddy Jimmy Mack.

"You had your chance, man, you had your chance," says Jimmy Mack.

"If I were tech savvy, I could Skype her."

On our fifth day on the continent, we fly with South African Airways to Cape Town. Upon arrival I am struck by the startling Tabletop Mountain, a most beautiful sight, located in the center of Cape Town. Stella, our guide, anticipating our awestruck impression, has arranged a tour. The car provides a magnificent view of the scenery; one of the seven wonders of the African continent, Tabletop Mountain is an earthly phenomenon, the Atlantic Ocean on one side and the Indian Ocean on the other. When the sun is setting on one side, it is rising on the other.

Tabletop Mountain, we are informed, is home to approximately 2,200 plant species—a flora lover's paradise. Baboons, small antelopes, and guinea pigs also live up here. Warm rain showers fall on one side of the mountain. On the other, pristine beaches flow unspoiled by man. It all looks as surreal as David Miller's "Paradise Beach."

The next day, we tour Robben Island, once a military base, later a leprosy camp, and finally a prison. In the end, criminals were moved to another prison and the island became a jail for political prisoners—particularly of the apartheid revolutionary war. This is where Nelson Mandela was imprisoned for almost two decades.

Stella introduces us to Mr. Thula Mabasso, a former inmate himself, who has arranged an overnight stay for us in the warden's village. Designed in the 1950s, these cottages remind me of life in the United States around the same time. Memories flood my mind and déjà vu washes over me as I think about the intimate talks Jeanette and I had in the cozy, art-deco lobby of her building. I've spent hours in this lobby, talking about my dismal childhood while she listened.

"You were terrified for a long time about not gonna up to her place," says Jimmy Mack.

"I was so enamored with Jeanette. Man, if I had gone to her apartment, all we woulda' done was make love."

"You sure about that? She wouldn't let you come up for a long time anyway."

"That's right."

"She must have been scared too," says Jimmy Mack.

The lobby was both an inferno and haven. It was a public space where we both felt safe emotionally and physically. We were so attracted to each other—I think we were both excited, in love, and afraid of our passionate feelings for each other. We used to talk a lot in that place. I told her a lot of intimate stuff.

"Smmhuh," says Jimmy Mack. "Like what?"

* * *

One day we cozy up in Jeanette's lobby for almost three hours, talking about my childhood. My marriage. My business. The whole works.

"I grew up on a farm," I tell her first, to try to ease into the heavy abuse stuff.

"You told me that. I did, too."

"People don't even know what a blended household is nowadays."

"What do you mean?"

"My mother, stepfather, four siblings, and four step-brothers made up our loud and sometimes violent house." I'm not gonna to call it a home. I don't even know what that feels like.

"Violent?"

"My stepbrothers were always fighting." There was never a peaceful moment. If it was, my emotions were always raw as liver. On red alert. "That's why I can't stand loud arguing today."

"Oh! no. I feel for you. Did they hit you and your blood brothers and sister?"

"Hit, kicked, pinched—but mostly made fun of me."

"What did your mother do about it?"

"Nothing, most of the time. Took their side and said I was older and probably had done something to make them pick on me. Only on very rare occasions would she defend us."

"What? That's horrible! And your father?"

"My absentee father? Nothing." Talking about him stirs up so many negative feelings in me.

"You mean he never came around to visit or see about his children?"

"No. Never." I feel depressed just talking to her about this.

"You must have felt awful, huh?"

"Still do most of the time. We lived only a few miles from him, and he never ever came around."

"It makes me sad to hear you say that. He didn't claim you?"

"I never knew nothing about it."

Wiping a tear from her eyes, Jeanette says, "I'm sad you had to grow up like that."

I feel like crying too, but I'm ashamed to. "Yeah, sure did. I still have nightmares. I wake up reliving things like that after all these years. See these sweat beads on my hands?"

"Yes."

"They break out like this whenever I talk about the past."

"Well, don't. No more today."

* * *

I get a firsthand view. One of the first things we witness is the torture tomb, and then we move on to Nelson Mandela's former cell. Eerie and teeny, it is a claustrophobic's death chamber. A cinderblock dungeon. I have to wonder, is his spirit hanging around?

"He slept on a paper-thin mattress for ten years until he became sick and was moved to a cell containing a cot," says Thula.

I can envision Mandela sitting there, his long legs dangling off the end of the cot, his robust body squashed against the cold concrete, anguishing about the state of his country and the danger Winnie and his family were in. "Could I have been as courageous?"

"Man, you jiving," Jimmy Mack sighs.

"Dr. King, a Birmingham jail, mass incarceration of black men, solitary confinement."

"Same old, same old," Jimmy Mack says disheartingly. Sitting down on his bed myself, I am overcome with tears.

"Nelson could have no visitors from within or without," Thula says, speaking as desolately as if it were happening today.

It's a good thing that we're wearing sunglasses. The quarry is brighter than sunshine on fresh snow. Unmercifully, neither Nelson Mandela nor his comrades were permitted to wear protection against this illuminating brilliance, and as a result, his eyes are damaged today.

As we stroll through the prison, I ask, "Where did he get the strength to hammer those rocks?"

Thula responds thoughtfully, "You know, Nelson was a boxer. He came from a strong family and the powerful Zulu nation. He knew how to pace himself—and most importantly, he was a cunning master." He winks at us. "Pretending he was working when he wasn't."

"To keep believing that South Africa would be free one day . . . Sounds like he had Job's faith." I sound like the deacon I profess to be. Maybe when I get back to the States, I will act more like a deacon. *Hypocrite that I am.*

"Man you don't even study the B. You're a Sunday morning deacon," Jimmy Mack reminds me.

I hum the Sam Cooke song quietly under my breath. *Working on the chain gang . . . Huh! Hah!* And to think that the backbreaking work was all for naught! Neither the cut limestone nor the opening it left was ever used for anything.

* * *

CHAPTER 26

"The real voyage of discovery
consists not in seeing new
landscapes, but in
having new eyes."

Marcel Proust

The culmination of our trip to South Africa is another elaborate ceremony, this time held in a spacious event facility. Stella explains the origin and the purpose of the ritual. It is a way to reconnect with our forefathers, a performance in tribute to our lost ancestors. Most African Americans choose to participate because it provides a spiritual connection with our past.

We are picked up in a German limousine, a car akin to the Mercedes Benz family. As soon as our driver stops, two maids are waiting to usher us into the mansion. A veranda wraps virtually around the entire house, which is decorated totally in white. White couches. White rugs. Even the accessories are colorless. The furniture is so pristine, I am reluctant to sit down. An irrational fear comes over me—I don't want to dirty the purity of the place, the spiritual essence of the gathering.

At the rear of the house is a large canvas tent under which a jazz band is piping out traditional music, its warmth spreading like heat from a potbelly stove.

Next to the band is a pretty woman with a shaved head, dancing. She is dressed in white and wearing bands of Ndebele jewelry. Her narrow waist is doing the "shout," a holy dance associated with the Pentecostal Holiness Church and born of the African continent. Her body shimmies and shakes, and I'm in every throb. I have the urge to shout with her.

In the middle of the room is a large table decorated all in white, from the lacy tablecloth to the embroidered white napkins. The meal is a cornucopia of food dishes, such as barbecued red sausage, smoked lamb *sosaties* seasoned with coriander and African spice rub, South African meatballs with toasted red tomatoes, and a large bowl of vegetarian stew with red beans and yellow and red peppers served with Basmati rice—the most delicious-looking food I've ever seen. The aroma of garlic, ginger, *malabar*, and "Mother-in-Law-Exterminator"—an unbearable combination of hot spices—drifts from the table. I feel like pulling up a chair to the buffet and eating all night long.

The dancers, a small women's group, perform street dances, as well as Sotho, Xhosa, and Shangaa, and utter traditional chants to the beat of a drumming combo. The South African Navy Band is playing music by Miriam Makeba: *Meadowlands* and *Phata-Phata*. My senses are hotter than either the spices or the dances.

"Doesn't take much for you," says Jimmy Mack.

Melanie and Martha sit on a long couch placed against the side of the tent, which is in a large enclosed garden. I move toward the table but am distracted by the dancing. Martha bogarts her way in front of the dancers and me. She prevents me from complimenting them.

Later in the night after I've eaten and drank my fill and been mesmerized by the dancing, we tread inside the house to the second floor, where a gallery of artifacts, masks, and old photographs are hanging. I study the pictures. In one is a group of people who look so much like me. My body freezes. They resemble my extended family in the States—uncles, cousins. One man is a mirror image—I could pass for his nephew or even his son. Awesome! I stand and stare for a while, and then move by it in a dreamlike state. I blow a kiss at the picture. I feel our spirits are speaking directly to each other. I think I see the man wink his eye.

Am I hallucinating?

Tears dripping from my eyes, I plop down on the Ashanti stool, a Ghanaian stool from the West African kingdom, designed especially for royalty and heroic warriors. These stools are sought after and sold throughout Africa. I weep because I know in my heart I have reunited with my estranged father's ancestors. I feel an overpowering connection to this man and unspeakable pride.

Melanie rushes over and rubs my arm. "What's wrong, Dad?"

Stella touches me lightly on the shoulder. "Don't be alarmed," she says to my family who's gathered around me, shocked. "This happens often. He's found a lost relative."

Martha is silent. Resentfulness and envy are written all over her face.

Stella gives each of us a white candle as we march reverently outside. As we light them, we chant the names of our ancestors.

"This is crazy," says Martha.

"Sounding like a gang banger," says Jimmy Mack.

To the left of the house is a man-made lake similar to a larger river where perhaps our ancestors first left on their journey of no return in waters from Angola and African countries south of the Sahel. Perhaps it was a night like this.

Our hostess offers prayers and thanksgiving to our ancestors.

A single tear rolls down my face.

* * *

The next day is our last in South Africa. I buy Jeanette a small South African mask—a piece small enough to put in my luggage. I had it created just for her by a local artist. I take care to choose wisely. It will go well with the paintings she has hanging all over her apartment.

"A little insurance piece," Jimmy Mack says laughing.

Affectionately, I say, "No, because I want to."

We eat a quiet dinner at the Market Theater. The performance is a play on AIDS prevention, and the talent is as good as any in the States. It reminds me of *Eclipse*, a play starring a Howard University graduate produced by the Woolly Mammoth Theatre.

We end the night early and prepare for our flight to Zimbabwe the next day.

* * *

CHAPTER 27

"A new place gives the opportunity to
see things in a new aspect and to choose
the setting for the new experience."

Marcel Proust

We land at Victoria Falls Airport in Zimbabwe and
book into a hotel overlooking the rolling water of
the Zambezi River and the nearby valleys and hills
just walking distance from the falls themselves. Although
smaller than the one in Jo'burg, the hotel overlooks a lush
garden as rich as a rainforest with Florida-like palms and a
beautiful array of the most colorful flowers, such as the deep
rose-colored Sachara.

Our tour guide, Nedai, briefs us on our itinerary for the next few days: nonstop touring, dining, and safari picture taking.

He assigns us our living quarters. All the bungalows are large and air-conditioned suites. Each unit is self-contained, with living room, kitchen, and two private bathrooms: one for Martha and one for myself. Thank God. We lack none of the amenities of the life we have briefly left behind.

By this time, having already seen it when I passed through customs, I am not surprised to see Robert Mugabe's picture hanging on the dining-room wall. Mugabe is certainly a despot, but seeing his photograph everywhere—even in the bathroom, over the toilet—is a powerful indication that we're on the African continent where black leaders are the norm. As tourists, we will experience none of the political unrest perpetuated by Mugabe, nor will we view any of the poverty into which he has grievously plummeted this country. Poverty is one thing that, by working hard, I have escaped forever. I am rich now. However, it is heart-wrenching to view it up close. Anywhere.

I go to bed and sleep like the baby giraffe I saw today on the grounds near our hotel.

At around midnight, I slip out of my hut and behold a constellation of millions of tiny diamonds in the sky. I'm breathless.

* * *

The next morning, I white-water raft down Victoria Falls and feel like a Navy cadet once again. The water cascades and splashes on my body like a shower in the midst of a summer monsoon.

My arms have been prepared for this adventure by years of track and field, officer's candidate training, and initiation in Omega Psi Phi. I'm speedy.

* * *

Having survived the storm in the haul created by Gunnery Sergeant Raleigh, I run and make my bed. Then hightail it to the mess hall.

I arrive before any of the other recruits. We mill around like a pack of wild dogs waiting for a meaty bone. This is our first formation, and honestly, we don't even know what we're doing.

"Form up, sweet potato pies!" Gunnery Sergeant shouts again.

"Yes, Gunnery Sergeant!"

Just like lamps on an Omega line, we try to march in perfect footstep formation, but we stumble and bumble like boy soldiers. Around the yard, over and over again. So many times that I get vertigo. For one hour and thirty minutes we perform vigorous calisthenics. We run for four miles in twenty minutes and forty-five seconds. We perform countless push-ups in two minutes—so many I can't remember. With neither food nor water, all under the blazing-hot sun, we jump through several unimaginable obstacles: a wall that makes China's Great Wall look like a white picket fence, thirty consecutive tires, a rope ladder, and a man-made mountain that makes Mount Kilimanjaro an ant hill. All are performed at a clocked speed. The most important obstacles are various swim tests, such as the "abandon ship jump" in which we are required to jump from a twelve-foot tower as if we are abandoning ship, and a five-minute "prone float"—floating face down for five minutes.

As I dive headlong into the water, I feel like the lucky candidate in my squadron because Grandmama enrolled me in swimming classes at the local recreation center in Carolina. I feel like a prized fighter training to avoid Sonny Liston. My sports conditioning and pledging experiences help, but before the new day turns old, I'm too tired to care. I flinch as I trip over another trainee, but I'm too scared to stop and apologize.

"Let me lay down the rules to you, brownies. You are in the Navy now—at least, tonight you are."

"What does that mean, Beamon?" asks my neighbor, Jefferson.

"The hell if I know," I mumble.

Gunnery Sergeant Raleigh continues, "Your body belongs to me; your soul, to the Navy. Do you get it? Cause I don't know how long some of you assholes will stick it out!"

"Yes, Gunnery Sergeant, sir!" we shout.

"This isn't a soft-ass college fraternity you enlisted in!"

"Yes, Gunnery Sergeant, sir!"

"What did you say?"

"YES, Gunnery Sergeant, SIR!"

"I inspect everything! Every day! Your dress clothes! Your rooms! Do you understand?"

"YES, SIR, Gunnery Sergeant, sir!"

"If one of you brats doesn't pass inspection, none of you pass inspection. Do you understand, Beamon?"

"Why is he picking on me?" I whisper to Jimmy Mack.

"YES, SIR, GUNNERY SERGEANT!"

"Say it louder!"

"YES, SIR, GUNNERY SERGEANT!" I bellow.

"You're heathens! You need to get some religion. Learn how to pray. I expect to hear you recite your prayers every night before you sleep and every morning before you hear my voice."

I do about sixty push-ups before I'm exhausted. I concentrate on a poem I learned while pledging Omega Psi Phi. I recall one of Dean Watson's flunkies saying that it would come in handy one day. I sure am glad I remember it now. It diverts my attention from the doggone push-ups. Soon, though, I hear the Gunnery Sergeant screaming again.

"YES, GUNNERY SERGEANT, SIR!" we yell. We race to the scuttlebutt and lap up water like thirsty bloodhounds.

The whole ordeal is torturous. I begin to lose a lot of weight. I find myself praying, Lord, I'm finally robust, and I want to stay that way. But looks are deceiving. Even though I am robust now, inside I feel tiny and scared.

At the beginning of officer candidate training, our platoon is assigned 316, a number that later becomes significant to me because it is the address of my beloved. We are given training manuals that include a schedule of our daily lives—hour by hour, regimented to the minute. Thinking back, I recall the university ROTC recruiter pitching me a much more flexible schedule with much more adventure and excitement than I've seen so far. It is a grueling schedule designed to make us into robots, and even with my past experiences, it's all I can do to keep up with the pace.

At the end of each grueling day, I realize that joining the Navy constitutes a foreign trade agreement not just the royal purple for the navy blue or the old gold for the white. The whole shebang. And the routine and the pressure start all over again the next day.

* * *

The next day's safari takes us near the border of the Okavango Delta Reserve in Botswana. I shoot photographs of flocks of birds, a lion pride, and a herd of giraffes. But along the way, I feel as though I am dream walking—here physically, but spiritually and emotionally almost eight thousand lonely miles away. Through the lens of my camera, I see the flashing dimples in her cheeks, the beckoning eyes, and the full, luscious lips.

At the edge of the game reserve, Nedai describes the animals as the driver moves gingerly around them. "The gazelles, known for their grace and beauty, have been in the park for five years. They roam in herds of about twelve," he says.

Click. I take a picture.

"Are they members of a family?" asks Matthew

"Yes, though some are more like neighbors or friends."

"Elephants—see the herd directly in front of us?"

"Yes," we say together. *Click.*

"We can drive within a few feet of them," says Nedai. "This is an extended family, for sure. Pregnant elephants stay with their families for protection and help in raising the baby elephants for the first crucial months of life."

"Still a lot of tusk poaching?" I ask. "For ivory?"

"Too much," he replies. "I'm afraid the species will die out. There is so much poaching that an elephant orphanage has been opened."

The safari is more than I imagined it could be. The terrain, the savannah, the animals are more real than a television production in HD. But somehow it doesn't ease my stress or the multiple conflicts playing polyrhythmically all over my body.

"The dancers reminded me of Jeannie," I whisper to Jimmy Mack.

"Every dancer reminds you of her," says Jimmy Mack.

"Not every one, now, come on."

"She's in your blood!"

"How so?"

"You know."

"You'll see what I'm talking about—like the dancers who performed at our welcoming ceremony."

"She's a triple threat—wet, wild, and warm. Hot! Hot! Hot!"

That afternoon after a tour to view the wild animals in the Matetsi Game Reserve, we eat dinner in a man-made riverbed shadowed by a canopy. The food is served buffet style, accompanied by waiters, like at an all-you-can-eat American restaurant. The menu contains a mixture of American and African foods with indigenous foods popular in the capital, Harare. The national staple dish, *sadza Ne Nyama*, is a cornmeal mix with a consistency and taste that remind me of Southern grits. Zimbabweans eat this with a red, tomato-based relish. We dip it in a stew containing golden pumpkin leaves, red beans, and corn from the cob. Though we debate about whether our stew tastes like buffalo or beef, we discover that the meat is ordinary chicken.

In the background, we hear world music: Bob Marley tunes and music by Thomas Mapfumo, a famous Zimbabwean musician who created *chimurenga* music that is reminiscent of jazz, played with the sax, drums, and the Southern-style hum-bucking guitar and the *mbira*.

Highly trained and well-armed Green Beret–type rangers guard us. Nedai and our driver say this is required to keep predators away—both human and animal.

To further protect us, bush fires rage like a three-alarm blaze. I watch the sparks fly, hear the wood crack, and feel Jeanette's fiery dancing in my loins. I am reminded of the last time I saw her hips and plump backside moving around her living room, dancing to the rhythms of "Spotlight."

"Oh, me!" moans Jimmy Mack.

I'm still feeling remorseful about the remarks I made to Jeanette before we left.

"Your mouth has a head of its own," says Jimmy Mack.

The words I uttered—*You better watch yourself, 'cause when the sunlight shines through your skirt I can see your thighs*—shock me to the extent that I am sure they came from someone else's lips.

"Lust," Jimmy Mack says, beating me over the head with my own words.

"Don't remind me," I snarl. They keep playing like an accordion in my head.

Laughing, with his head pointed to the sky, Jimmy Mack says, "You'd better watch yourself."

I am certain that a fever has taken over my brain, and I can't cool it down.

"Jasper. Jasper! The waiter is asking you a question," scolds Martha. "What do you want to drink?"

I've been daydreaming. I ask for another rock shandy—
it tastes similar to syrupy Carolina lemonade.

* * *

On our final day, I dare to take a ride over Victoria Falls in
a hot-air balloon. To my surprise, it is the thrill of my life. I
float like a red, orange, and yellow Chinese kite, the Year of
the Dog. It feels better than the first time I did a daredevil
ride, releasing my hands off both handlebars of my bicycle.
But do I dare try it again? It is too risky and I am too old.

Still, the view—a combination of wildlife and
landscape—is nothing less than heavenly. I look out over
roaring waterslides and lands unsettled and untouched by
man. I take pictures from that height. It is an exhilarating
experience. I feel like a kid dipping and tumbling down a
giant waterfall at a fall carnival in Carolina. The water
splashes in my face; I shake my head and take a deep breath.
I feel light-headed and free as we float in the air. This is
how I feel when I am with Jeanette. My troubles vanish the
moment I hear her voice, see her face. I feel free to enjoy my
money and live the life I've strived so hard to obtain.

After landing, we spend a few hours shopping in the
Artist Market of the Tonga—the smoke thunder people. I spot a painting that would go well in Jeannie's living room. I wish I had the room (and the gall) to carry a
large, intricately carved mahogany sculpture home for her.
Impulsively, I buy the painting, which is populated with figures similar to Haitian art, an orange explosion of primary

reds and yellows. I discreetly have Nedai ship it back to her in the States. I feel ill at ease buying tangible things for her, not only because Martha might find out but because ninety percent of the time I express my feelings for her by just giving her money. I suppose it makes me feel more powerful doing it that way.

"Lots of money," sings Jimmy Mack.

Being in Africa is a life-changing experience for me. Like most African Americans, I feel an incredible closeness to my brothers and sisters here. And seeing the striking picture of what I hope are my paternal ancestors was more than I could have dreamed of. I hope to carry this love in my heart forever. It is everything I have fantasized about since I was a child.

As I contemplate returning, I have a deeper meaning of who I am as an African American man. I hope I can take that feeling with me. I hope it can inspire me to be a better and stronger man by pursuing psychotherapy and discovering and becoming the person that I am—the one God wants me to be.

I buy several African carvings—one for the church. I will have my name as the donor and the description of the piece inscribed on a plaque. I'll hang it in the Peter L. Farmer Memorial Library. The other pieces, a spring stone sculpture titled, "Coming From the Fields," depicts an elderly woman with two children clinging to her dress, holding a bowl of food. It evokes memories of my grandmother. I see a mirage—Richard and I hungrily begging for peanuts. It cost me $34,000 and will hang in my home, and the other one is for my beach house. I also bought a couple of talismans for good luck; something tells me I am gonna to need them. I buy some African fabric for my sister, Barbara, and dashikis for my brothers. I hate to leave, but I must return to my life in the United States and deal with all the issues hanging over me.

* * *

CHAPTER 28

"The whole object of travel is not to set foot on foreign land; it is at the least to set foot on one's own country as a foreign land.

G. K. Chesterton

Back in the States, Hugh Masekela's trumpet still blasts in my ear, and the flavors of *braaivleis* and *pap*—roasted meat and porridge—linger on my tongue. The smell of coal-burning Soweto stoves loiters in my nose. Vivid images of gleeful children playing with ingeniously made wire toys flash through my head. The spirits of my people rage in my heart.

My schedule is tied up with various church meetings. The most important is planning for the pastor's first installment service, which requires many of the church officers' approvals (including mine). But this time things seem different. On Sunday, I shake my fellow deacons' hands, and it feels as though I am palming my African brother's. The flow of centuries of blood connecting us finger to finger.

The celebration is very significant for many reasons; this is the eighth pastor in the history of the church and one I selected. I survey the congregation and imagine that these are my father's family members. That I do belong. Maybe, just maybe, I can stand up to the criticism and the sarcasm from folks—even Trustee Anderson.

"Maybe," says Jimmy Mack.

I want to see Jeanette right away when I get back in the States, and I call her house as soon as I can. She isn't home on Sunday—probably attending church and taking yoga. I leave a voice mail message: *I'm back, and I have several things I've got to do before I get over to your house. I'll try you again ASAP.* I am anxious to seek her forgiveness for the gross mistake I made before I left. I am serious about seeing Doctor Moore. My thoughts about that are even stronger since I've been to Africa.

The next day I send her an e-mail:

> *I am back from Africa. Had a great trip. It was a life-impacting experience. I will call you sometime today for sure. I haven't forgotten what I said.*
>
> *… Jasper*

I'm determined to get a divorce and to be with my soul mate. I also have a follow-up doctor's appointment relating to my anxiety attack. But Martha is keeping me busy with all manner of activities.

Late that afternoon, I receive a cheerful e-mail from Jeanette.

Hi Jasper,

Glad you are back and that your trip was wonderful. I'm relieved that you are sticking to your word about getting help. Looking forward to seeing you and talking about the trip, too.

Jeanette

"You need to stay home today to meet the telephone repairman," Martha says.

"You got to do this and you got to do that," mocks Jimmy Mack.

I don't bother to object. Anyway, this will give me time to speak with Jeanette without my wife's prying eyes all over me. Still, sometimes I think that she tampers with the phone or the network on purpose, just so she can assign me something to do.

"Riiiiight, Jasper," laughs Jimmy Mack. "Martha does it so she can 'keep' you out of trouble!"

"You know it's something she might do!" I insist. "She wants to keep me from seeing other women."

"Too late, baby, for that. Where there's a will, there's a way," says Jimmy Mack.

"She knows I'm really unhappy with her," I say.

"Is she that perceptive?" asks Jimmy Mack.

"Call it perception. I call it suspicion. But her abusive behavior has left me no other choice. And after all, we've been married more than thirty years. I've changed, and she just isn't what I want or need anymore. I realized this the moment I fell in love with Jeanette. I'll set up an appointment to meet with a couple of lawyers she recommended."

"Which firm?" asks Jimmy Mack.

"Hogan Lovells."

"They're good, man."

"They won a one-of-a-kind case for Jeanette, and she has been raving about them ever since."

"Okay." I feel like a chicken just thinking about talking to a lawyer.

"No time like the present," says Jimmy Mack enthusiastically.

"You got that right." I flip open my phone and dial Hogan & Lovell before I lose my nerves.

"Good. When's your appointment?" asks Jimmy Mack.

"They squeezed me in for this Friday at eleven a.m."

"This Friday? You go, man!" says Jimmy Mack.

I call Jeanette immediately. Her phone rings and then clicks into voice mail. I leave her a message about all these things I want to discuss with her—seeing Doctor Moore, my appointment at Hogan Lovells.

"Yeah, you say you gonna do these things," says Jimmy Mack. "You better stick to your word this time. You hear me! You've said you were gonna do something so many times before. . .."

"I am serious this time."

"Okay," Jimmy Mack replies.

On Wednesday, I call Jeanette again as quick as I can on one of our house phones. It cracks and pops like static from a remote radio tower. I don't know what's happening...

maybe Martha has been tampering with the phone. *Really, I wouldn't put it past her.*

"Old lady rigging the phones," suggests Jimmy Mack. "Could be what all those repairs were about?"

Luckily I finally reach her—the first time since my return from Africa.

"Hi."

"Hi, Koko," she sounds excited. Almost as much as I am to hear her sexy but guarded voice. "You're back."

"Yes, almost a week now. Didn't you get my e-mails and voice mails?" I ask.

"Yes, and I wrote you back several times."

"I'll check my inbox today, but we've been having a lot of problems with the Internet."

I switch my attention back to Jeanette. "What?" I say.

"Did you liberate Zimbabwe?" Jeanette asked.

I laugh. Jeannie has such a great sense of humor.

"No, but I made an appointment to meet with the lawyers. Debbie—aaaahhhh . . . Wait a minute. I have their names right here."

"Debbie Boardman and Adam Levin," she says before I can find my notes. "Did you really?" She sounds excited. "I am so proud of you."

"And Doctor Moore, too."

"You did. . . *crackle crackle* . . . ? Unbelievable . . ."

"Huh? We have a very bad connection."

"Did . . . *crackle* . . . a good . . . *crackle*?"

"What? Yes, we had a very good time, thank you," I reply. Jeanette must be puzzled by the tone and the business like demeanor of my conversation. I hope she knows why I am using this clandestine language. I want to tell her all about Africa and what happened to me there, but something is wrong. I think Martha is eavesdropping on my telephone conversation. She's worse than the infamous J. Edgar Hoover.

Watch yourself! Lulu's bark conveys to me.

I listen for a second. *Is that Martha coming?*

"Oh! My phone is gonna out. I'll call you back as soon as I can," I say, and I hang up like a suspect covering his tracks. I reach over and rub Lulu's pretty golden fur. It feels smoother than a lion's mane.

That night, I can't sleep. While Martha is taking her shower, I tiptoe downstairs to my office and peck out an e-mail to Jeanette by the nightlight. I hit the send button when suddenly Martha comes marching down the stairs, snooping like a bird dog. She appears in the doorway and is all over me like kudzu. But at least I got the message out.

> *Just a quick note. I was somewhat constrained when I was talking with you on the phone. I think Martha is on to me. Do not think that my feelings have diminished or that I'm no longer concerned over the pain I've caused you. I have been reading a self-help book, too:* A New Earth: Awakening to Your Life's Purpose, *by Eckhart Tolle. Next I'm gonna pick up* Black Pain. *So you see, I am trying. That's all for now.*
>
> *… Jasper*

I have promised Jeanette that I would atone for the things I said before I went to Africa. *And I will.*

"No more hemming and hawing?" asks Jimmy Mack.

"No more," I say timidly.

Friday morning, I go for my meeting at Hogan Lovells. I am so nervous and excited at the possibility of my freedom from Martha, I arrive thirty minutes early. This is a tremendous step for me. I don't like lawyers. I don't like law offices. But I'm trying to be a big boy. I push out my chest, square back my shoulders, and hit the button for the thirteenth floor.

"Good job, Jasper," says Jimmy Mack.

As I exit the thirteenth floor though, I almost vomit.

At what price freedom? I ask no one but myself.

"What is the expression? The rule of the law?" asks Jimmy Mack.

"Yeah. I've got a lot riding on this."

"Don't tell me. I know. Money?" says Jimmy Mack.

"Right."

I enter the conference room where I see two hotshot divorce attorneys, members of the twenty-something generation, waiting, ready to go. They're so young. I hope they know what they're doing. I'm sure glad one of them is a woman because of my issues with those of the opposite sex.

They offer me a continental breakfast, which is laid out on the buffet table in a private dining room. It is enough food and drinks to serve a party of thirty. I fix a cup of strong coffee because my nerves need an infusion of caffeine real bad. I sip it slowly...then they call me back in the conference room.

I go over my financial portfolio, including my three houses, bank accounts, and secret credit union accounts that I haven't told them about yet. When Jimmy Mack startles me.

"I know who the bad cop is, Jimmy Mack."

"Who?"

"You know."

"Come on . . . tell me."

"I'd rather not say. They may pick up on it."

They question me as if I have committed a felony.

Adam Levin jumps on my case right away. "We need to know the truth about everything, Mr. Beamon. I don't like surprises," he says.

"Bad cop," says Jimmy Mack.

Wow, I think. *I am the victim here!* Aren't they gonna help me keep as much money as I can? Who said I wasn't gonna to tell the truth?

"What Adam means, Mr. Beamon," says Debbie Boardman in a firm but sweet voice, "is that we need to know about all and any of your assets. Bank accounts, investments, stocks, bonds, real property, and personal property, anything like that."

I'm terrified! If Martha knows about *everything*, I'm gonna to lose a lot.

"To get your fair share, Mr. Beamon, we need to know about everything," Ms. Boardman repeats. "Believe me— we'll fight to the bitter end." She says pounding her fist, that delicate fist, lightly on the conference table.

"Oh my."

"Tell the complete truth," Mr. Levin insists.

"All our money is lumped together in one bank account," I say, my voice dripping with regrets. "Most of it is mine."

"Most?" Levin sounds like a defense lawyer cross-examining me. "Do you mean *all of it?*" he interrogates me further. "Didn't she work, Mr. Beamon?"

My heart is speeding at about a hundred miles an hour. "Yes, she did, but I made the majority of it," I say.

"How much are we talking about here?" asks Levin.

"Fifty-five million dollars."

"Whew!" they both whistle.

"What an entanglement," Levin emphasizes as he jots down some notes in his iPad.

"Anything else, Mr. Beamon?" asks Ms. Boardman.

"Well . . ." I hesitate. After a long sigh, I sit up straight in my chair and speak breathlessly. "I have a secret account and a few investments at the Navy Federal Credit Union."

They scrape the information out of me like a graffiti-cleaning crew scuffing grime from a Times Square sidewalk. The meeting lasts for an hour and thirty minutes; at the end I feel as if I've had an examination for prostate cancer.

"Man up. You know she's not gonna to take this like a kitten," says Jimmy Mack.

"I know. I know. Don't keep scaring me. It's gonna to be acrimonious," I say.

"You can bet your money!"

The firm's research team is reviewing the divorce laws as they pertain to PG County and Maryland. "I am hoping it is not a fifty-fifty state," I say.

"Anyway, it's gonna to be a knockdown, drag-out," Jimmy Mack laughs.

"Jimmy Mack, leave me alone—you might dissuade me."

Things never have been good between Martha and me—not before nor after gonna to Africa. A change is way over due. But let's be honest—my main concern is losing as little money as I can.

* * *

CHAPTER 29

"Every dog has his day."

The next day, I am driving to Jeannie's house when Martha calls to order me back home.

"Get your ass back here! *Immediately!*" she says, screeching like a peeper frog in spring.

"Why? What's gonna on?" I reply.

Click.

Hell, I think. My worst nightmare is about to come true. I speed dial Jeanette's telephone number.

"I was on my way to your house, but . . . I have to go back home."

"What's wrong? I sent you an e-mail. Did you get it?" asks Jeanette.

"No." My heart stops. "Let me open my mailbox and check." I pick up my phone and search through my inbox frantically; swerving, I almost hit a long-distance truck.

"I don't see it," I say, my voice quivering. My brain is detonating… alarms gonna off all over my body.

"Okay, well, I'll tell you what I wrote. Jasper, I don't want to talk about any of your issues. Not about your sexual problems: the guilt, the shame, the erectile dysfunction and general anxiety, not Martha or your church. I've got things I need to do. Those are *your* issues."

"Anyway, I forgive you for accusing me of wearing clothes that arouse your sexual desire. But you've been back for weeks now. It's too late for you to come over here to talk about anything. I am tired of talking and listening and counseling. Just sick of being the co-dependent in this relationship."

"I've been back a week," I say defensively.

"Two. I'm gonna to New York for a book conference. Don't put me in a negative mood. I need to stay focused," says Jeanette.

"I hope you succeed, Jeannie. I'll call you later. Good luck in New York."

I think I hear her say, "Good luck on becoming a man."

"Ouch!" Jimmy Mack says.

"My birthday is July 3. Come to New York and celebrate with me. You can get back home before you turn into a pumpkin," Jeanette says bitterly

Is she testing me?

"Messing with you," says Jimmy Mack.

"I can't—I have to account for all my time!"

"Are you in prison?"

This woman has a way of getting to the real issues with me. I think I'm a man. I fathered a son and a daughter.

Doesn't that make me a man? But deep down—not even that deep down…

I know what she is talking about. Truthfully, I'm as flaky as fish scales and as powerless as a slave.

"It takes more than a sperm to make a man," my loyal sidekick says.

"Thanks, Jimmy Mack."

"No problem, sperm donor," he teases.

I drive back to my house like a teenager on speed, zooming around the curves on two wheels and pressing the pedal to one hundred miles per hour.

Martha attacks me before one-foot lands on the carpet. Could a black man stopped by the cops have been more frightened?

"What in the hell is this?" she says, pointing to my computer.

I am horror-stricken. Out of my mouth comes a word only a baby could interpret: "Whhhaaaattt?"

"You know damn well what!"

"Nooooooo."

"These e-mails!"

"E-mails?" I say to Martha.

"Oh, God!" I moan.

Sensing my demise, Lulu rushes into the room, barking and yapping at Martha. "Yap, yap, yap!"

"Shut the fuck up," Martha says to Lulu, who darts under a chair, disappearing completely.

I decide to go on the defensive. "You read my e-mails! You broke into my mailbox!"

From underneath the chair, Lulu is whining nonstop and her tail is bumping the floor. *Thump. Thump. Wallop. Wallop.*

Martha lunges into the right side of my head. The sound causes her to panic and lose control of her bowels.

"*You* left it open, fool! Who's Jeannie? Who's Jeanette?"
I throw up a wall of silence.

"Who *is* she?" Martha repeats vehemently. "You heard me, motherfucker."

"Calm down, Martha, calm down. This is not what it looks like. I was just helping her with a business proposal."

"Business proposal, my ass. You liar!"

"She's just a friend of mine." I don't know how much she knows about my relationship with Jeannie, so I talk sparingly. I don't know how many e-mails she has read, though I have tried to erase them as soon as I've read them. I know from past experience, though—from when she's caught me with other women—that she needs to run out of steam. Still, her tirade makes me feel like I'm back in Viet Nam.

"A friend? What kind of fucking friend do you write messages like this to?"

"Like what?'

"Like these: 'Are you okay?' You sound pathetic, fool! 'I miss you. I haven't heard from you in two days. I know that I will never heal until I do right by you.' Or how about 'Hello, Jeanette—my sunshine. You are perfect for me. You're so intriguing.' THAT'S WHAT!" screams Martha.

"She's been sick—been having a bad time."

"You're gonna to have a worse time! If you're having an affair, I will take you to the cleaners—I'll take every damn penny you got, man!"

Oh—not my money!

I can't divorce this woman. And now I realize I can't see Doctor Moore. What's she gonna to say? I'm too scared. I will have to give Martha fifty percent of my hard-earned money. Lord, my "transformation" lasted about two seconds—as long as it takes a Boeing 757 to hit the asphalt and glide into a 360-degree turn on the runaway at Reagan National Airport.

"Calm down, Jasper, calm down," says Jimmy Mack. "I wish you had done the disappearing act—off to a tropical island."

"I wish I had, too."

"I told you. You could be at Club Med lying under the palm trees in the Ivory Coast by now," says Jimmy Mack disgustedly.

Wheezing like I'm having an asthma attack, I reply, "You right, man."

To Martha, I say, "No! It's nothing like that! It's not like that at all!"

"Well, what am I supposed to think? Where were you gonna just now, anyway?"

"To . . . the bank?"

"She ain't gullible," shouts Jimmy Mack.

"You liar! You bald-faced, bald-headed liar! I'm gonna to call that woman." She heads upstairs, ranting and raving presumably to search for information about Jeanette. A few minutes later she stomps back down, pulls up my shirt, and snatches my cell phone from my pants belt, frantically flipping through the call log until she sees Jeanette's number.

I follow her, stuttering pathetically. "I . . . I . . . I'm . . . I'm sorry, Martha. No, please, Martha . . . don't call Jeanette. I . . . I didn't have an affair—we never had sex."

"Not because you didn't want to," says Jimmy.

And of course, he's right.

* * *

Later that night Martha is taking a much-needed bath. My cell phone rings incessantly. I fumble, grab it, and stumble out of bed.

"Hello," I say weakly. I hear the dreaded voice of Trustee Charles Anderson.

"Deacon Jasper F. Beamon. We need to talk."

I get that ominous feeling I got when Jeanette sent me the first e-mail, my heart sinking like the *Titanic*.

"The deadline e-mail," says Jimmy Mack.

"Yes, Trustee Anderson," I mumble.

"You need to settle this with me, or I'm gonna tell your wife tomorrow. You have been running and dodging, and ducking your feet too long. Don't play me cheap, man."

"Give me s-s-some t-t-time," I stutter as sweat blobs drop on my nightshirt.

"I've given you enough already. Meet me tomorrow in the church parking lot at twelve noon, or Martha will know everything there is to know by five p.m."

"I'll try to be there."

"Be there. This is not the time to get smart with me. Let me read you a few lines to refresh your memory."

I can't meet you at the Ritz Carlton tonight. My wife is performing at the Kennedy Center. They found an extra ticket for me. Forgive me, but you know how much I want to see you.
...Jasper!

"Think that might sound familiar to your wife, the piano player? And then there's this!"

Here's a "little something" to show you how sorry I am. Forgive me for not being upfront, but you just don't know how much I care about you.

"That little something was five thousand dollars, Deacon. Remember that?"

"Stop it. Stop it," I whisper. *I can't take any more.* "Do we have to talk about this now!"

"No time like the present," he says, laughing. "Are you having another panic attack?"

"I'll call you first thing in the morning."

"Don't call—be there!" he says, his voice booms through the telephone.

I put the blanket over my head and slide way down under, as deep as I possibly can.

* * *

CHAPTER 30

"Everyday our work brings
us marriages of deception,
compromise, and convenience."

Precious Ramotswe (A. McCall Smith)

I *am in a crisis. I am in a crisis. I am in a crisis! Oh my God! Oh my God! Oh my God!*

"You need a cup of bush tea," snickers Jimmy Mack. For Precious of the *No. 1 Ladies Detective Agency*, that's her favorite way to calm down.

I didn't sleep five minutes last night. I punch in Jeanette's number.

"What's wrong?" asks Jeanette.

"I left my e-mail open, and my wife read our e-mails."

"Oh, shit!"

"She was gonna to send you an e-mail, saying that I can't communicate with you ever again, but I persuaded her not to do it."

"That's a joke, Jasper," laughs Jimmy Mack. "Get real! That woman's crazy. You can't convince her to do anything!"

"Don't send me no e-mails!" Jeanette screams. "What are you gonna to do?"

Gasping for breath, I manage to say, "I'm gonna to be alright. I'm gonna be alright."

"Good for you! Good for you! That's exactly what you deserve!" screams Jimmy Mack. "You could have avoided this mess."

"I can't communicate with you anymore."

"Is this what *you* want to do?

SILENCE.

"You lied. You said you were gonna to get therapy. You led me on. You consulted two divorce lawyers. You lied. Remember what you said? 'I won't heal; still I'll do right by you.' Isn't that what you promised, Jasper?" yells Jeanette.

Be calm, Be calm. Be calm.

I pace around and around the den, paralyzed, as all hell is breaking loose. In one ear, I hear Jimmy Mack scolding me, "God took her away from you!" And Martha is cursing and shouting, louder than a yowling hyena, "You weird dog!" In the other ear, I hear Jeanette advising me to seek help: "You need to call Doctor Moore."

She is pissed.

"You're in an abusive relationship," she rants. "It's only gonna to get worse! Just like I said."

I hear her, but I'm too scared to even think about seeing a psychiatrist.

She's not gonna to let me go, I think. *I am gonna to lose my money. Martha's never gonna to let me go.*

"If you don't call under these circumstances," says Jeanette, "then when will you?"

SILENCE.

"Coward!" yells Jimmy Mack.

Lulu whimpers.

Jeanette slams the phone down.

In my mind, I hear it over and over, the last thing Jeanette said, repeating her mantra: "You need to call Doctor Moore!"

I drop the phone. It lands on the floor and cracks the edge of the glass coffee table. I put it back on the hook. It rings immediately. I am panic stricken. I really don't know what to do, but my survival instinct warns me not to cross Martha.

I hope that wasn't Rebecca calling, playing one of her adolescent pranks. That's all I need. Gagging, I run to the bathroom and bend over the commode. My entire breakfast—bacon, eggs, bread—splatters all over the toilet and the bathroom floor.

I wipe the foul-smelling waste from my chin and rinse my mouth. My mind is spinning. *I'm gonna to do everything I can to placate her, or I will end up in financial hell.*

God! Living with a jealous woman is torture. Even in the twenty-first century, men don't openly admit they are victims of domestic violence. We see it as a sign of weakness to admit or even consider seeking professional help. Allowing a woman to physically beat you, verbally abuse you and control you, and—*Lord forbid!*—be in command of your money is grounds for public ridicule. I am terrified of becoming the laughingstock of my community and church—if I'm not one already. Maybe people are laughing behind your back.

I'm ashamed to talk about it anymore.

I hear Martha in the den, dialing the telephone.

Martha, being the brazen women she is, leaves a strange message:

"This is Jasper F. Beamon's wife. The three of us need to meet. We want to talk to you."

Oh no!

She's calling Jeanette.

What in the hell is she talking about? I ask myself. I'm too damn scared to stop her. But Jeanette knows me better than that anyway. Oh, hell no, I do not want the three of us to meet or TALK. But I know darn well what Martha wants to do: threaten her or pay her off before she puts our business in the streets. If the church finds out, we both will become the laughingstock of our church and our professional communities.

I can't stand the thought of public ridicule. I still remember my stepbrothers and those racist Navy bastards jeering and calling me ugly names.

"Maybe she thinks she can bully Jeanette like she does you," says Jimmy Mack.

I wish I could bury myself in the backyard or run away for good. I know Jeanette doesn't tolerate drama queens. I'm terrified and embarassed. I feel like crawling down the sewage.

I wish I had a friend to talk to.

"A BFF?" asks Jimmy Mack.

Much to my dismay, Martha storms into the kitchen, almost knocking the hinges off the swinging door, picking up right where she left off. I can hear her banging the pots and pans as if she's playing several percussion instruments.

Alone at last, I rock back and forth in my easy chair, barely breathing. This does me absolutely no good. Lulu runs to me and jumps up in my lap.

"Woof, woof."

A few minutes later, I am walking around the yard. *How did I get here?* Lulu is trailing me at every twist and turn. I try to think of the best lie—the best way to get out of this crisis.

A few minutes later Martha comes outside, and she starts picking on me and fighting again.

"I'll sue you for a divorce! You think you were poor growing up? Just wait until I finish with you!" I move to the right. She blocks my path.

She raises her hand to me, and I run under her arms and fly back inside.

I knew it. I knew it, I repeat to myself.

I knew this day would come! I avoided it the best I knew how.

Suddenly, I realize that giving up Jeanette is like losing all my money—that she is worth more to me than fifty-five million dollars. That I'd rather throw away fifty-five million dollars than lose her.

I stop in my tracks. I am panic-stricken. But I can't do anything about it. My anchor is gone. I am drifting down the Rappahannock River on a deflated inner tube.

Back inside Martha pins me against the wall and picks up an antique lamp. She throws it, missing my head by an inch. I trip over the red leather armchair and stumble to my feet, heading back upstairs where I ball up into a corner, chanting. Martha follows me and opens a drawer. She snatches a red sieve-edged knife. Closer and closer she inches toward me, until she is standing directly over my head. I lean back as far as I can against the wall, clutching my hands around my face like a protective helmet. I am paralyzed by fear. I begin to hallucinate.

* * *

On the eighth day, the sun shines for a few hours. Through my binoculars, I observe a threatening situation. I step out of the bridge to confirm if what I see is real, then check with Bridge Officer Harris.

"Officer Harris, I see a potential situation about five hundred yards off the starboard. Check it out immediately!"

"Yes, sir, Officer Beamon." In minutes, he returns with the confirmation. "The Congs are firing on grounded SEAL Team Seven marooned on My Khe beach as they scurry to their ship."

I feel like chicken shit—terrified of violence, the blood I might see, the horrendous racket that's coming for sure. Terrified of making a disastrous mistake, I am forced to give the command. "Destroy the enemy immediately."

The officers and the entire gunnery crew feed and fire the forty-millimeter guns in the front and aft of the *Taussig*, launching a twenty-one-inch, six-hundred-pound, blood red "live fish." Simultaneously we drop a fifty-five-drummer depth charge directly in their path. We finish out the attack with twin-mounted, five-inch, thirty-eight-caliber guns and two wide-inch barrels firing ammunition so ferociously, the gunpowder blows in the gunners' faces and knocks them off their feet.

The Viet Congs are cremated like grains of sands on a beach.

Seconds later, I hear the loud engine of a Huey overhead. I glance upward. It is swooping down over the SEALs. They latch on to the Huey and are airlifted to their waiting ship in ten minutes.

After this successful rescue in Vietnam, we will return stateside. Shortly thereafter, Admiral Gravely intervenes on my behalf to ascertain that I receive my due: the Medal of

Honor. I am lucky—no, blessed is a better description—to have had the opportunity to serve under his command.

But right now, the uproar playing in my house is worse than the Vietnam attack or the bombing of Hiroshima. For two consecutive days, even in my sleep I hear it. I am sweat-drenched in nightmares. I reel. I rock. I gasp for breath. I clutch my hands around my head like war armor.

* * *

I dodge the knife.
"DON'T CUT ME, MARTHA!"

* * *

CHAPTER **31**

"The violence done us by others is often less painful than that which we do to ourselves."

François de Rochefoucauld

I slip past Martha as she raises the knife to stab me. I run as fast as I can, screaming like a victim of the Jamestown melee, my patent leather shoes clicking and clacking like Savion Glover's tap dancing. Diving into our third guest room—the room farthest away from Martha's—I lock the door and hastily shove the heaviest chair under the doorknob.

"I have a good mind to pour a pot of scalding hot water on ya!" Martha threatens through the door. "Don't sleep too deep!"

"She knows how to scare you," Jimmy Mack mocks.

I sleep fitfully all night long, tossing and turning, an agonized soul in the throes of a mental breakdown. Each time I awake, I hear Martha's voice threatening to do me bodily harm. She's on the telephone, reliving this nightmare to my daughter, spilling her gutted heart out. Cursing me out. Plotting revenge.

"Your good-for-nothing father is having an affair! I am gonna to kill him!"

I believe her.

I have no doubt that Martha is capable and ready to carry out these threats. I shake and tremble in my bed. But it never occurs to me to call the police or to seek help for myself. I am too ashamed and too afraid. After all, I'm a man. Men handle their own problems. What would people think? I should know how to handle my wife. I feel all alone in this world. This is, after all, the house I bought with my own money—but I am the one being abused. I know deep inside that this is not normal behavior. I've experienced this before.

* * *

"Get in your squad! Line up, ladies!" he yells.

"Yes, Gunnery Sergeant!"

"Drop that sea bag and drop it quick," says Gunnery Sergeant Raleigh.

"What?" I'm confused. "What's a sea bag?" I ask.

"Your bag, princess!"

Oh! My luggage, I dare say only to myself. Is that what you're yelling about? All this commotion over a piece of luggage.

Does this man know how to speak without screaming? I wonder.

Gunnery Sergeant Raleigh is a fire-breathing dragon, his mouth foul and hot as molten iron. To our innocent and over-wrought bewilderment, he wants everything done at light-ning speed and to his specificity. For what reason?

"I'm gonna scare the dickens out of you, make you work harder than you ever thought possible, and prepare you for any Navy emergency!" He marches up and down the line, inspecting us from head to toe. He pulls out various recruits, including my squad mate, Roy Jefferson.

"What's wrong with your shoes, Jefferson?"

Jefferson quickly looks down at his shoes. He jerks his neck back up and stares at Sergeant Raleigh with the dumb-est look on his face.

"Those laces aren't gonna tie themselves!" says the Gunnery Sergeant.

"Yes, sir, Gunnery Sergeant!" Jefferson screams so loudly that my ears ring as if I've just left a heavy metal con-cert. He ties his shoe laces so tightly, one breaks. The entire platoon roars with laughter.

"SHUT UP!" Gunnery Sergeant orders. "You're all responsible for each other. When one person breaks the rules, you all get punished. If any one of you fails inspec-tion, all of you fail. That goes for everything: ironing your clothes, making your beds! I mean everything! I practice the one-for-all rule. Do you understand me? Give me ten laps, sweet peas. Around the mess hall, speedies."

"Yes, Sergeant, sir!"

"You verbally demoted me. If any of you pussies does that again, you will all push those sweaty bodies up until these United States elect a black president."

"Yes, Gunnery Sergeant, sir!" we shout.

The next day at zero-six hundred hours, we are out in the yard again. The sun is just rising in the northeast sky.

He orders us to line up again, in groups of tens. "The tallest to the shortest!" Then he struts through the rows, acting like the Incredible Hulk.

"This is how I want you every morning! Formed up! Do you get it?"

"Yes, Gunnery Sergeant, sir!" we sing out.

With all the constant yelling, some of the others look shell-shocked, ready to go AWOL right now. Take me with you. I grew up in an environment just like this. Lisa, my guardian angel, has told me in no uncertain terms how it has affected me: *Being exposed to yelling and screaming has caused changes in your neurons and the brain cells responsible for regulating emotions. You will always be sensitive to intense sounds. The main difference is that here, unlike at home, everybody is yelled at.*

Hey, I know how to deal with this, I think. Suck it up!

The purpose of the Navy indoctrination, we are told that night and throughout the many moons to come, is to train us to work as a team during combat or emergencies.

"I want your asses out here in formation in one second, and I'm counting now! I need you to follow orders! Stop looking like a bunch of shipwrecked debutantes!" he barks.

Death can't be any worse than this.

* * *

Morning comes, and it feels as though I was awake ninety percent of the night. This "morning after" is a disaster too. I'm a mummy in my bed, afraid to move. Martha starts her tirade again, bringing yet another person into the drama.

"He left his e-mail box open. There were over a hundred messages between them, some he tried to delete! They were intimate and detailed. The bastard has been carrying on with her for a long time." Pause. "Yeah, you're right. Involved deeply with that *whore!*"

It must be Rodney on the line. Martha has threatened to call every member of our church, our clubs, my fraternity. She says she'll relay the circumstances over and over again—how she found my e-mails to Jeanette, how much money I gave Jeanette, and my abominable thirty-year relationship with Rebecca.

But to do so would bring *her* way down in their eyes, too. And furthermore, I reason prayerfully, I'm sure she is too ashamed to admit she can't keep me satisfied.

Still, I am meek as a lamb. Maybe I should call Doctor Moore? An appointment with a therapist doesn't sound so bad right now—better yet, hospitalize me in a mental institution—get me away from her. And yet somehow, Martha's threats frighten me too much to take that step. *If I do seek therapy it will inevitably lead me to a divorce, which will chop my money into half.*

While Martha is preoccupied, I force myself out of bed and head to the kitchen to brew a pot of coffee. I try to eat breakfast, pouring myself a bowl of Rain Forest Gone Wild cereal. I only wish I were that far away. I need my strength to get through the day, but I can't swallow a crumb. The best that I can do is to gulp down the hot, tasteless coffee.

I ponder my carelessness, turning to my companions.

"How could you leave your mailbox open?" accuses Jimmy Mack.

"I don't know."

"You old fool," he says.

Did I subconsciously leave my mailbox open? Did I want her to *force* me to stop seeing Jeanette since it is something I didn't want to do or have the courage to do myself? Am I that COMPLEX?

"Yea, just that sick" says Jimmy Mack. "What do *you* think?"

I swallow hard, not knowing what to say

Long pause.

"I don't know," I say agonizingly.

"Don't say I didn't warn you to get your stuff together."

Lulu is the only one on my side. She knows that something horrible has happened, and she is sticking by me like only a dog can, letting out an occasional whimper in sympathy.

I analyze my behavior over and over again. How could I have been so careless, so stupid? My soul has already left my body. These horrible days, the accusations from Martha, the recriminations, the regrets about Jeanette, my involvement with Rebecca and my fears—day slips into night and night into day. I barely know what is happening. This crisis has taken its toll on me. I am losing weight like I am on a starvation diet. I comb my hair and a lump the size of a baseball falls out of my head. When I look in the mirror, I look like a scarecrow.

But I am back to my old ways of behaving. I don't see how I can get into therapy. I am just too scared, too lazy, too shaky, and too embedded in this marriage. I promise Jeanette one thing and do another. I'm as shaky as a leaf on a tree in a hurricane. When I'm in trouble, I make all kinds of promises, but after the crisis passes, I DON'T FOLLOW THROUGH. I said I was gonna to see Doctor Moore more times than I have fingers and toes.

* * *

CHAPTER 32

"The price you pay for your
enslavement is your self-respect,
self-dignity, and self-esteem."

Iyanla Vanzant

A thousand-pound rhinoceros is sitting in the middle of my chest. Severe pain spreads outward from the center like high-voltage electricity to my neck and down to my shoulders and up my arms.

My breath is short. I clutch the Bible as sweat pours down my arm like dishwater. Loose pages of my notebook containing the sick and shut-ins list and the "Concerns of the Church" bulletin sprawl on the floor, unfolding around my feet like a Chinese fan. I slyly pick them up avoiding the glaring eyes of Trustee Anderson. My chest is tighter than a blood pressure cuff.

Lisa whispers, *"One of the main symptoms of a heart attack, Jasper."*

It feels like the whole congregation is glaring at me. *Do they know?*

It is Sunday morning—not just any Sunday, but Communion Sunday. Today is a busy one. There are seven babies to baptize, twenty new members to receive the Right Hand of Fellowship, and communion to serve. It is on this day that I have the most responsibility, on this day that I must appear before this sedate, holier-than-thou congregation many, many times. Don't get me wrong; this is one of the reasons I joined this church. I am rich. I am status conscious. Belonging makes me feel good.

The communion table is dressed totally in white. The wine and the miniature whole-wheat wafers, both of which will work wonders on my body, are lying on the tablecloth. I need something right now to set me straight—help me to cope.

The sanctuary is full to capacity. I see some very attractive women in this church, and it is difficult at times to remember I'm a married man or to act like one. *The trouble with life as noted by John Barrymore, with whom I have many things in common, not the least of which are: abandonment by our fathers, serving in the Navy, and a love of women. There are too many beautiful ones in this church.*

Down, dog.

The one thousand faithful seeking to see and be seen, and if they meet God at the altar—well, hallelujah! That's even better, too. Why I think of this now is a mystery my brain can't even answer.

"Aw, shucks. Who are you to talk?" says Jimmy Mack.

Elderly churchwomen—"mothers," as they are called—all dressed in white are seated together in their special pews, looking holier than the Virgin Mary. They sway and hum, keeping their bodies in tempo with the processional hymn played by Martha, the choir director, my wife. President of the Black Millionaire Wives Club.

I race to the church's administrative building, down the stairway, and to the deacons' office to collect myself. I try to ignore the stabbing pain in my chest and the wrenching pain in my heart. This isn't too hard for me since I am an expert at numbing my feelings. I've had enough pain anyway, what with the shingles and the panic attacks. Both of these are the result of my current crisis, recurring post-traumatic stress disorder—a reaction to my years in the Navy and to the war zone of my childhood. I've had several of these bouts, and they come on just when I'm trying to avoid having one. Maybe I'm just panicking again now . . .

The economy is creating additional havoc in my mind too. Just when I feel I've accumulated enough riches, society has done a 180-degree turnaround on me. Money, now considered vulgar, was the one thing that made me feel good about myself.

"What in the heck am I gonna to do?"

"Hell, I don't know," says Jimmy Mack. "You worry too much about what other folks think."

"We're in church, man! Watch your mouth."

"Okay, sorry."

So far I've lost millions. Maybe I shouldn't worry, but losing that much money made me suicidal.

"You went a few days in the nut house."

"PIW." But then again, if Donald Trump is worrying, shouldn't I? Although, with my poor mental health, I certainly don't need a reason for anxiety . . .

"Lord, if just one more thing . . ." I say.

"You know what your doctors told you," says Jimmy Mack

"Relax. Relax."

I need to remember what happened the last time. Not to overreact. *It's probably just a panic attack.*

"The longer you wait, the harder you'll fall," Jimmy Mack declares. "You love to procrastinate about everything."

"Yeah, yeah, I know."

"This could be it—the big one. You've been under a lot of stress lately and sick several times. You need to go to the hospital now. Don't wait!"

"I'll try to make it to the end of the service."

"Okay, hard head. You've been sick so much lately— you could die this time."

I don't feel up to all this today. The cowardly mess I made of my relationship with Jeanette haunts me day and night. She's the love of my life, and I denied her—denied that we were even involved. How sleazy can I get? And here I stand, a deacon in this church for more than thirty years . . . That's why they call us dogs. My guilt is sticking to me like fleas on a hound dog's back. *Shame on me.*

Back in the baptism hall, I prepare the baptism pool, letting the water flow like Pharaoh's rain into the Nile River. Then I stir it with my middle finger. Shivering, I raise the thermometer several notches.

Glad I caught that, I think. Folks would blame me if the water were too cold, and I'd feel humiliated.

I imagine my own body being dipped into the water, as a verse from that old-school song "Misty Blue" comes to my mind:

> *Just the thought of you turns a flicker into a flame.*
> *Oh baby! I should forget you! Heaven knows, I've tried.*

"Everything is A-OK," Jimmy Mack says.

Heading to the stairway, I hear the choir singing, "Nobody Knows the Trouble I See."Just as I clear the steps about to head into the sanctuary, I walk straight into Trustee Anderson.

"You've got until tomorrow at twelve o'clock to meet me."

I run into the sanctuary as if I am filled with the Holy Ghost. Jerking and gasping for breath like a dying man, I plunk down in my chair.

The late arrivals slip quietly into their velvet-padded seats. If this were St. Mary's Catholic Church, they could relieve their shame by confessing. Instead, they straighten their backs. They are the pride of a powerful African kingdom and recipients of its prosperity. They begin to sing along. They ask for God's forgiveness for their tardiness, as well as their perpetual Saturday night sinning.

The choir sings a communion song, "Nothing but the Blood." How could I possibly be thinking of her at this moment? Thinking of her at all while I'm in church? But I am.

I miss her, I say to myself, in agony. *I want to see her. I want to see her now.* The pain is overwhelming. *I love her.*

"No, I can't. I'm a married man."

I love her. I'll get a divorce.

"No, I can't. I can't lose my money."

This is getting the best of me.

I remember Jeanette's words: *God looked down and saw your needs.*

"That's what she told you?" asks Jimmy Mack.

"Her exact words," I say.

If I can just make it to the benediction, I can escape into a Sunday afternoon of football fantasy.

"Right. Escape into another Sunday of oblivion," says Jimmy Mack.

The church secretary reads the usual list of church announcements, "Bible study Wednesday night at seven p.m. Choir rehearsal every Tuesday at six thirty p.m. The guest speaker for next Sunday is none other than the powerful Right Reverend K. Benjamin of Ever Ready Baptist Church. And I'm glad y'all elected the president. Now let's support his economy plan. Let him clean up you know whose mess.

The church roars like fans at a football rally.

The choir sings another song. I sing along, too: "He has moved so many mountains right out of my way."

It is time for prayer. It is time to collect money. It is a good thing they don't call on me to pray. What would I pray for? *Lord, heal my broken heart . . . ? Lord, don't let me lose my money . . . ?*

I am a deacon. They gave this job to me because I am rich. I was proud as a June graduate when I got it. My presence will encourage church members to pay their tithes and donate more money to the church. Money begets money, as the old saying goes.

I count the church offerings—ten thousand dollars. This is small change to me. *I hate to count change.*

"Everybody isn't as blessed as you," says Jimmy Mack.

I return to my spot on the pulpit just as the time comes for me to read scripture. Suddenly, I feel as though I'm in a fog. I hear someone call my name.

"Deacon Beamon, Deacon Beamon, Deacon Beamon," a voice whispers in my ear.

I jerk my head up and realize everyone is looking at me. Waiting for me.

Did I fall asleep? I wonder.

I pull myself together and stride to the podium. I place my Bible gingerly on it. I turn to the verses that I need to read, coughing and pretending that I have a cold. I feel Martha's eyes burning into me like a red-hot curling iron. Tyrant that she is, it would kill her if anyone embarrassed her—especially me. I know I had better get a grip, or she'll come down from the choir loft and get a grip on me.

As inconspicuously as I can, I loosen my tie.

This one thought sets me off: *I hate her.*

Lord forgive me.

"You can't move without smelling her fucking breath and that cheap-ass Rose Garden perfume," says Jimmy Mack angrily.

Oh my God, you're swearing too much.

"Good morning, Mount Mariah," I say.

Then I think, *Did I say that already?*

But the congregation responds politely, "Good morning."

"Good morning," I repeat myself, forgetting.

I read the first line of the Scripture. Then I read the second verse—two times. I pray silently as my heart thumps like a base drum. But as I raise my head to steady my brains, something compels me to look up in the balcony. I think I see . . . No, it isn't. Maybe I need to change my eyeglasses. I pause.

Is it time to get bifocals?
Did I conjure her up?
Am I hallucinating?
Maybe it's somebody that looks like her.

"No ifs, ands, or buts. It's her!" says Jimmy Mack.

Jeanette is sitting in the front row of the balcony, wearing a red hat tilted provocatively to the right and covering her eye ever so slightly. I blink my eyes and look up again. It is her. It's Jeanette! Those come hither eyes . . .

My God!

"There in all her splendor, I might add," says Jimmy Mack.

I can't even think, much less continue the Scripture reading. Yet I must.

Stop the tsunami! I pray—the one raging inside of me.

The choir begins to sing.

Rock of Ages cleft for me . . .
Let me hide myself in Thee.

I snap my head back down. Lift it and watch her sitting like a goddess. powerful, sexy, commanding her throne. I am a fly caught in her web, although we are the only two who know who she is.

I try to read the next verse, but I'm tongue-tied and trip over the words.

"You are like whitewashed tombs, which look beautiful on the outside but on the inside, are full of the bones of the dead and everything unclean." I read the verse slowly, wishing mightily that I could thrust my head in a gas oven...

I steal another quick glance at her.

Yes, Lord, that's my beloved alright! Oh my God, what am I gonna do?

"First, calm down. And then, act like you normally do," says Jimmy Mack.

I hear the choir sing the preparatory song, "Jesus Saves." As I stride back to my chair, I get one last glance of Jeanette. She slithers out of her seat and walks seductively toward the stairs.

*   *   *

My next memory is of the paramedics pushing me on a stretcher toward the ambulance. *Are they taking me to a leprosy colony? God, I must be seeing things.*

"That's where you need to be," proclaimed Jimmy Mack.

I am ashamed of myself before these sophisticated folks. The hypocrisy, misplaced values . . .

*   *   *

Shortly after I get settled into my hospital room, the phone rings. Martha answers it.

DEAD SILENCE.

Martha turns to me and angrily says, "She hung up on me. I bet I know who that was."

Barely able to breathe, I say, "Not now, Martha."

An hour later, my cell phone rings from the bedside table. Martha jumps up and answers it.

"Martha Beamon," she says, Listens. Then she almost slams it down. I hear her say, "Hello Trustee Anderson."

I faint.

* * *

Five hours later, I wake up in the intensive care unit of the hospital, breathing laboriously.

"Mr. Beamon, you have had a serious heart attack," says the doctor. "Your left and right ventricles are blocked. We're gonna to operate and give you an angioplasty as soon as you are stabilized. But first, we want to give you a cardiac catheterization."

Later that night, I do some serious soul searching. I pray.

God, please heal my body. I'm not ready to die. Give me another chance. I know I asked before, and you kept your promise. I've been a stubborn fool. If you heal me, I promise you I will get the therapy I need and tell the world about it. I will encourage more men to do the same thing. I avoided doing it when I got back from Africa, but I won't put it off any longer if you heal me just one more time.

* * *

"God took his time answering you this time," says Jimmy Mack.

Two months have passed.

My operation, luckily, is successful. But my recuperation is long and painful. I am hospitalized for a month and remain on semi–bed rest for another month.

I never do go to therapy.

As soon as I am released from the hospital, Trustee Anderson pays me a home visit. In the end I pay him one million dollars not to tell Martha about my affair with Jeanette, not to sell that chapter of Jeanette's book to the *National Enquirer* or to tell the church hierarchy about my "minor indiscretions," as he called them.

"You believe that stuff about the *Enquirer*?"

"That's what he said."

"Sucker!" laughs Jimmy Mack.

My decision to stay with Martha has taken a toll on me. I'm a bald-headed eagle and an anorexic on a soda cracker diet. When I look in the mirror, I think it's Halloween.

I try to live my life within the confines of Martha's strict requirements, which means I rarely go anyplace alone. I always tell her where I am gonna, and when I will return. As an extra measure of my imprisonment, I wear something almost akin to an ankle bracelet, an electronic monitor, which lets her know where I am at all times. To be honest, the abuse has gotten worse.

"She told you. Jeanette told you," says Jimmy Mack.

Furthermore, she cancelled my cell phone number and forced me to get a new one. Jeanette, Rebecca—none of my female acquaintances can call me. Jeanette has the home telephone numbers, but she hasn't called.

"Fool, do you expect her to?"

"No," I say sadly.

Martha still plans all my social activities, including regular outings with the same six, tired old couples. All of the excitement and joy has evaporated from my life. No more fun, no excitement with Jeanette, and no more hot sex with Rebecca.

"Your life is so serious now, man," Jasper Mack interjects. "You might as well be dead." *You look it.*

Even Lulu's playful and affectionate manner doesn't help me at all. I feel lifeless and empty inside like all the blood has drained out of me. My self-esteem is as low as T-cells in an AIDS patient.

"Jimmy Mack, I'm sure I would've made out better with Jeanette."

"Oh! Stop," says Jimmy Mack. "I've heard enough."

I read in the newspaper that Jeanette's documentary was very successful. After it was posted to YouTube, it spread like cholera. Got 300,000 hits immediately. She won the Independent Spirit Award for Best Documentary Feature. I saw her on *Oprah* discussing the film with her producer. She received funds from a Swedish JAK, a cooperative bank that doesn't charge interest but provides loans to small business and other creative endeavors in exchange for buying membership shares (somewhat like our credit unions), to supplement what I gave her. Now her documentary is being used by mental health professionals, clinicians, and hospitals worldwide.

She told Oprah that she is considering publishing a companion novel to the film, perhaps a book on Kindle or . . . what do they call it now? E-publishing. Since that fatal Sunday when I saw her at Mount Mariah, I haven't seen her.

* * *

Three months after my heart attack, I receive a letter from Jeanette telling me she has plans to publish the book very soon. Gave me the opportunity again to review it—twice. But I acted like my usual self.

"You didn't read it?" asks Jimmy Mack.

I send her an e-mail:

Jeanette,

My wife and I have read your synopsis. We congratulate you on your work and wish the best for you in all your future endeavors. We have supported your work through business development consultations and generous resources. We prayerfully and respectfully request no further communications.

... Jasper

"Man, you sorry!" says Jimmy Mack. "You lied, denied, and asked for prayer and respect in the same breathe—like father, like son. You know you were crazy about her and would have given her more money if Martha hadn't caught you! You make John Edwards look like a choir boy."

"Jimmy Mack, as soon as I heard her voice, you would spasm."

"You know that is right. And I don't even want to know what you did the second time she contacted you."

"She sent the letter to the church (in care of Pastor Wheeler). I never even answered her," I say angrily.

"You fool."

"I am worried about the contents of it."

"I hope she tells EVERYTHING she knows about you. It'll serve you right."

"I tell you one thing, she didn't let me stop her from moving on . . . succeeding."

"Good for her, buster."

* * *

Last night I had a nightmare that she had changed everything in her book.

"Even your relationship with Rebecca?" asks Jimmy Mack.

"Even that . . . ah . . . ah . . . after Rebecca was married many years later, I kept bird-dogging her jelly." I was out of pocket every day... with her...five days a week. I told Jeanette that, too.

"I don't have anything to say," says Jimmy Mack, shaking his head. "Now that is sinful."

* * *

Several months later, I read in the local paper that Jeanette has published that novel. It did so well, she received an impressive (at least by my standards) offer from a traditional publisher, and a major motion picture producer plans to make a movie of it too.

I'm as proud of her as I am scared.

I guess the significance of that red dress was to remind me of the power she still has over me. She was rubbing it in and trying to show how fine she is, too. Maybe even make me jealous or regret breaking up with her.

"You got to admit that she looked gooooood," says Jimmy Mack. "You know something else, Africa didn't do you a damned bit of good," Jimmy Mack continues disgustedly.

"Not so far," I say. "Not yet. I didn't love myself. Nobody else did."

"Lying again! Jeanette loved you unconditionally."

But I couldn't accept the real me. I controlled my feelings for Jeanette because I wanted to keep my money, to be the "good" father, the faithful husband, and the pious deacon. Most important, I was terrified of scorching in the inferno of the fire dancer.

"You want your cream and you want to lick it too," says Jimmy Mack.

How did I wind up like this? How did I get myself into this fix?

My story begins fifty-plus years ago, when I was a boy growing up in the tobacco fields of Carolina. I'm a wealthy man now and a nice guy too, albeit an unfulfilled one—an alcoholic's empty whisky bottle. I didn't get any breaks growing up. That my biological father never claimed me, even though he lived only a few miles away up the road, just a mile from the new interstate highway, and my mother never nourished me—played a crucial part in who I am today.

Needless to say, his absence and her neglect took a toll on my three siblings, but mostly on me. I'm convinced to this very day those relationships—or lack thereof—are the reason why I'm a complex man.

"Oddball," says Jimmy Mack.

I wailed when I entered this world. But I wasn't born afraid.

* * *